K.C. COP
NO TIME
—— FOR ——
DONUTS

BOB HARTMAN

ISBN: 978-1-955403-23-8 (sc)
ISBN: 978-1-955403-24-5 (e)

Because of the dynamic nature of the Internet, any web addresses or links contained in this book may have changed since publication and may no longer be valid. The views expressed in this work are solely those of the author and do not necessarily reflect the views of the publisher, and the publisher hereby disclaims any responsibility for them.

I want to dedicate this book to my wife Cindy, my children Ryan, Tracy, and Aysha. Also, to my family and friends, on and off the Kansas City Missouri Police Department. As well as to the memory of, two of my best friends, Officer Mike Wheeler and Civilian Steve Gohlmann.

These short stories are actual true events, in which I was personally involved. They occurred between 1982 and 1995 while I was serving as a Police Officer, Detective in the Bomb and Arson Unit, Homicide Unit, the Burglary and Auto theft Units with KCPD. These incidents are taken from my memory of the events as they took place. They are not in any way, meant to hurt or cause discredit, to anyone or anyplace described or resembled in these stories. I wish to make it known that my personal comments in each story, may be a little on the redneck side, but they are not meant to be racist, or sexist, but humorous. Even though most Police Officers humor is sometimes considered sick, and differs from that of other people. We use this humor as a tool, to handle the many mental stresses we deal with each day.

I would like to request that all the non-Law Enforcement readers, try to place themselves in the Police Officer's shoes, while he is handling these true incidents. Then to think to themselves, what would someone have to pay you to go through that, or even if you would. would also like to remind the public, that we Law Enforcement Officers are just as human, as anyone else. We have families, and problems, were not perfect or super human beings. We like to be judged as individuals, not all good, not all bad.

I would like to thank, all the department member's, victims, witnesses, citizens and suspects involved in these stories. Their stories gave me the inspiration to write these stories, as well as those that encouraged me to write them, Special thanks to Det. Jim Browning, for helping me come up with this title. But above all GOD, for watching over me, and letting me live, as well as learn through it all. My hopes and prayer's, are that this book may save someone from going through, one of these incidents. Also, that it might give someone a small understanding, of what these victims' have gone through.

!!!WARNING!!!

I have been advised by non-Law Enforcement readers, that they wished that they had not read some of these stories. They really did not want to know what really happens out on the streets, they appreciate their sheltered lives to much. These stories may change the way you see everyday life. Some of these stories are written very graphically, just as they would be written in my Police reports. This is so that the Judge and Jury can get a small understanding of what it was like, for the victim to go through these incidents.

CONTENTS

____

CHAPTER 1

____

THE UNBELIEVABLE AND HUMOROUS

1. I Said to The Nude Female, Isn't It Cold, She Said, I Don't Know Did You Touch It.
2. Shit and Fall Back Into It.
3. Unexcited Nurse/Bartender.
4. A Gay Guy, Pointed at Me, "And Said, Are You Trolling."
5. Gay Male Runs towards Me with His Arms Out, I thought Where Can I Hide.
6. She Said, "What's the Matter Are You a Leg Man."
7. I'll Stab Myself, OUCH!!!
8. The Sergeant and the Skinny Dippers.
9. The Kansas Police Officers Stated, we know you Drug Him across the State Line.
10. Hey, Darcy Look What I found, He Was At Least 10" Soft.
11. Rape in Progress, No Room in The Car.
12. Surprise, Same on Both Ends.
13. Nude Lady Covered Head to Toe, With Her Own Shit.
14. Hanna Banana, she said, He Was Gay, But She Would Change Him.
15. She Was All wet, so She Thought 1 Should Be Too.
16. She Had Already Patted Him Down, and then I told her that He Had V.D.
17. What's That Bobbing in Your Lap?
18. Officer Want A Blow Job.
19. Breaking in At Liberty Memorial.
20. Scared Christian Devil Worshipper.
21. Cocaine and Rubber Bullet Burglary.

22 thru 45. Drunk Driver Arrests, Short Stories, and Comments.

46. The Stalking Brownie Burglar.

47. Have You Seen a Car prowler, OH!! ! It's You.

48. Drunk Driver Pinned in Car Wreck, Not Even Scratched.

49. She Was and 11, and she Wore A see through Dress in Court.

50. Her Bloody Dress, His Bloody Face, Her Time of the Month.

51. He Ran Because, He Didn't Have His Driver's License, but I Wasn't After Him.

52. Sex in the Park Elephant.

53. Look What I See, a Venus Fly Trap.

54. $200 Dollars A Night, And She Comes with Batteries.

55. I Went to a Halloween Party, As One of The Three little Pigs.

56. The watch Dog Ate the Cigarettes, Not the Burglars.

57. Here Come Da Pigs.

58. His Gold Tooth Made Him Do It.

59. Ok, You Got Me To Bend Over, But Why Scratch Up My $300 Cowboy Boots.

60. These Clothes are not clean; I'm going to Kill You.

61. The Smiling Grabber, Your Name Is Karen Isn't It.

62. The Burglar That No One Could Find.

63. Preacher With holster For Bible, In His Pocket.

64. Teacher Need to Go, Well Why Didn't She Say So.

65. They got More Than They Wanted, When the Woman Turned Out to be A Man.

66. Saved by the Observant Ambulance Attendants.

67. Return of The Gorilla Balloon, No Questions Asked.

68. Auto Theft Suspects Hiding Under porch, With Evidence Stuck to Them.

69. Held Hostage with Bear Traps, While Guarding House.

70. Stolen Abandoned Van, Tracked Back in The Snow.

71. Tracks in the Snow Leading to a Tree, Now I Wonder Where He Went.

72. Kiddy Drug House, Food Stamp Pay Checks.

73. Your Husband Was Caught Having Sex, With A Female Impersonator.

74. Catching a Bat with Tupperware.

75. Flashlight Blinding Foot Chase, Crash.

76. Nude in Tanning Bed, "It Just Quit, But I Need Work, And I Will Fix It for You."

77. Pro Wrestler, you're too Big to Fight, I'll Shoot You.

78. Prostitute Takes everyone's Pants.

79. He Abandoned the Gas Station, Because A Prostitute Took His Money and Pants.

80. Sprit Festival Slam Dancers, Or Cap Stun Victims.

81. She Hid Her Shoe Laces Where!!!

82. Uninvited Guests Covered in Slime.

83. He was carrying her limp In His Arms.

84. He Was Having a Vietnam Flashback.

85. Ninja Goofy.

86. Radar Officer Needs Help.

87. He Was an Adult at Midnight; He Stole at 12:20AM, So I Sang Happy Birthday.

88. He Blew Up His Own Butt, To Scare Her into Coming Back to Him.

89. They Shit all over the School Nurse's Office.

90. He Was Okay Until 1 Woke Him, Then He Had to Go to The Hospital.

91. Women Can't Run with Their Pants Down Either.

92. Drunk Female, Kisses Kids That Stole Her Purse.

93. Her Blood and Hair Were on The driver's Side Of The Windshield.

94. Vice President Quayle.

95. Sophisticated Flasher.

96. He Even Stole Their Pots and Pans.

97. The Sergeant, got up on the Bar table, And Blew His Whistle.

98. The Ironing Board That Attacked Me.

99. He Calmly stated, if You Don't Stop, You'll Break My Wrists.

100. My Pain Loving Instructor.

101. My Flaming Flares, Were Sticking Out of The Hood of His Car.

102. Dumbo, Hammer, and the Predator.

1.   I Said to The Nude Female Isn't It cold, She said, 1 Don't Know Did You Touch lt.

I was patrolling the Westport area at about 2 a.m. One rainy morning, when I came upon a vehicle sitting in front of a house with its lights on, and its windshield wipers on high speed. I did not think much about it at the time assuming it was just someone in a car waiting for someone else. However, when I passed by again at 4 a.m., the car was still there, the lights were still on and the windshield wipers were still going at high speed. Although it had stopped raining an hour or so earlier. Upon checking the car out I noticed a very attractive 24-year-old white female occupant stooped over the steering wheel. It appeared as if she was passed out, dead or whatever, so I stopped to check. Upon approaching the car, I noticed a pair of leopard-skin panties lying on the seat next to this person. It only took another second to realize that she was wearing nothing from the waist down and her legs were wide open. I knocked on the window to hopefully get her attention and wake her up but to no avail. So, I opened her car door, and I put my hand on her arm and shook her, then I said, "Ma'am, are you okay?" There was no response. After noticing that she was breathing okay, and that she was beginning to respond, I shook her again and said, "Ma'am, aren't you cold?" Her response was slow so I shook her again and said, "Ma'am isn't it cold?" She suddenly looked up into my eyes, looked down at her naked crotch and then back up at me and said, "I don't know did you touch it?" Of course, that was the last thing I had expected to hear from her. I am sure I must have turned several different shades of red. Later on, I determined from questioning this person that she worked as a call girl. She had been with a male "friend" in the car earlier engaging in whatever they had been doing. The next thing she knew she was alone in the car, asleep, without her panties on, and I was walking her. I asked her to make herself more presentable and leave the area. An indecent exposure charge would have been an option here, but that charge is only for someone who appears indecent, and she certainly did not seem indecent to me. I think that's only when they are ugly!

2.   Shit and Fall Back Into It.

One summer night we received a call about skinny-dippers at Troost Lake up north of the river. Upon our arrival there we observed approximately eight college kids swimming nude in the lake. It was apparent that they had seen us coming, they were running out of the water trying to quickly dress, and get to their cars. We stopped several of them, but one 24-year-old white male swam across the lake and got out on the other side. We yelled for him to come back, but he kept going. After questioning these students, all white males and females in their twenties, it turned out these were students from a college somewhere in Kansas, and they were just out having fun. We merely asked them to leave the area as we normally do. We were unable to find the person who swam across the lake so we recovered his clothes and went on our way, hoping we would be getting a call shortly about a nude man wanting his clothes. Approximately five hours later I was patrolling another area in the northern part of the city. I discovered a truck in a furniture store parking lot, with the rear end of the truck partially in a creek bed. I checked the truck and found there was a white male asleep in the front seat wearing only a pair of overalls. I woke him up, and asked him to exit the truck; the first thing I noticed was that he smelled as he had shit on himself. Upon questioning this person, it turned out that he was the same person who had swum across the lake earlier that evening. This male informed me that when he got out of the lake, he was freezing cold, naked, and of course embarrassed. This male stated that he headed to the nearest place of shelter, which turned out to be a nearby Baptist Seminary. At the seminary he found a pair of very large coveralls on a clothes line and puts them on.

He then started looking for a place to lie down, because he felt intoxicated. He eventually found this truck, and got in it to get out of the cold air, however when he noticed the keys were in the truck, he decided to start the truck to get warm. He then realized someone might hear the truck running, so he drove to the furniture store parking lot. He backed the truck into what he thought at the time was a hidden place, because all he wanted to do at this time was get some sleep. Sometime during the night, he had gotten out of the truck, and walked up an aluminum ramp to a storage trailer in this same parking lot. He was checking this shed out, when a combination of his nerves and the alcohol he had drank, caused him to need to have a bowel movement, which he did on the aluminum ramp. While he was trying to pull these large coveralls back up however, he lost his balance and fell backward sliding on his back down this aluminum urine and shit covered ramp. He explained then that, that was why he smelled like he did. This gives a vivid new perspective to the old saying "Shit and fall back in it." So, basically this guy had left one situation that would have allowed him to go on home with no penalty. Then traded it for a stealing and auto theft charge, both of which are felonies, in which he was convicted. Nice thinking!

3. Unexcited Nurse/Bartender.
    Another story about the interesting times I had while patrolling the Westport and Plaza areas. About 4 am each morning after all the bars had been closed for a while, I would do what I called my rounds or wake up calls. My wake-up calls consisted of waking up all the drunks and parkers and getting them on their way one way or another. This was in order to keep them from being robbed, which at that time was becoming more common. On this winter morning as I was making my rounds, I located a 26-year-old white female nurse from a local hospital, and a 28-year-old white male bartender from a local bar. They were sitting in a pickup truck with all the windows fogged up, in the Westport area. I awakened this couple and asked them to move out of the area because of the threat of being robbed at that time of the morning. I then left and a couple of hours later I drove by the same area and there was this

same pickup truck parked just a couple of blocks down from where it had been earlier. I went up and knocked on the window of this pickup truck and got no response. The windows were all fogged up but I was able to wipe one off a bit and I looked inside. I observed the nurse sitting nude, in the driver's seat and the bartender sitting nude in the passenger seat, with his head lying against the nurse's shoulder. This male had his finger in the nurse's vagina; however, both of them were passed out. I got no response from knocking again so I opened the   passenger door, and I started shaking the male trying to wake him. All of the sudden, I heard a noise like a cork popping out of a wine bottle as this male's finger popped loose from this female's vagina. It was obvious that they had both passed out in the middle of a sexual act (not a very arousing one, apparently). The couple was requested to make themselves more presentable and leave the area. I remember thinking to myself at that time wondering how someone could fall asleep doing this.

4.   A Gay Guy, Pointed at Me And Said, Are You Trolling.
I remember I was walking down the street in the mner city, in an area known for its homosexual activity. This was during my new officer break-in period, and I was with my break-in officer. It was a really cold winter night, and I was wearing long-johns under my uniform.

I remember stopping a couple of obvious homosexual pedestrians that were walking down the street acting as if they were soliciting for prostitution. As I was talking to one of them when he looked down at my crouch and said, "Are you trolling?" I remember just looking at him, not really understanding what he was talking about, and then he pointed down at my unzipped uniform pants. Luckily, with long underwear on, I guess I really could not tell, however I was extremely embarrassed, and my break-in officer made sure everyone at the police station knew about this incident.

5. Gay Male Runs Towards Me With His Arms Spread Wide open, "WHERE CAN 1 HIDE !

    There was another time with this same break-in officer and another officer that we went to a disturbance in an apartment building. I was walking down the hallway with the other two officers walking behind me. At the other end of the hallway a flamboyantly gay 20-year-old white male came out into the hallway from his apartment. This male says in an excited female like voice, "Oh, Oh, officers, then he stopped and looked at me. I should have known I was in trouble then. This male then becomes extremely excited and says "OHHH," as he spreads his arms out wide as if to give me a hug, as if he la-mew me, and I was his long-lost friend. Talk about wanting to crawl in a hole! I do want to make it clear, that he did not really know me; he only thought I was someone he knew. By the time I got that straightened out my break-in officer and my assisting officer were bursting out in uncontrollable laughter. This of course continued until we got to the police station where they were able to get other officers to join in. It should also be noted that this male became so excited that he said, he forgot why he called the police, and that it did not matter now, it was not important anymore.

6. She said, What Is The Matter, Are You A Leg Man.

    I remember one summer going to a disturbance at a swimming pool. When we got there apparently the persons causing the disturbance had left because nothing was happening.

    However, there was a 23-year-old white rather good looking, large breasted female who came up to us wearing a skimpy bikini. I could not help noticing right away that right above her swimsuit top was a tattoo on the top portion of her breast; it appeared to be something that looked like a horn. Apparently, she had been talking to my partner before she came up to me, and she had shown him this tattoo. She then asked me if I would like to see the rest of her tattoo, because I guess she had noticed that it attracted my attention. Trying to be a gentleman, (as always) I said, "No, but thank you anyhow." She responded by saying, "What is the matter, are you a leg man?" Well, years went by, then one day I ran across this same woman again, I was off duty, and she remembered me! She said, "Are you still a leg man?" I said, "No, not really," and before I could say anything more, she exposed the portion of her breast that I had not seen before revealing a unicorn. I still see her around occasionally and I tease her about that unicorn.

7. I'll Stab Myself, Ouch!!!
    I remember getting an Emergency call one night in the Northland area in which a 17-year-old white male had stabbed himself. The call was from the young man's 16-year-old girlfriend. She had been talking to him on the phone about wanting to break up with him, and he had stated that he would stab himself if she broke up with him.

    She then said that she was sorry, then all of a sudden, she heard him say "ouch" and he said he had stabbed himself. Upon our arrival at this location, the young man opened to door, and said that he had stabbed himself with a 1 " blade knife, and it had penetrated into his stomach. He did this while on the telephone because he wanted to should his girlfriend that he was serious. After he had actually stabbed himself, it hurt so much that it made him say, "Ouch." He was taken to the hospital and we suggested some mental treatment for him, to his parents. He was in so much pain after the ambulance and medical personnel where done poking around on him, I do not think he will ever do that again.

8. The Sergeant and the Skinny Dippers.
    I remember an interesting incident that happened one night in the midtown area when I responded to a complaint about skinny-dippers in an apartment pool. Upon our arrival we observed a number of both male and female teenagers skinny-dipping in the pool. The funny thing was that the sergeant who responded with

us told them all to stay in the pool, and then he told the males to get out and get dressed. Then he told the females stay in the pool until the males were out. Then one by one he gave each female permission to get out of the pool and get dressed. I believe he must have been just checking for weapons, to make sure they didn't have anything concealed. Ha Ha."

9. The Kansas Police Officer Said! We Know You Drug Him Across The State Line.

We had an incident one evening near 39th & State Line. It was snowing and there was a 47-year-old white male drunk, lying in the middle of the road passed out. He was not quite in the middle of the road, he was actually on the Kansas side, and he was so big that I drug him out of the street to the closest curb. I then asked the dispatcher to notify Kansas City, Kansas and have them come and check him out. I used an ammonia capsule to wake this drunk up. I then stood with him, until the Kansas City, Kansas Police arrived. When they arrived, they stood this drunk up and his pants and underwear both immediately fell to his knees. He had urinated and shit in his pants. The Kansas City Kansas officers insisted that he had been on the Missouri side and I had dragged him across the road, so that they would be stuck with him, but I really had not. The worst thing about this is that they had to put him in the back seat of their patrol car and take him home. To this day when I see these officers, they still accuse me of dragging that drunk across the State Line.

10. Hey Darcy, Look What I Found, He Was At Least 10 Inches Soft.

I was working in the Westport district one night doing my 4 a.m. wake up rounds. On this one morning across the street from a popular historic bar there was a car parked, which was usual because they are normally all gone by that time of the morning from that area. Since this was unusual, I checked the car out. I looked in the passenger side of this car and observed a 25-year-old white male with his pants, and underwear down to his knees, sitting in the driver's seat slumped over sleeping. This situation in Westport was not that unusual, however when I first observed this male, I had to take a second look because he was hung like a horse. He was a very well-endowed person (at least 10 inches), and he was passed out. Darcy one of the Westport K-9 Security Officers was nearby so I called her over, gave her my flashlight and said, "Darcy, look and see what I found." She looked into this vehicle and it startled her she was not sure what it was that I wanted to show her, or what she really had just seen.

She appeared to be amazed, and she took her time checking him out. She called several of her other security friends over. By the time she was done, there were about six people standing around there, several males and several females. I woke the guy up and asked him what was going on, why was he sleeping with his pants down to his knees. He stated that he really did not know! That he had had a girl he had met in the bar with him and she was performing oral sex on him, and the next thing he knew I woke him up. All the security officers were cheering and laughing when I woke him up. He was arrested for indecent exposure.

11. Rape in Progress, No Room in Car.
     Another strange incident happened during the same time period in the Westport area.

Three of us Police Officers were talking to a number of male and female Westport Security Officers. All of the sudden another Westport Security Officer ran up to us and said there was a rape in progress behind one of the bars. We all then hurried to that location and I was the first one to arrive. I was in a parking lot directly behind the bar, approximately 4 feet above the alley. I looked down and saw a very attractive 23-year-old white female lying on her back nude on the cold asphalt, rock and glass covered alley. A 25-year-old white male was on top of her with his pants pulled down just to his knees, having intercourse with her. It was extremely cold outside, and I remember thinking to myself, that low life. I jumped down off the retaining wall and put my gun to his head and I pulled him up off her while stating to him, you're under arrest. I was expecting the female to be crying and trying to cover herself. However, to my surprise, she just said "What's the matter, Officer," as she just lay there nude with her legs wide open. I had to ask her to get up and get dressed, I guess it had to be because she was so intoxicated or something. I asked the male what was going on and he stated that they were having sex in the alleyway, because she wanted to. He stated that her girlfriend was already using their station wagon to have sex in with someone else. I asked the female why she had not gone home, used the grassy area or had him lie something down for her to lie on. This female stated that she guessed she had not thought about it at the time.

12.   Surprise, Same on Both Ends.
I had another incident near a bar that was frequented by gay individuals, in the mid-town area. I had been making my wake-up rounds and I was checking this parking lot when I observed a vehicle running in the parking lot after everyone else was gone. I looked in the passenger window of this vehicle and observed what appeared to be a couple performing oral sex on each other, in the "69" position. From what I had seen through the passenger window, I knew it was a female I had seen having oral sex performed on her. I went around to the other side of the vehicle and knocked on the window, with the intention of trying to get the male out first. However, it was the same scene on the through the driver's side window. It turned out to be two gay white females in their mid-twenties performing oral sex on each other. They were asked to find a more appropriate place.

13.   Nude Lady Covered Head to Toe with Her Own Shit.
I went into work one night at North Patrol and I was assigned to relieve my buddy by taking over the paddy wagon. The first thing

he told me was that there was a lady in the back of the patty wagon, whom he believed had shit in her pants.

He also stated that she needed to be taken down to Police Headquarters because she was belligerent and drunk. He did not tell me that he had seen her pull down her pants and shit in the back of the wagon while he was driving. On my way to get the patty wagon from the downstairs detention area, I noticed bare footprints in the hallway of the detention area that smelled like shit. However, I had not tied it together yet. Upon my arrival at Police Headquarters I opened the patty wagon door and out stepped a nude white female. She was about 40 years old, covered with shit from head to toe, in her hair, on her arms, on her legs, on her face. She had apparently taken her clothes off in the back of the patty wagon, after she fell in her own shit while trying to stand up back there, while we were moving. After she got her clothes off, she apparently again fell several times and had rolled around in her own shit. I quickly told her to step back up into the patty wagon and I shut the door as fast as I could. I then called for a female detention officer, and after explaining the situation to her. She brought a paper suit for the woman to put on. With the female detention officer present this time I again opened the patty wagon door and the woman stepped out of the paddy wagon. She wiped off her face with the paper suit the detention officer gave her to put on, and then she threw it on the floor and just stood there. The detention officer then got another paper suit and puts it on her, then took her to the female detention «ea. Of course, I had to go to a car wash and wash the patty wagon out.

14. Hanna Banana, She Said, "He's Gay, But I'll Change Him."
A female officer and I were dispatched on a disturbance call, however by the time we arrived, the disturbance was under control, and we were not needed. It was pouring down rain, and 2 a.m. in the morning, when we left this call. As we were leaving, a car went down the street at a high rate of speed. This car went out of

control and spun in a circle in the middle of the street, and then it took off again. We went after the car with the red lights and sirens on. This car did not pull over until it pulled off the street into a driveway. The driveway of a beautiful home, a miniature mansion divided onto apartments. The driver of this car was a 21-year-old white female and the passenger was a 19-year-old white male. When the car parked the passenger took off running for the apartment building, where he went into an apartment. The female also took off running for this same apartment door; however just as she got ready to shut the door, I was able to grab her shoulder and pull her back out. I asked her what she taught she was doing, and she stated, "Oh!" As if this was the first, she realized that I was after her. I told her I was trying to stop her because she was speeding and driving carelessly. It was very obvious that she was intoxicated, by her blood shot eyes, stagger, and liquor breath. I then escorted her out to the police car where my assisting female officer searched her. As this female officer was searching her, she felt something strange around this female's waist, she asked her what it was. This is where this incident really started to get bizarre, instead of answering the female officer's question, this female lifted up her dress, revealing her pantyhose that she had rolled up around her waist. I then transported this female to the Police Station. Where I gave her a breathalyzer test that showed that she was quite intoxicated. I asked her the required questions for my reports. Which were, have you been taking any drugs or alcohol, or if she was on any prescriptions. She said, "You mean like injections?" I said yes. She said, "The only thing I want to be injected with is my boyfriend's peter." She then went on to tell me that her boyfriend was gay, but that she was trying to change him. They had been to a gay bar earlier and were on their way home when I stopped them. She stated that her boyfriend really only liked men, but he would have anal sex with her, as long as she performed oral sex on him.

They were planning to be married in June and she told me she would like me to come over after the wedding. She said that she wanted me to dance with her on her verandah and then to make love to her afterwards. This female was wearing a nice, pair of leather gloves that appeared to be quite expensive. While we were sitting there, she took her gloves off and her hands were caked with mud. I asked her why her hands were covered with dried mud, she replied that she had been potting plants, and when it was time to go out drinking, she just put her gloves on. When I asked her, her full name, she stated, she wanted to be called Hanna Banana, because it was like a part of her name. She was obviously mentally ill and her family was notified. This female's family was very thankful; they had not realized that she had stopped taking her medicine.

15. She Was All wet, so She Thought 1 Should Be Too.
Another incident happened in the city when Kansas City was having a lot of flooding. I was driving the paddy wagon with a prisoner in the back of it taking him to the Metro Patrol Police Station for booking. I was driving around some real deep water in the area of 55th and Troost, when a female Police Officer, who was standing in this water up to her waist, flagged me down. I thought she must have an emergency, because she was standing next to a vehicle that was occupied by two very heavy-set black females both in their twenties. These females had apparently driven into this deep water and stalled their vehicle out. Because the Female officer was frantically waving, I was thinking that something was wrong with one of the occupants of this vehicle, and it was an emergency. So, I slammed on the brakes and jumped out of the patty wagon, running into the water to help her. I said, "What is wrong?" She said, "These ladies are stuck in the flood water and they need us to push them out." I said, "You asked me to come into this water that is clear up to your waist, and it was not even an emergency?" She was just a small thing, so the water was higher on her, but it was only up to my knees. The two women had not even gotten out of the car yet, so they were not even wet. I got in back of their car and helped push the car out of the water. The women started the

car, turned around, and drove right back into the water going the opposite direction as if they were going home. I would not push any further, I informed them that they should have ordered a tow truck or pushed the vehicle out themselves as everyone else does. I reminded that female officer of that situation every chance I got. I told her that I owed her one. I did, however, get her paid back, or rather she did it to herself.

16. She Had Already Patted Him Down, Then 1 Told Her He Had VD.
This same female officer called me to assist her with a car check in the Plaza area one evening. When she was patting the 22-year-old white male driver of this vehicle down, she reached into his pant's pocket and found a bottle of pills. They were marked tetracycline. There was also a letter inside the pill bottle that stated that this male was being treated for venereal disease, and he should notify anyone he has had sexual contact with. She was still patting this male down when, I read the letter out loud to her all of the sudden she jumped back and she went hysterical. I think she thought she was going to catch every disease in the world. I told her that this was a pay back, even though she did it to herself. It felt pretty good.

17. What's That Bobbing In Your Lap?
On the Plaza one night I found a 20-year-old white male sitting by himself in a car on a dark street. I stopped to find out what he was doing.

He was sitting in the driver's seat of the car, with a blanket over his lap. I thought he was just playing with himself or something. I asked him what he was doing, and he told me he was waiting for someone. I asked him for some identification, and he took it from his wallet which was lying on the dashboard. He handed me his driver's license, and I went back to my patrol car to run a check on it. As I was waiting to get a response back from the dispatcher, I was keeping my eye on this white male, I then noticed the blanket moving up and down in this male's lap. I had not realized that there was someone else in the car previously. I then went back up to the car and asked the male to lift the blanket up, which he did with a big smile on his face. Under the blanket was a 19-year-old white female performing oral sex on him. Even after he lifted the blanket off her she did not stop what she was doing. I finally tapped her on the head and stated, "Please stop -while I am talking to you." She finally stopped and gave me some identification. I checked them with the dispatcher and they were both wanted on warrants. Then they were both taken to jail. Some people just cannot stop for anything.

18. Officer Want A Blow Job?

Another incident that happened in Westport. A large crowd was gathered, it may have been St. Patrick's Day or something special. There were lots of disturbances and fights. One guy in particular had been in a bunch of fights, and he had been running from us. We finally caught up with him, but it took five of us to hold him down so we could get him handcuffed and shackled. I was holding a leg and other officers were holding other body parts. All of the sudden I felt a tugging at my right arm and I looked up to see a beautiful white female in her early twenties. She was tugging at my arm, saying "Officer, Officer." I then explained to her, "I am right in the middle of a disturbance here, where trying to hold this guy down." Then to my surprise she asked, "Officer do you want a blow job?" Of course, I just turned back to what I was doing and she went away. Why would someone say something like this when you are in the middle of a fight? That is just typical of the things' people do in Westport.

19. Breaking in At Liberty Memorial.

When I was first breaking in as a new Police Officer, my break in officer made me drive through the Liberty Memorial Park. At that time, the Liberty Memorial Park was primarily frequented by Homosexuals and was crowded shoulder to shoulder with cars and pedestrians. I was not familiar with this area, but he made me drive through it, (I guess to see how I would react). Inch by inch I drove through the crowd and all of a sudden two males in their twenties jumped in front of the Police car. One of the males jumped up and wrapped his legs around the other one's waist and gave him a long kiss on the lips. I had never seen anything like this before, (I must admit I felt nauseated at the time). My break-in officer just laughed, and told me to calm down. After a few moments, the males moved out of the way and I was able to finally get out of there, it was a very uncomfortable feeling. I have experienced a lot since that time, and I now can treat homosexuals just like everyone else, (as long as they do not touch me).

20. The Scared Christian Devil Worshipper.
Occasionally I work as a Police Officer on off-duty jobs for special events, and in this case, it was at the city auditorium. I had been hired to be responsible for the security of a Christian comedian who years earlier had been a priest or some type of leader in a devil-worshipping community.

The comedian was extremely concerned that the members of the devil-worshipping community were after him because he had left them to become a Christian. He requested that I stand next to him at all times. Inside his dressing room he did not want me to move away from the door that was only a few feet from him. He insisted that I always be within two to three feet from him. He informed me that there had been many instances where these devil worshipers had been after him, and he believed in the supernatural. Well as far as I was concerned when I accepted the job to protect him, I was going to do so to the best of my ability. I walked him to the stage, and I was only a few feet away from him. I kept my eyes on him and the crowd throughout his whole show, and nothing happened. After his show however I walked him to his limousine, and then it was my job to walk in front of his limousine and escort him to the overhead exit door out of the auditorium. When I got to this door, I called on my walkie talkie to the auditorium security booth to request them to push the button to open the overhead door. I called several times and there was no answer. The comedian then called for me to come back to his limousine window to ask me what was going on, because he was becoming very scared. I explained the situation to him and he begged please just do something to get the door open. I tried the walkie talkie again and this time there was an answer, I requested them to open the overhead door. However, the overhead door still did not open, so I called the auditorium security again on my walkie talkie. The auditorium security people said they had pushed the button and the overhead door should have opened. By this time the comedian was convinced that this had something to do with the devil worshippers or supernatural powers, and he started to panic. He yelled, "Open the door! Get the door open now! I've got to get out of here now.!! I explained to him that the door had to be opened by the auditorium security, I had no control over it, and but that they were doing everything they could. I then again explained to the auditorium security the situation I was in and amazingly the overhead door opened and the comedian was out of there like a streak of lighting.

21. Cocaine and Rubber Bullet Burglary.
I was dispatched to a residence up north of the river, where prowlers were reportedly inside the residence. Upon my arrival I was contacted by a 31-year-old white male who had been hiding behind a neighboring house. This male was holding a double-barrel sawed-off shotgun loaded with rubber bullets, which I immediately took from him. This male was extremely excited and apparently high on drugs, however after I got him under calmed down. He told me that someone had broken into his house by using the garage door opener in his car that was parked in his driveway. This male stated that he was upstairs in his residence when he heard voices downstairs. This male stated that he broke out a window upstairs with his shotgun and yelled for someone to call his girlfriend and he yelled out her telephone number. One of

his neighbors had heard him but he did not do anything, so this male ran outside and went over to another neighbor's house where he called his girlfriend. This male then told his girlfriend to bring him another shotgun with more rubber bullets. Upon my first contact with this male I had noticed that this male was not making any since. However, I had one of the assisting officer's watches this male as the other officers and I went to check his residence for prowlers, at his request. I located this male's garage door opener in his car but it did not work on the garage door, so it could not have been used to open the garage door as the male claimed. We then checked this male's residence as he requested, but we found no prowlers in the residence. However, we did find numerous guns and narcotics lying out in plain view. Since these items observed were contraband, we recovered them and we found contraband in almost every room in the house. We found a double barrel shotgun in the living room loaded with 5 rounds of #4 buckshot, 15 other shotgun rounds were found next to it in a jacket pocket.

Lying on a closet shelf inside a closet with the door wide open was an extremely large plastic baggy of white powder that was tested and found, to be almost 99% pure cocaine. In our check of the residence we also discovered a .380 automatic pistol loaded with a full clip, and a live round in the chamber. I also located another .380 automatic pistol, some .44 caliber cartridges and a .44 caliber revolver in a leather shoulder holster. I located another double barrel shotgun, another shotgun, mace, a black electronic shock-type device with nitrogen cartridges, a lot of shotgun shells, as well as rubber bullet shotgun shells, there were numerous rounds of ammunition of all makes and sizes. We located a couple .9mm pistols, handcuffs, an electric stun gun, holsters, a loaded .22 caliber revolver, balance beam scales for weighing drugs, plastic baggies, white powder in small baggies, large jars of blue and yellow tablets, and an aircraft registration in the resident's name. I taught that this was really strange that this resident owned an airplane. Because it showed on a W-2 form that he had lying out, that he had only made $7,000 working part-time in a local tavern, for all of the previous year. This male also had a fully dressed new Harley-Davidson motorcycle in his garage, two freezers, all new high dollar stereo unit and furniture, clothes. This male also had a large room full of marijuana and marijuana plants, black lights for growing plants, numerous large plastic bags of dried marijuana plants. In this residence we also found numerous phone numbers and names of people who owed this man money. We arrested this resident and recovered all the contraband and weapons for his and our safety. It should also be noted that this resident's girlfriend did arrive and in her vehicle was another double-barreled shot gun and rubber bullets, which the resident had requested her to bring. Upon recently checking this males arrest record he does not show an arrest for that date. I do not know if he became a Federal snitch, or what, but this was the largest amount of drugs I have ever recovered.

22 thru 45. DRUNK DRIVER ARRESTS, SHORT STORIES, AND COMMENTS.

Drunk drivers are always a joy. Alcohol has a strange effect on people. You might have to fight a drunk driver at night and then the next day you might find him to be the nicest person in the world, someone you might want to take home to meet your family. Alcohol changes them.

22. This 25-year-old white male driver refused to take a breathalyzer test. He stated that he had only had two drinks earlier. I had followed him to a Quik Trip after noticing him cut another vehicle off in traffic. There was only a white male clerk and a black male in the Quik Trip at the time this male staggered into the store. I waited until this driver came out of the store. When he observed me in the parking lot, he became extremely nervous and instead of going to his car he went straight to the pay telephone outside the Quik Trip. I told him he was, under arrest for driving under the

influence of alcohol or drugs. Which I determined by his breath, his bloodshot eyes, his slurred speech, and his staggering when he walked. I asked him why he was drinking and driving. He stated that he was not driving, then he made the statement, "You must have bad eyesight on you buddy if you say you seen me driving." He said his brother was driving and again said that I must have bad eye sight. He said his brother was in the Quik Trip when I arrested him. I asked this male if his brother was a white male and if he worked at a Quik Trip. This male stated that his brother was a white male but that he did not work at a Quik Trip. There were no white males in the Quik Trip, other than the clerk and a black male. I knew that he was the one driving when I saw him pull up in his car by himself, and go into the Quik Trip.

23. This 21-year-old white female blew a .19 on the breathalyzer. The legal limit for alcohol in Missouri is .10. She had run her new Ford Escort off the road, hit a sign, and overturned her car. She had gotten a bloody nose in the accident, and it was obvious that she was intoxicated, and possibly on drugs. However, she denied that she had been drinking, prior to the alcohol test. One month later, after totaling this car, this same female won a new Chevy Camero, in some type of drawing. I learned this after I stopped her for driving this new car through back roads} where 4-wheel drive vehicles normally frequented. When I stopped her, she had only had this new car about one month, and it was almost totaled. The seats were torn and burned with cigarettes, the dash was broken where someone had stolen the stereo out of it, and it smelled like a brewery. The car had gotten this way because of the back roads she was driving on, her drug use, and the only people she hanged around with were 16-year-old or under, who it was quite obvious that she was buying alcohol for.

24. This 32-year-old white male had been observed by several citizens to be driving recklessly the area. He blew a .16 on the breathalyzer. When I observed him, he was driving at a high rate of speed; he

had cut in front of oncoming traffic causing two other vehicles to run off the road, to keep from being hit by him. When I stopped him, he stated that he had not beam • drinking, however he had the strong odor of liquor on his breath. I asked him the standard questions we have to ask to fill out the paper work for a drunk driver. I asked him if he was ill, He stated, "Yes, I am sick and tired of your questions." I asked him where he had been drinking, He stated, "At a friend's house, but really it's none of your business." All during this time he was using continuous profanity and was being very belligerent. I asked him if he had gotten a bump on his head recently, and he said yes, he had gotten one when I made him get into my police car. It should be noted he never was in my police car. However later he changed his story and said that he had gotten a bump on his head from the paddy wagon door. Towards the end of this interview, when I informed him that I would need to send him to the hospital by ambulance. I told him that he would have to pay for the ambulance, and he would still be charged with drunk driving. He finally, confessed that he really did not get a bump on his head. He then stated that he had said that he did, hoping I would take him to the hospital and he would get out of the drunken driving charges. This is just one example of an incident in which a drunk driver said that he had had nothing to drink and then it was later proven that he had.

25.   This 27-year-old white male refused to take the breathalyzer. I had pulled him over for speeding and careless driving. He had agreed to take the breathalyzer test several times on the street, however when we got to the police station, he said he would only take the test if his lawyer was present. Since this is his right, I told him to call his lawyer, right away and I led him to a telephone. He then stated that it was too early in the morning to call his lawyer, and that he would call him later in the day. The breathalyzer test has to be administered immediately to accurately indicate the amount of alcohol in the system, at the time the person was operating the vehicle. I told him that I could not wait several hours, and he needed to take the test

or call his lawyer then. However, he would not change his mind, even after I informed him that this would be considered a refusal to take the breathalyzer test, and he would lose his driving privileges. It should be noted most lawyers will advise their clients to take the breathalyzer test, because it would be easier to deal with then, a refusal being an automatic loss of driving privileges.

26. This 42-year-old white male blew a .19 on the breathalyzer test. He was stopped after I observed his vehicle pulling out of a parking lot, in the middle of traffic, causing cars to swerve to avoid a collision. His car was straddling the white center line and was all over the road.

    I stopped him and asked him how much he had to drink, after I smelled liquor on his breath. He answered, "Oh, eight to ten beers/' then he shouted, "Christ, I love beer!" I am supposed to note on my reports if the people I stop make any unusual actions or statements. This male made several unusual statements, he said, "I am drunk! I really fucked up! Why don't you just kill me!" I notified this male's wife of his statements and she responded to the police station, where she bailed him out of jail. This male's wife then stated that she was signing him into a treatment center right away; she had had all she could stand.

27. This 22-year-old white male blew a .10 on the breathalyzer, which is the legal limit, however, he was extremely out of it, and had to have been using some type of drugs. He was very belligerent and cocky. His driving had almost caused several accidents, even when I pulled him over; he ran the front tire of his vehicle up onto the curb. I asked him to take a breathalyzer test and he agreed, however when I asked him to blow into the breathalyzer tube, he held his tongue over the hole of the breathalyzer tube. I was not able to get a good sample, but it was still enough to get him convicted of drunk driving. I had asked him when he stopped drinking, and he replied, "After I finished my last beer."

28.   I drove by a bar north of the river and observed this 22-year-old white male being helped to walk, by a 24-year-old white female. I was just curious so I slowed down and sure enough this female escorted this male to the driver's side of a car, and helped him get into the driver's seat. By the time I got turned around, this male was driving up the street in the oncoming traffic lane. It took a while but I got him to pull over when he recognized the red lights in his rearview mirror. He voluntarily took the breathalyzer and he blew a .162. I asked him the standard drunk driving report questions, such as, "Are you ill?" He stated, "Yes, because I cannot post bond." I asked him, "Are you hurt?" He stated, "Yes, my heart is broken." The woman that had helped this male walk and get into the driver's seat of the car showed up at the police station. She wanted to bail this male out; she turned out to be his wife, who also appeared intoxicated. The wife had apparently driven their car to the police station after I took him to jail. I informed her that she was not real smart, and then I had her call someone to come get them.

29.   This 22-year-old white female was observed north of the river driving at a high rate of speed. I paced her with my police car at about 70 mph in a 40-mph zone. She appeared to be intoxicated so I requested that she take a breathalyzer test, which she did and she blew a .167 on the breathalyzer. I informed this female that she would be receiving a driving under the influence and a speeding ticket. Then I asked her how much she had had to drink, she said she had three drinks. All of the sudden this female became rather indifferent in her attitude after she made the above statement. She blurted out, "I don't drink, I wasn't drinking, and I was almost home." I guess at this point she realized that I was not buying any of her excuses. Then she smiled real pretty and said, "Come on officer you are not really going to do this, are you?" But of course, I was, and I did charge her with drunk driving and speeding which she was convicted of. I also explained to her that the area she had

been speeding in was a very heavy traffic area and I was tired of taking accident reports there because of drunk drivers hurting innocent people.

30. This 20-year-old white male north of the river refused to take the breathalyzer test. I had been called to a local drive-in, north of the river, in reference to a man passed out in his locked car blocking the drive-up window. Upon my arrival I observed this male parked right out ide of the drive-in's take out window, with his car radio playing very loud. I beat on his car window for about fifteen minutes, while trying to unlock this car by other means.

When this male finally woke up, he did not open his eyes he just started moving his body in time to the music. After approximately five more minutes the male opened his eyes, seen the police standing there and then he stated "Wow Dude." Then this male just sat there looking at us as if he was only imagining us. I hit his window a couple more times and he rolled the window down, at which time I reached in the window and unlocked the car door, then I pulled him out of the car. When I got him to the police station, I informed him not to drink any water, not to smoke anything, not to chew gum or put anything in his mouth (which is the procedure prior to taking the breathalyzer test). As I was escorting this male to the breathalyzer for the test, we had to pass a drinking fountain, which I was not even thinking about. Immediately this male took a drink of water, before I could stop him. I was going to again have to watch this male for 15 minutes to make sure he did not put anything in his mouth prior to the test, which is also procedure. I had to tell him at least three times that if he puts anything else in his mouth it would be considered a refusal to take the breathalyzer test, which he stated he wanted to take. This male stated that he understood after he had tried to smoke a cigarette and chew gum. This male then asked to use the restroom, and I was thinking now he is finally cooperating and he surely could not get in trouble in there. After he had been in the restroom for a few minutes, I went in to check on him, and there he was drinking from the sink in the bathroom. I considered that a refusal. I asked him why he had gotten so drunk, and he said it was because he kept having bad dreams.

31. This 25-year-old white male blew a .17 on the breathalyzer test. I stopped him after I observed him driving erratically and very fast, he had hit the curb four times. When I got him stopped, he said he had not been drinking for hours. He also said that he was taking medication because he was very sick. I asked him the standard drunk driving form questions, one being do you have diabetes, his answer was he did not know, and that it had not been determined yet. He also stated that he suffers from alcoholism, but that he would beat this drunk driving charge in court because, he had not had anything to drink for hours. He was requested to take a breathalyzer test, which he agreed to, however even after being asked not to smoke or put anything in his mouth several times. I caught him smoking a cigarette, and chewing gum in this jail cell. I then informed him that he had been warned several times and that his smoking and chewing gum would be considered a refusal to take the breathalyzer test. However, I did wait another 15 minutes after taking everything away from him and I gave him the test. When he got the results however, he then started crying and whining, and he stated that he wished he could die.

32. This 25-year-old white male north of the river blew a .13 on the breathalyzer. I observed him carelessly driving at a high rate of speed in a residential area; he was straddling lanes, and not signaling his lane changes or turns. I tried to stop him right away, but he kept going until he got to a residence where he pulled into the driveway and tried to change positions with the passenger. In doing so, he left the car in gear and it started rolling backwards, almost striking my police car, which was parked behind his car. When this was happening, I had already gotten out of my police car, and I was walking up to his vehicle. Luckily the passenger

who was now in the driver's seat, got the car stopped in time. When I questioned the original driver, he told me that he had not been driving but that the passenger had been driving and he was just getting ready to change places with him. The passenger was confronted with this because I just wanted to see what he had to say, but all he did was put his hands up as if he was not going to say anything. I advised the passenger that he made the right decision not lying to me. However, I also let the driver know that I did not appreciate him trying to play me for a fool.

33. This 20-year-old white male north of the river blew a .14 on the breathalyzer. I had been dispatched on a suspicious party call. Upon my arrival at this location I observed a pickup truck with the engine running and the transmission in reverse, 25 feet off the road in a ditch. The driver was lying across the front seat with his head on a pillow and his foot on the brake. Several attempts to wake him up were unsuccessful, even with ammonia capsules placed under his nose. Eventually I was able to wake him up; I believe he was under the influence of both drugs and alcohol. I asked him if he remembered how he got in this ditch, and he stated that he did not. I asked him why he had not turned the engine off or taken the transmission out of gear, and he stated he did not know. I also asked him if this happens frequently, and if that was why he carries a pillow, he did not like that question at all. I asked him how much he had to drink, and he stated about ten drinks. This male also stated that I should not worry about how much he had to drink, because I was in trouble and his father was going to hear about this. I then asked him who his father was and he stated that his father was an Air Traffic Controller at the Kansas City International Airport. I have to tell you I was really scared, I think I am still shaking in my boots after that one.

34. When I observed this 24-year-old white male north of the river he was in a bar parking lot getting out of the truck. He had been a passenger in the truck and now he was changing places with the

driver. I observed the truck pull out of the bar parking lot and into traffic at a high rate of speed as if he did not even look to see if anyone was coming. This caused traffic in both directions to swerve over to the side of the rode to avoid and accident. I stopped this male, who was obviously intoxicated and I had him transported to the police station where I questioned him. This male stated that he did not even remember driving, stopping, or anything. This male stated that the last thing he remembers was that he and the passenger had four or five drinks at the bar and then stopped to get something to eat at a restaurant. This male blew a .20 on the breathalyzer. When I asked him if he was operating a motor vehicle he stated, "If you say I was, I guess I was. " He was very cooperative, I really believe he could not remember if he was driving or not. I also asked the original driver why he let this male drive and he stated that it was because he already had too many drunken driving charges pending, and his friend had a clean record. I then informed this male that he was a real winner, and I sure would not want him to be my friend.

35. This 19-year-old white female north of the river went through a stop sign and into traffic without even slowing down. I attempted to pull her over, however I had to follow her for two more blocks, with my red lights and siren on before she would stop. When she finally stopped, it was also obvious that she was intoxicated, by her slurred speech, blood shot eyes, and the smell of liquor on her breath. I requested that she take a breathalyzer test and she agreed at which time she was escorted to the police station. The breathalyzer test showed her to have an alcohol level of .19. She stated that she had been going to her grandmother's house. I asked her if she had been drinking and where and she stated, "I just was, that's all I can tell you." She then stated that I would not see her anymore. I told her this is great you learned your lesson and she would not drink and drive any more, (but boy was I wrong). This female then stated that I would not see her anymore because she was going to commit suicide because of this. However, it should

be noted, that she had controlled her suicidal tendencies for at least another couple of months. Because I saw her in the police station when another police officer arrested her for drinking and driving.

36. I observed this vehicle leaving a Quik Trip north of the river. This vehicle was being operated at night with no headlights on. The vehicle was only going about 20 miles per hour, but it was all over the road. The driver was a middle-aged white male.

I attempted to stop this vehicle using my red lights and siren; however, he refused to stop for about five more blocks. Then he only stopped for a stop sign. It was as he did not even realize I was behind him, so I jumped out of my police car and I ran up to his vehicle. I opened his driver's door and pulled his emergency brake on. I then turned his vehicle's engine off and pulled him out of the car. He had during this five-block refusal to stop, pulled in front of a vehicle causing it to come to a complete stop. When he was crossing a bridge, he had swerved and caused yet another vehicle to swerve to avoid being stuck by his vehicle. Although this male did blow his breath sample toward the breathalyzer tube from three inches away, it registered an alcohol level of.24 on the breathalyzer. This male became very belligerent at the police station and he wanted to fight, so he had to be restrained. At one point during this time this male looked up at me and said, "Do you want to die, I have a surprise for you." Then for some unknown reason he started to repeat this while looking at me, "Are you all right, are you all right," he said this over and over about a hundred times. I guess it must have gone over my head because I could not figure out what he meant by this, but I know that I really did not care either. This male continued to be very violent he kept trying to kick and hit me and other police officers. Finally, we had to even more securely restrain him and take him to police headquarters. Then as I understand it, he won himself a trip to the mental health hospital from there.

37. I observed a vehicle crossing the center line several times up north of the river, and I noticed that the windows were all iced up on the vehicle. I do not know how the driver could even see outside. When I got the car stopped, after I had followed it for six blocks with my red lights and siren going a 23-year-old fairly attractive white female got out of the vehicle. I requested that this female have a seat in my patrol car because it was obvious that she was quite intoxicated. I asked this female for her driver's license and she stated that she had left it at home. She told me her name, but it was later determined to be a false name, which she gave because she had several drunken driving related warrants out for her at that time. She was given the breathalyzer test and her alcohol level was .12. She realized at this time that I had figured out who she really was by her social security number, and she knew she was in big trouble now. She then started crying, and said officer can I talk to you in private. This is where the big red flag pops up in an officer's head, and they want as many witnesses around as possible, to keep them from being sued or losing their job. I informed her that our business would need to be conducted in the presence of all the other officers, who were also working their arrests. She then looked around, then leaned over and whispered in what I will admit was a very sexy voice, "Officer is there anything I can do for you, to get me out of this mess." I do not know if that would have been considered attempted bribery or not, but I knew it meant real trouble. I acted as if she had not said anything and I continued with my arrest proceedings, which really pissed her off.

38. I was dispatched to a gas station up north of the river on a 27-year-old intoxicated white male wanting to pump gas into his vehicle. However, the gas station attendant felt that this male appeared so intoxicated that the attendant refused to turn the gas pump on for him and the attendant then called the police. By the time I arrived at the gas station the male was driving his vehicle out of the gas station. I contacted the attendant and he pointed this male's vehicle out and I started to try to catch up with this vehicle

when he quickly accelerated squealing his tires. This male's vehicle then hit the front bumper against the curb at which time I turned my police cars red lights and siren on however he refused to stop. This male then zig zagged his vehicle through traffic trying to get away from me. When this male finally decided to pull over, he was requested to take a breathalyzer test in which he blew a .18.

This male also made several statements to me including that he had nerve problems. This male stated, you cops, judges and lawyers all get a percentage of these drunk driving arrests, and you are all on the take. I asked this male the year and make of the vehicle he was driving. He stated that he did not even remember if he was driving his car or his truck. He really did not remember.

39. I was dispatched to a disturbance north of the river where a 23-year-old white male had been involved in a disturbance at one of the local bars. The bartender had refused to serve him and had informed this male to leave because he had been fighting with a girl in the bar. Apparently, this male's vehicle had hit something in the parking lot as he was leaving, because there were small trees stuck in the front grill of his pickup truck. Upon my arrival I was informed by the dispatcher that the bartender had called her back and he stated that this male was now driving his pick-up truck out of there parking lot. I observed a pick-up truck pulling out of the bar parking lot at that time that matched the description of the pick-up truck the bartender said this male was driving. This male drove his pick-up truck right down the middle of the road straddling the white line. I turned my police vehicles red lights and siren on and then tried to stop him. This male drove for about a block and a half, and then he just stopped in the middle of the road. He then got out of his pick-up truck and started walking back toward my police vehicle. As this male was walking towards my police vehicle however, his pick-up truck started rolling backwards he had left it out of gear. I had to yell at him at which time ran back and got his pickup truck stopped

before it hit my police vehicle. This male only blew a .11 however he appeared to be very high on drugs. I asked this male several questions and he answered very angrily, he stated that he had only had three beers, later he said four and then he went back to three. This male stated that he was an FBI informant and that this drunk driving charge did not mean anything, I was wasting both of our times. I guess he thought that if he was an FBI informant that he could get away with anything. He was wrong and he was charged and convicted.

40. I was patrolling my area up north of the river. I observed a 32-year-old white female hit a 12" curb as she tried to go around a corner on her Harley Davidson motorcycle. This female went flying off the motorcycle as it spun in circles on the asphalt. I immediately ordered an ambulance however this female had only received abrasions all over because she was wearing all leather. This female appeared intoxicated and she was extremely belligerent. I asked this female to take a breathalyzer test however be restrained and taken to the police station. This female refused to take the breathalyzer, she refused to answer any of my questions and she stated that she wanted to contact her psychiatrist before she answered any questions. This female stated that she was not going to talk to anybody or say another word, until her psychiatrist arrived. I asked this female if she meant her lawyer and she stated no my psychiatrist. She refused and she just tried to walk right past me while stating "I'm going home." This female was not asked any more questions, just charged with drunk and careless driving.

41. I observed a middle-aged white male up north of the river pulling out of a parking lot. He was quickly accelerating and squealing his tires, until he observed me at which time he slowed down. I followed this white male for a few minutes just to see how he was driving, and if he might be intoxicated. When he observed that I was following him he must of became scared because he all of the sudden accelerated faster as if to elude me. I turned my police cars

red lights and siren on and this male finally did pull over about 4-1/2 blocks later. This male then quickly got out of his vehicle and started to run off, but he was apprehended immediately by myself. I could immediately tell that this male was intoxicated so I requested that he take a breathalyzer test. This male blew a .17 on the breathalyzer.

When he was asked questions for my reports at the police station he stated, "You don't know who I am, I personally know the prosecutor." Then he stated that he had had 6 DUTs, and he knew what he was doing. He stated, "I'll also get out of this one and I'll sue you." This male was charged with careless and drunk driving as well as failure to stop for a police officer.

42.   A middle-aged white male north of the river was observed driving erratically and at a high rate of speed, and with only one headlight operating on his vehicle. This male was observed driving this way behind some closed businesses I had been checking at which time. I tried to stop this male by turning on my red lights and siren. He did not stop until he tried to get out from behind the buildings. There was a car blocking the other end of the driveway blocking him in. This male was also obviously intoxicated. He stated to me that he had already lost his driver's license, and that he did not need to go through this again. This male was requested to take a breathalyzer test and he blew a .17 on the breathalyzer. This male stated that he had lost his driver's license for a prior DUI, and he really did not need to take this test. I then asked the male to sign his name on the Miranda waiver stating that I had read him his rights, which he did but he signed it fuck you.

43.   I observed this middle-aged white male north of the river as he was getting into a vehicle. It was obvious he was quite intoxicated, he could barely walk. I pulled up next to this male's vehicle and I asked him not to drive but to get some friends to take him home or something. This was a business area where there were plenty of

telephones and people. I observed this male get out of his vehicle and walk to a pay telephone, so I drove off after he thanked me. However about 10 minutes later as I was driving at another location, I observed this same male driving his vehicle in the oncoming traffic lane. I immediately stopped this male and took him to the police station where he blew .18 on the breathalyzer test. During the questioning of this male, he all of the sudden just stopped talking and he stated that, "This is a bunch of bullshit." This male was very cooperative, then very uncooperative. Then he was belligerent, and then he was apologetic. The man appeared to be extremely intoxicated.

44. This 33-year-old white male north of the river only blew a .076 on the breathalyzer however he appeared to be extremely intoxicated or high on drugs. I first observed this male driving his vehicle down the middle of the street causing me to swerve to the side of the street to keep his oncoming vehicle from striking my police car. By the time I was turned around this male must not have seen me because he was now parking his vehicle in the middle of the street blocking both lanes of traffic. This male then got out of his vehicle with a screwdriver in his hand and he went into the parking lot of a used car dealership. I stopped this male right away before he could do anything. I asked this male what he was doing and he said he was car shopping. I asked this male why he parked his vehicle in the middle of the street and he stated someone else was driving, "There was no one else in the car." I patted this male down for weapons and I found some marijuana and possibly hash in this male's coat pocket. The male then immediately stated that those were not his drugs in the car or in his coat pocket. I thought that this was very nice of him to tell me he had drugs also in his vehicle that also did not belong to him. When this male realized what he had said he refused to answer any more questions. This male was extremely intoxicated or high on drugs. In his vehicle I found several speakers, a lot of knobs to radios, zigzag papers, a 4-10 shotgun, a zap gun, and a bag of marijuana. This male was

quite obviously there to steal car radios. His only problem was that he was so messed up, that he parked in the middle of the street.

45. I stopped a middle-aged white male bar owner from north of the river. He was stopped because he pulled out in front of myself and another vehicle at a very high rate of speed. When I stopped this male and questioned him about why he did this, he stated that he was very proud of this. I asked him how much he had to drink and he said a bunch of shots. He refused to take a breathalyzer or answer any other questions other than he said that he was at another bar drinking and he deserved to get drunk sometimes. He stated that he thought this whole thing was funny, he stated," you can't do anything to me; I'm not going to jail, or anywhere but home. " Then he urinated in his pants, and just smiled. He then stated, "I am drunk and I deserve it sometimes." I informed this male that if he did not take a breathalyzer test, he would automatically lose his driver's license. This male then became very belligerent and stated," I don't need a driver's license, arrest me, I'll ride my bicycle to work from now on." This male also was trying to threaten me, I guess. When I was finished with him, and I started to leave he made this statement to me, "I will be waiting for you at my bar tomorrow night. "I always thought it was quite interesting the things these intoxicated drivers will say. A lot of them say the same things over and over you just hear it from all of them. For instance, you cannot do this; you did not read me my rights. Here's my driver's license, with usually $20 or $100 attached to it. What can I do to get out of this? I only had one beer. Why aren't you at the donut shop, why aren't you out catching murderers or robbers and stuff, instead of messing with people like me.

46. The Stalking Brownie Burglar.
As a Burglary Detective I investigated a burglary up north of the river. This burglary involved a 57-year-old white male and an attractive 36-year-old white female. They had broken off their relationship approximately one month earlier because the male

was an excessively jealous person. The female just wanted the male out of her life. The male however could not accept this and he had been stalking her since that time. This male had been hanging around her house and work, calling her at all times of the day and night. There were signs that the male had been waiting outside her house. There were cigarette butts by the comer of her house, as if he had been standing there, watching her movements. This male even painted a heart on the female's driveway, on the day of this burglary. On the day of the burglary this male had come to this female's front door with some brownies he said he had made for the female's kids. This female had no idea the male was coming over but she wanted to get rid of him. The female told the male that she was getting ready to take her two boys out of town and that he would have to leave. After the male left the female put her car in the garage so that if the male would return, he would think that she left. However about one hour later while the female was upstairs taking a shower and her boys were downstairs watching television, this female heard a noise at her front door. The female then started down the stairs towards the front door thinking that her boys had locked themselves outside. However, all of the sudden she heard a loud popping sound and the front door came open forcefully and this same male walked in. When this male observed the female standing on the stairs he was in shock. The female asked the male what he thought he was doing and the male stated, "I came back to get my brownies." The female then told the male to take his brownies and leave. The male would not leave however he just asked the female why she was hiding from him, and why did she say she was leaving town. The male then stated, "I love you, I want you back." The female then stated to the male," please leave, get out of my house right now." The female also noticed in this male's hand he was holding an 8" tool of some type, a pry tool which he had forced the door open with. The male had then left the scene when the victim reported this to me. However, I was able to get a warrant for this male's arrest and the victim was able to get a restraining order against the suspect.

This male still repeatedly called the victim after this trying to get her to drop the charges. This male never did get the message that the female did not want anything to do with him. This case was settled out of court where the male agreed not to bother the female anymore and she dropped charges. The female stated that she did not want to see this male go to jail; she just wanted him to leave her alone. This however only lasted a couple of months, the female had moved to a surrounding city and the male is now stalking the female there as well as trying to intimidate her neighbors.

47.   Have You Seen A Car Prowler, Oh"' It's You.
I was dispatched on a car prowler north of the river. As I was driving down the street a couple of blocks from where the car prowler was supposed to be, when I noticed a 17-year-old white male underneath a pickup truck working. I could see this male underneath the rear end of the pickup truck turning a wrench on the wheel nuts of the underneath spare tire.

I did not really think much about it at the time. I checked the area and I could not find any car prowlers. Then I stopped to ask a male working under a pickup truck if he had seen anybody prowling cars or anything. This male stated just a minute, and then he came out from underneath the pickup truck. When he saw my uniform, he just threw his wrenches down, and he took off running. Well, I guess I felt pretty dumb right then, but I had found my car prowler. The foot chase was on this male was taking wrenches from his pockets and throwing them back at me as he ran. I pulled my gun out at that time and I ordered the male to stop. This male did not stop and I had to chase him for 2 blocks then he all of the sudden he stopped turned around and tries grabbing for my gun. I did not have time to put my gun in my holster. I was not going to fight him with the gun in my hand, so I threw my gun to the side, and I tackled the male. I got the male easily into handcuffs after we wrestled for a few moments. However, when I picked this male up off the ground, I noticed that my gun was laying on the ground underneath where this male had ended up lying. It was not a real good move on my part but it kept the gun out of his hand for the time being. It turned out that the male had been trying to take the spare tire off this pickup truck. He had removed the lug nuts on some of the pickups' wheels and he had tried to get several other parts off the pickup truck.

48. Drunk Driver Pinned In Car Wreck, Not Even Scratched.

I was dispatched to a traffic accident in the North East part of town. Upon my arrival I observed a very small foreign car that had the type of seats that you had to pull the whole seat forward to get into the back seat. This accident involved this small car striking another car and then striking a light pole. The front end of this small car was crushed; the other larger car that the little car struck was barely damaged. No one was injured in the larger car, so I went to check the driver of the small car. The driver of this small car was a 42-year-old extremely intoxicated white male. This male was pinned in his car; the back of the driver's seat had come forward during the accident. There had been a case of oil behind the driver's seat which had slid underneath the driver's seat, pushing it forward pinning him. This case of oil was holding the driver's seat forward, which was pinning the driver up against the dash the windshield and the steering wheel. The male was pinned in his car and he was screaming that he was hurt. I had to order the fire department to cut this male out of his car. The fire department personnel had to cut the metal away from the center driver's side of the car to get to this case of oil. When we got this male out of his car he stopped screaming and he started to walk away.

I stopped this male and I asked him if he was all right, and he stated that there was nothing wrong with him he was going home. This small car was crushed; there was almost no way a person could live through that unless they were drunk. He was not even scratched, but he was taken to the hospital to be checked out. He was arrested for drunk and careless driving.

49. (She Was an 11), and She Wore A See-through Dress in Court.
I stopped an intoxicated 23-year-old white female in the Plaza area. She did not look like much that night; she was wearing dirty and raggedy clothes. I stopped this female because she was driving very fast and carelessly in a little Volkswagen and she was driving all over the road. When I stopped this female, she was very belligerent, and she stated that she had not driven a vehicle with a clutch for a long time and that was why her driving was so bad. It was quite obvious that she was intoxicated by her slurred speech, staggering and the smell of liquor on her breath. I requested that she take a breathalyzer test but she refused. I advised her that she would automatically lose her drivers' license for refusing to take this test but she did not care. I wrote her tickets for drunk and careless driving. She was convicted in city court for drunk and careless driving and the state had temporally revoked her driver's license. However, when it came time to go to state court, to determine whether she would get her driver's license back. It was a real warm sunny afternoon, and this female walks into the court house wearing a white see through cotton dress with no bra. She also had just some light-colored bikini panties under it, she was an 11. She looked so gorgeous that the prosecutor came up to me and said, "You know we can't do this. He said that there was no way we could take her in front of this male judge looking like this and ask him to take her driver's license away from her." Then the prosecutor stated, "This is one we should probably let go" and he did.

50. Her Bloody Dress, His Bloody Face, Her Time of the Month.
I stopped this white male and a white female in their late 40's, because the female was driving at a very high rate of speed and all over the road. It appeared as if they were making out or something while she was driving. The female was driving and the male was sitting in the in the middle of the front seat. I pulled them over and when they stopped the female driver immediately got out of her car and started walking back towards my police car. This female

was wearing a real long white cotton dress. I immediately noticed that she had one of her panty hose legs on and one off, hanging down between her legs. I asked this female to return to her vehicle while I did a record check on her, when she turned around the whole back of her white dress was all bloody. Well I thought that she must have gotten carried away and forgot that it was her time of the month. When the female returned to her vehicle the male passenger got out and started walking back towards my police car. This male had red all over his face that looked like blood and I think I figured it out at that time. They were having a little bit of oral sex and I don't think he realized it was that time of the month for her. It was a pretty gross situation, it was so bad that she only lived a couple blocks away so I made her park her vehicle there and walk to her home, because I wasn't going to deal with this.

51. He Ran Because He Didn't Have His Driver's License, But I Wasn't After Him.
I was dispatched on a code 1 emergency call involving a car accident one night which happened on the border of Kansas City and Independence.

As I was crossing the bridge on Truman road with my red lights and siren on a pickup truck which I was getting ready to pass all of the sudden pulled in front of me and slowed way down. It was a two-lane bridge and so I went over to the right lane because I wasn't sure what he was doing but I had to get to this accident to check for injuries. I again attempted to pass this pickup truck but he again pulled in front of my police car like he didn't want to let me get bye him. The dispatcher just then advised me that Independence Police officers where at the scene and I could slow down. Because the Independence Police were at the accident scene already, I went ahead and tried pulling this pickup truck over. The pickup truck would not stop but as we drove right past this accident where the Independence Police were this guy in the pickup truck swerved and almost hit an Independence Police Officer. The Independence

Police Officer had to jump up on the trunk of his police vehicle to keep from being struck. I had advised the dispatcher of what was going on and she had another car assist the ambulance at the scene of the accident. The accident consisted of two cars that struck each other and one of the drivers was severely hurt. Several Independence Officers joined the chase, there was about six police cars following this pickup truck into Independence. This pickup truck started taking side roads then all of the sudden it pulls into a yard and 17-year-old white male jumps out of the pickup truck and runs for the front door of the house. Independence Police Officer however drove his police car right across the yard and cut this male off at his front porch. The Independence Officer then gets out of his police car and grabs the male by his long hair and jerked the male backwards but then he continued running. This Independence Officer had a whole hand full of hair which was no longer in this males' head. Another officer then tackled this male and we were able to get him under control. I then asked this male why he pulled in front of me when I was on an emergency call and why he ran from us, he stated, "oh, my uncle lives here and he doesn't have a telephone, I didn't have my driver's license with me and I thought you were going to arrest me so I wanted to make sure my uncle knew where I was at so he could post my bond". This male was charged with careless driving and trying to elude the police. I believe this male's biggest problem was that he was paranoid from smoking marijuana.

52. Sex in the Park Elephant.
We were having a lot of problems in a park north of the river. There is a cement elephant in this park and we were always getting complaints from parents of kids who were up there on the elephant playing. Because these kids were finding underwear, used condoms and sticky stuff all over up there. Apparently at night this is a location where parkers go to have sex. The elephant has a large seat on top of it where it is fairly secluded. We started checking the park each night because all city parks are supposed

to be closed at 10 p.m. One-night officers were dispatched to this park on a disturbance in the park. Upon their arrival they observed a 22-year-old white nude female in this elephant seat trying to cover her up. This female was extremely unattractive; she stated she had gone to the park elephant to have sex with an unknown 25-year-old white male whom she met at a bar. The female stated that when she took off her clothes and performed oral sex on the male, he grabbed her clothes and purse and left her stranded there. I do not know what is so attractive about this park elephant for sex. They also use the concrete penguin in this same park for a restroom. These things make it really unattractive for kids who want to play in that park. We were eventually able to identify the male who did this, and the female got her clothes and purse back. The male was charged with stealing. This male stated the most embarrassing thing about being caught was that she was so ugly.

53. Look What I See, a Venus Flytrap.
I was checking a Northland bar one early morning and it was just after daybreak when I observed four male juveniles probably around 10 years old. These juveniles were in this bar parking lot looking into the driver's side window of a vehicle parked there. I could see that there was a pair of bare feet sticking out of the open driver's side window of this vehicle. These juveniles would look in this car window and start laughing and then run back away from the window then back up to it again. I was very curious what these juveniles were not only doing up this early but what they were looking at that was so funny. As I drove over to check these juveniles, they took off running. I looked in the same car window the juveniles had been looking in. I observed an approximately 30-year-old white nude male sitting in the passenger seat asleep. There was also a heavy-set white nude female in her early thirties lying on his lap asleep. She had her feet hanging out the window, and she was lying face up. This female was nude, and her legs were spread apart. This was a really gross sight, because it looked like when this female would take a breath her vagina breathed right

along with her. Her vagina looked like it could be a Venus flytrap. It looked as if you could touch it with a nightstick or something and it would *guck it right in there, arm and all. It was a really scary sight; it was so scary not even bother to wake them up. I did not want anything to do with this one; however, I did hit my siren a couple of times before I pulled away.

54. **$200 Dollars A Night, And She Comes With Batteries.**
I stopped a 24-year-old attractive white female for speeding and driving all over the road one early morning on the west side of the city. The first thing she asked me when I approached her vehicle was, if I knew this police officer and that police sergeant. All these people, in different area Police Departments, as well as the Kansas City Missouri Police Department. This female stated that she was dating a couple of them. I normally take into consideration, however things changed. This female then told me where she had been all night. She stated that she had been drinking at a private hot tub party with a rich male over in Kansas and she was getting $200 a night to do this. She stated that she had warrants out for her arrest because she had written some bad checks and I told her she needed to go to the police station with me. She asked me if I would call her police sergeant friend from another police department, but I told her she could call him herself at the police station. I noticed on the back seat of this female's car she had a large sack of different sized new batteries. I asked this female what she used all the batteries for, she very proudly stated," Oh, vibrators and toys and stuff, $200 a night I charge these guys to spend the night with them." This female then stated that the man she had just been with was a very high official some place in Kansas and she had just spent hours with him in his hot tub. This female did not appear to be intoxicated, so I did not request that she take a breathalyzer test. I did write her tickets for speeding and careless driving. She had a state warrant for fraud checks, so she was turned over to the county jail. I really have problems with name droppers, if you do someone a favor once they think you are there best friend

and will help them out of anything, so they always mention your name. I think that is what this female thought she was doing by mentioning all the names she was naming. Stating that she was with a high official from Kansas, she thought she would get out of going to jail.

55. I Went To The Halloween Party As One Of The Three Little Pigs.
I was working off-duty at a Halloween party one night for a large company downtown that was putting this party on for their employees. All night long people kept coming up and asking the three of us police officers working the party what our costume was, or they said they liked our costume or whatever, we were in uniform. After a while of this, I became tired of it because most of the people saying this were intoxicated and they thought it was more humorous than it really was. So, after a while when they asked me, I said I was there as one of the three little pigs and they got quite a kick out of that. It went on throughout the night, "The three little Pigs."

56. The Watch Dogs Ate The Cigarettes Not The Burglars.
One of the first burglaries I worked as a detective was in the northeast area of town. I was out driving between some interviews when I heard Police Officers being dispatched on a burglary in progress two blocks away from where I was at. When I arrived at the scene, my plan was to just watch to see if I saw anything suspicious, until the dispatched officers got there. However, as I pulled up one block away, I observed three white male juveniles running out the back door of this residence. There were three Doberman Pinchers in the back yard of this residence. The Doberman pinchers were not bothering the boys at all. These boys were dropping cartons of cigarettes as they ran out of the back door of this residence. These boys had taken six cartons of cigarettes from the residence, but instead of biting the boys the Dobermans were chewing the dropped cigarettes up. These boys went over the rear fence an into some woods, they did not even know that I had observed them. I

informed the officers coming of this and we surrounded the area. We did catch a couple of the boys right away. We had several long foot chases with the third one who knew the woods better than we did. However, I was finally able to catch this third juvenile by hiding by his house after the other officers left the area. Eventually this juvenile came walking out of the woods thinking he was home free, boy! Was he surprised? These boys had committed (4) burglaries that day. When they were convicted in juvenile court they were given (7) years for each burglary a total of 28 years. This was busted down to them only being charged with one burglary which meant they only had to serve 7 years each. It turned out that only one of the boys had to serve that sentence because he was sixteen and certified as an adult, the other two boys were fourteen and fifteen. I know the sixteen-year-old was out of jail before he turned seventeen (less than one year). He was the only one that had denied being involved in these burglaries; when I saw him do one with my own eyes. I believe the other two juveniles were sent to juvenile homes, where they had to spend a couple of years. Their confessions to the burglaries helped me solve several more we did not even know about, as well as getting people's belongings back. I do not believe this sentence helped this sixteen-year-old at all because I have heard his name many times since as being involved in some kind of thefts. I have not heard the other juvenile's names since that time. I think a lot of this sixteen-year-olds problem was, was that he was very proud of his father who had and has since served time in prison for burglary.

57. Here Come Da Pigs.

It's always interesting to go in to the city housing projects. The drug dealers usually have control of them. The people that are living in the projects that have to live there, but do not mess with drugs have to almost stay in their homes like prisoners.

If you do use or sell drugs, its survival of the fittest. The drug dealers have so much control over these places, that it's cool for the children to help the drug dealers not the police. These projects also have a great communication system. Because there is really nothing to do in the projects. Most of the people just sit around on their porches or inside their apartments looking out the windows. They are watching to see if anything is going to happen. Which it usually does when they become bored, someone will get drunk and beat up their wife, girlfriend or someone. Or there will be a shooting, stabbing etc... This is the only entertainment they have. Since everyone is always looking outside when one person sees the police coming, they will yell, "Pigs, " here come Da pigs. Then pretty soon you hear somebody else yell here come Da pigs and then everybody starts yelling Pigs. The whole housing project knows we are coming so there is no such thing as a surprise. This gives the drug dealer's time to hide their drugs and everyone else time to clean up their act, as well as the people with warrant's time to run. I wish we had that kind of communication in our police department.

58. His Gold Tooth Made Him Do It.

I was working the inner city one night when a 24-year-old black male came into the police station and asked to talk to a detective. Since I was the only Detective working that night, the desk clerk sent him to lucky me. This male informed me that he was involved in gang activity, he had aids, he did robberies, burglaries, stolen cars and he murdered people all because of a gold teardrop he had on his front tooth. This male stated that he was forced to be a member of the Crips and the Bloods gangs, and they forced him to be a male prostitute. The gang leaders made him do these things, or they would make him kill his own girlfriend. This male continued to talk and say things that made no since at all. During this time this male seemed to be having mood swings, he would be very violent and then very nice. I asked this male if he thought that he was a danger to himself and others, and he stated, yes. Some of the information this male had given me I felt was very legitimate. This male also admitted that he was currently on and was addicted to water (PCP), as well as he sold it. This male was taken to the Mental Health Center, where he agreed to be taken. Believe it or not a lot of good information on one gang was obtained from this male. I have experienced that on several occasions' people on drugs for some reason come to the police to tell on themselves. It must be an unconscious request for help, which I try to see that they get.

59. Ok, You Got Me To Bend over, But Why Scratch Up MY $300 Dollar Cowboy Boots.

I had an incident on the Plaza one night where I had arrested a 41-year-old nicely dressed white male drunk driver that was 7' something tall. This male would not cooperate with me when I tried to pull him over with my red lights and siren. When he did finally pull over, I requested that he go to the police station with me to take a breathalyzer test. I also informed this male that I did feel he was intoxicated because he was driving carelessly all over the road. I opened this male's car door and requested that he get out of his vehicle and come with me to the police station. This male refused to get out of his vehicle so I reached in the open driver's side window and pulled his ignition keys out, which he tried unsuccessfully to stop me from doing. This male then tried to close his car door and roll up his window. The patty wagon driver showed up about the time that I was trying to hold this car door open so that this male could not lock himself in. With the patty wagon drivers help I finally did get this male out of his vehicle. I then requested that this male try to walk a straight line, which he refused to do. So, I asked him to say his ABC's and he also refused to do that, he wouldn't cooperate at all.

I then informed this male that I was going to have the patty wagon driver take him to the police station for a breathalyzer test. This male then stated, that he wasn't going anywhere with us, and he sure was not going to take a breathalyzer test. This male then tried to walk away; at which time I grabbed his arm and he swung his fist at me. He was so intoxicated that he missed me; however, I had

had all I was going to take from this guy. The patty wagon driver and I then tackled this male and put handcuffs on his wrists and shackles on his feet, because he kept trying to kick us. The next problem we encountered was that this male refused to get in the patty wagon; he was so tall we couldn't get him to bend over.

I asked this male several times to cooperate with us or he would get hurt, but he just laughed. The patty wagon driver must have experienced this before because he knew just what to do. The patty wagon driver all of the sudden punched this male right below the belt, which quickly bent him over. We then shoved him in the patty wagon and took him to Police Headquarters. Later on, one of the headquarters detention officers advised me that this male had on brand new $300 cowboy boots, and that he was pretty upset because our shackles had scratched them up. This was his only complaint, he was charged with drunk driving, careless driving and resisting arrest.

60. These Clothes are not clean; I'm going to Kill You.

I was dispatched to a disturbance one night in the inner city. Upon my arrival I observed a 27-year-old black male a 24-year-old black female arguing loudly in the middle of the street. This female was holding an attack dog by a leash, it was growling and barking it was very apparent that it wanted to bite this black male. This male had a knife in his hand as he was confronting this female. I asked the male to drop the knife, and then I asked the female to lock her dog up. In doing this I was able to get the two of them separated so I could calmly talk to them and find out what was wrong. It turned out that these two were husband and wife. The husband had given his wife $2.65 to go to the laundry mat and wash his blue jeans. This male stated that when his wife came home from where ever, with his jeans they were not clean. The male wanted his wife to tell him what she did with the money he gave her. This male stated that he asked his wife if she spent this money on drinking, a boyfriend or what she had spent the $2.65 on. This male stated that his jeans were not clean and he knew when a pair of jeans were clean, because he had spent (6) years working in a prison laundry, and he knew when something was clean. This male stated that he was going to kill her because of this, and if she wouldn't have had that dog he would have. When I asked the female her side of the story, she stated that she did wash her husband's jeans; she had nothing else she could use $2.65 for. This female stated that she had apparently stayed there at the laundry mat and talked to long to one of her friends, and that was her husband's real problem. This female further stated that if she hadn't had her dog, she felt that her husband would have tried to kill her. I guess you should know when things are clean when you've been working in a prison laundry that long. This male and female both appeared to have had too much to drink, so I requested that one of this male's friends let the male stay at his house overnight, or until this male calmed down.

61. The Smiling Grabber, Your Name is Karen Isn't It.
This is a story I thought was quite humorous. A friend of mine (a.k.a.: Cheeseburger) was telling me this story at about 2:00 p.m. on this date. My friend informed me that earlier that day he and another friend (Curtis) had been in his tow truck and they were giving this 20-year-old white female named Karen a ride. Cheeseburger stated that he did not really know Karen but he knew her sister well.

Cheeseburger stated that Karen was going to rent a room in his mother's house. Cheeseburger stated that Curtis was driving his tow truck and Karen was sitting on the seat between them. Cheeseburger stated that they were going down the road, and all the sudden Karen gets a big smile on her face and reaches over and grabs Curtis between the legs. Cheeseburger stated that this surprised both of them, and Curtis was having problems driving. Cheeseburger stated that Curtis asked Karen to stop and let go, however she just kept smiling and squeezing like she didn't understand what he was saying. Curtis finally stopped his tow truck and got out to get her to stop squeezing him. Cheeseburger stated, that Curtis informed Karen that she was not going to be riding with them if she was going to act like this. Cheeseburger stated that Karen immediately calmed down and she was ok again. Cheeseburger stated that everything was fine until later when they were outside in his yard driving a riding lawnmower and Karen wanted to ride it. Cheeseburger let Karen drive the riding lawnmower but after a while she refused to get off of it. When Karen finally stopped and got off of the riding lawnmower, she got a great big smile on her face. Only this time she walked up to Cheeseburger and grabbed him between the legs and won't let go. Cheeseburger stated that again they were shocked at what she was doing and he was going crazy trying to get her away from him. Karen again finally calmed down and she was just fine. When Cheeseburger told me this story, I thought that it was a pretty strange story. Well I thought that this story would have ended there, however about 4:00 a.m. the following morning I was dispatched to a 7-11 Store. This call was to handle a disturbance involving an unknown female getting into and locking herself inside a males pickup truck after he left it running outside this 7-11 store. Upon my arrival this male came out of the store and pointed to a female who was sitting in his pickup truck with the doors locked refusing to let him in. This male stated that he had started to go into the store an as he was doing so this female got out of the passenger side of the car parked next to his pickup truck. This male stated that this female then left her car door open and got into his truck and locked the door. This male stated that he had pleaded with this female to unlock the door and get out of his truck but she wouldn't. I walked over to this male's pickup truck and the female was acting as if she were driving it down the road. I knocked on the driver's door window of this pickup and the female unlocked and opened the door right up. I asked this female what she thought she was doing in this male's truck. This female stated that she was just sitting there listening to the radio. I asked this female to get out of this male's pickup and then I led her to the sidewalk in front of the store. There were about eight people gathered around watching all this happen. When we got up on the sidewalk, I asked this female what her name was and if she had any identification. This female all the sudden smiled this great big smile and grabbed me right between the legs in front of all these people. I pushed her away really quick and I said, your name Karen, isn't it? Sure, enough it was Karen, the female Cheeseburger had told me about. I would have never dreamed this would have happened, what a coincidence. I immediately handcuffed Karen's hands behind her back. As soon as I put the handcuffs on Karen she calmed down and she became the sweetest, nicest girl. I took Karen to The North Kansas City Hospital to have them check on her mental condition, and over there she was just fine. At the hospital we were sitting in the waiting room for about 20 minutes and all this time Karen had been very polite and cooperative as if she didn't understand why she was there. I was kind of feeling sorry for Karen so I took the handcuffs off of her. We were just sitting there waiting for Karen to be seen by a doctor, when Karen slowly reaches down and takes her shoes off, then her socks, which she neatly tucks inside her shoes. This was not a real problem for me however Karen then stood up and pulled her shirt off over her head. I thought to myself, Oh My God Karen please don't do this to me. Then I told Karen to put her clothes back on, I know she was going to take all her clothes off. I had her put her shirt back on and I handcuffed her again.

We were sitting there again for another 20 minutes and Karen's just as cooperative and as sweet as she can be. A nurse finally came into the waiting room and she informed me that I should take the handcuffs off of Karen now. I removed Karen's handcuffs and the nurse leaned over and very gently asked Karen if there was anything she could get her. Karen all the sudden got that great big smile on her face, and before I could warn the nurse, Karen reached out and grabbed the nurse by the breast. This really made this nurse very unhappy, so the handcuffs went back on again.

I was finally able to get Karen evaluated, so I could figure out what to do with her, put her in jail, for not letting the male have his truck or leave her at the hospital). The doctor at the hospital had me take Karen over to the North Kansas City Mental Health Center where he had her admitted. The doctor said that Karen was acting like this because she had not been taking the appropriate amounts of medicines prescribed for his mental illness. The doctor also stated that these actions Karen was carrying out, most likely were the result of childhood sexual abuse. Of course, Karen never rented a room from Cheeseburger's mother.

62. The Burglar, No One Could Find

I had been dispatched on an alarm call at an inner-city automobile upholstery shop one early morning. Upon my arrival there, there was another police officer already there, and she had arrived just seconds after the call came out over the radio. This officer stated that the only thing she had immediately found wrong with this business, was a small hole in a glass window in the garage door. This officer watched this garage door as I checked the rest of the building, even though we did not believe the hole was big enough for anyone to get in through, and that this was most likely a false alarm. I checked the front of the business and upon looking into the office area I could see that the cash register was open and laying on the floor with papers all around it, like it had been knocked off the counter. The officer had arrived at this business almost immediately and I had arrived just moments later. Neither of us seen anyone at or near this business at that time. I could find no point of entry into this business, however the cash register on the floor told a different story. I then had the dispatcher call the owner of this business and ask him to respond to let us inside, so we could also check there, just in case there was someone in there. When the owner arrived, we quickly checked the building and found no one inside. However, the owner stated that the cash register was not on the floor and the garage door window was not broken when he locked the business up. The owner also pointed out that his alarm system consisted of an electronic beam which was about 3 feet inside of the garage door and it led up to the front door. The owner stated that something had to have passed through this beam in order for the alarm to have gone off. I just knew that somebody had to have been in business, but how did they get away without one of us seeing them. Somebody had to have gotten in the business through this small hole in the garage door. I had the dispatcher request the Canine Unit have someone respond to also check the building. The police dog searched this business and found a scent by the broken window but he could not find anyone in the building. I knew somebody had been in this business, but it didn't make sense how they could have gotten out so fast. I decided that I wanted to check this business just one more time. This time however as I was searching, I seen the strangest sight. There was a roll of carpet on a low shelf with a pair of tennis shoes sticking out of it. I then called for the other officers to show them what I had found. I really wanted to have the police dog come back and get this person out of the carpet, however he was already gone. We unrolled this roll of carpet and inside was a 33-year-old Hispanic male that had just gotten out of prison for burglary two weeks earlier. Somehow this male had crawled through that small hole in the window glass and he had somehow rolled himself up in this roll of carpet, and then got it back on this shelf.

This male was skinny and tall but it still seemed impossible. The police dog was not able to get this males scent because of the strong smell of the brand-new carpet. If I wouldn't have luckily seen the bottoms of this male's shoes, he would have gotten away with this burglary, but not this time. I remember this male begging me to please not take him to jail, because he had just gotten out of prison and he wanted to. see his kids some more. This male was returned to prison shortly after this.

63.   Preacher with Holster for Bible in His Pocket.

I was dispatched to an inner-city liquor store one late evening to received information. Upon my arrival the liquor store owner informed me that a black male in his late fifties had been in his liquor store and when this male reached into his pocket to get his money, he had pulled out a small revolver from a holster that was in his front pocket. This business owner observed this without this customer seeing him, and when this guy left the store the owner called the police and wrote the guys license plate number down. I checked with the dispatcher and with the license plate number I was able to obtain the address this license plate was registered to. I then went to this address with an assisting officer. As I was approching this address the vehicle and the male that the store owner had described pulled in the driveway of this residence. However, when this male got out of his vehicle and observed my police car he ran into his residence. I knocked on the front door of this residence several times then after a few moments this same male opened his front door. When this male did finally answer his door, he asked me what was wrong. I asked this male if he would step outside so that I could talk to him, which he did. I informed this male of what the store owner had seen. This male stated, "No, no, I'm a preacher, I don't carry a gun". I then asked this male to let me pat him down for a weapon, which I did, and I found a small holster in his front pocket. I then asked this male why he carried a holster if he didn't carry a gun. This male stated, "oh, I've got a small miniature bible and I carry it in there". Well, there wasn't much I could do about this, but I did warn him not to carry his gun even if he was a preacher.

64. Teacher Needs To Go, well! Why Didn't She say so.?
    I had been sent to run radar in the area of two northland schools, after a speeding teenage boy hit and killed another boy on a bicycle. This neighborhood was up in arms about this and they wanted a lot more police to patrol the speed of the motorist driving up and down this street. I really hate to do traffic enforcement, because I wouldn't-want someone to give me a ticket if I made an

honest mistake, that's why they call accidents, accidents. Since the local citizens requested that I be there, and they wanted me to write tickets that's what I did. I had stopped a 30-year-old white female for going down this street 15 miles per hour, over the posted 25 mph speed limit. I asked this lady for her driver's license, as she was getting it out of her purse, I explained to her that the reason I stopped her. I explained to this female that she was speeding and that we had a child killed at that location by a speeding motorist. After this female angrily handed me her driver's license, I walked back to my police car. I checked this females name through the computer, and she had no record so I wrote her a speeding ticket, then I walked back to her vehicle to get her signature on the ticket. This female signed the ticket then I gave her, her copy at which time she stated, "I hope you're happy". I asked this female what she meant by that statement. This female stated that she was ill and she had diarrhea, and that was the reason she was speeding, she had to go to the restroom. Then this female stated, "I hope you are happy, I went in my pants".

You know, all this female had to say was that she was ill, and I would have told her to slow down, but keep going (some people don't give us a chance to be discretionary}. This female turned out to be a school teacher at one of these local schools and that was where she was trying to get to, to use the restroom. Well, with this female being so smart mouthed, she got her ticket and I guess I was happy.

65. They got more than they wanted When the Woman Turned Out To Be A Man.
There had been. A black 24-year-old homo-sexual male that always hung around the Westport area as a prostitute. This male dressed like a female, he looked like a female, he acted like a female and he had a body. This male even had breasts like a female because he was taking hormone shots; his only problem was that he wasn't genially equipped as a female. He would solicit mostly Johnson

County white males, and he would give them oral sex or he would let them have sex with him in his anus. He would tape his penis to his stomach so that if his customers would put their hand in his crotch area, they would not find anything. Occasionally this male's customer would find out that the was a male and they would not be happy so they would try to beat this male up. This male was also very strong and he had plenty of street fighting experience. On this night I was dispatched to a disturbance in an apartment complex parking lot in the Westport area. Upon my arrival I observed this male's vehicle and this male fighting with three white males. This male was taking on all three males at once, and doing a pretty good job of it. My assisting officer and I got the four of them separated then I asked one of the male customers what was going on, even though I was sure I already knew. This customer stated that the three of them were invited to get oral sex from this female so they went into the parking lot. Apparently one of the male customers had put his hand in the groin area of this male prostitute as this male customer was engaging in anal sex with this male prostitute and as this prostitute was performing oral sex on one of the other males. When this male customer touched this groin area of this male prostitute and found more than he wanted to find, (a penis), the fight was on. Well, this black male was able to take care of himself pretty good however the fight was on when we were called by neighbors by all the noise. All three of these males had had some type of sex with this male prostitute. Another one of these males stated that they had loaned this male prostitute money and they wanted it back. The male prostitute stated that these three men had paid him to have sex with them, (which he did) and now they wanted their money back. As this male prostitute knows I could have arrested him for prostitution at that time, however just like in the majority of these cases, the males are too embarrassed to want to show up in court. The males were embarrassed to admit they had sex with a male, and their parents, wives or girlfriends might find out about this. These males refused to assist in the prosecution of this male prostitute.

This male prostitute was not charged with anything at that time, but he was just asked leave the area. This same male prostitute has since died of aids, and just think of how many people this male had possibly infected.

66. Saved By Observant Ambulance Attendants.
I stopped a drunk 27-year-old white female one night up north of the river. This female was driving at a very high rate of speed, she had no headlights on and she was driving all over the road. This female did not pull over right away, when she finally did pull over, she pulled into the parking lot of a business and parked her car. I asked this female to step out of the car which she refused to do.

I then asked her to roll her window down so that I could talk to her, which she also refused to do. I knocked on the window several times thinking that she was going to drive off again. This female finally did roll the window down but just a little bit. I explained to her that I needed her to get out of the car because I believed she was drunk driving. I had requested an assisting officer however there was no one close. I was finally able to convince this female to come out of the car, and when she opened the car door, I grabbed her and made sure she came out. She came out of the car and I turned her around and put her hands up against the roof of her car. Because this female was acting so strange, I did just a general pat down of her to see if she had any weapons on her. A pat down by a male officer on a female means just their pockets, lower legs, arms, hair and their waist. As I was patting this female down, she pushed back with her hands off of her car and she came backwards into me almost knocking me over. This female then tries to turn around and hit me. When this female did this, I pushed her forward against her car. However, this time I used my body to hold her against the car while I was bringing her arms behind her back so that I could put handcuffs on her. I informed her that she was under arrest at that time. I arranged for a patty wagon to take this female to the police station. This female refused to take a breathalyzer test, however I did write her tickets for drunk and careless driving. This female then made a formal complaint with the desk sergeant against me. Her complaint stated that I pushed my body up against her, (when I pushed her up against her car), like I was trying to have sex with her from the rear. This female stated in her complaint that she only liked women and she didn't appreciate a male doing that to her. In the police department, police officers are guilty until they prove themselves innocent, when a citizen makes a complaint. I believe the reason for this is that the police department would rather pay someone to settle their cases out of court. I really thought my goose was cooked, because it was my word against hers. However, I got lucky, because one of the cities ambulances that serves the northland area, had parked in our police station parking lot to wait for their next call. As I was leaving the police station to get back in service, the ambulance driver called me over and asked me what I had done with this female. I asked him how he knew about this female and he stated that he and his partner were parked across the street at a 7-11 store, and they saw this whole thing. The ambulance driver stated that he saw the female push back against me, then he seen me slam her back up against the car, at which time I handcuffed her then waited until the patty wagon arrived. The ambulance driver stated that they were going to come over and help me but I had handled the situation before they could even get out of the ambulance. I requested that these ambulance attendants tell the desk sergeant about what they had seen, and they did. They informed the desk sergeant that they did not see anything that would lead them to believe what this female said had happened. This case was investigated and I was thankfully found not guilty. All it takes is a word, somebody saying something like this and you are in trouble. Thank God, those ambulance attendants were there.

67. Return Of The Gorilla Balloon, No Questions Asked.

As a Detective in the inner-city area, I was assigned a case of a theft from a haunted house down in the bottoms. On this particular incident one of the haunted houses had a real large gorilla balloon on the roof of their building. One late evening somebody stole this gorilla balloon and I had to go up on the roof to look for evidence. I observed blood where someone had cut themselves, while cutting the metal cables that held the gorilla balloon down. I took samples of this blood but I really didn't have a lot to go on. This gorilla balloon was valued at $5,000 dollars, and it was just a rental. As I was investigating this case, I put the word out to all the other haunted houses. I informed the other haunted house owners to pass the word on to their employees about this theft.

The renters of this gorilla balloon just Wanted this gorilla balloon back, no question asked, because it was a rental. After I put the word out, one of the police officers who had worked these haunted houses for years and he knew almost all the employees, told me he had also put the word out. This police officer stated that he told all the employees that he came into contact with, that he expected that gorilla balloon to be in the back of his pickup truck before the night was over.

This Police officer also informed the employees that he would park his pickup truck in a dark alley behind one of the haunted houses, and that if the gorilla balloon showed up there would be no questions asked, however if it did not show up, they would all be in big trouble with him. This police officer checked his pickup truck every couple of hours, and on one of these occasions the gorilla balloon showed up in the back of this police officers pickup truck. The gorilla balloon was all sliced up and it wasn't any good for anything, however it did show up. I never did get anybody to admit to me exactly who took the gorilla balloon. However, this other police officer and I had heard rumors since that time that an employee of one of the other rival haunted houses did this as a gag. This was a very expensive gag, but I feel that we put enough pressure on all the haunted house employees, that I don't think this will ever happen again.

68. Auto Theft Suspects Hiding Under Porch, With Evidence Stuck To Them.

Auto theft is a very big problem all over the city but it is a bigger problem in the inner city. On this particular case we were looking for an Oldsmobile that had just been stolen. This stolen car had been gone only for about 15 minutes, when I observed it sitting in the middle of the street running with both of the front doors open, about 7 blocks away from where it had been stolen. I checked this car and I found that the passenger rear side window had been broken out, the steering column broken, some of the lug nuts had been taken off of the wheels and the trunk had been pried open. Since this car had only been gone for about 15 minutes and this much had been done to the car, the suspects wouldn't have had time to go too far away. We started spreading out looking around for suspects, when I see two black males run out of some bushes and go behind some houses. I started to run in that direction but they had too much of a head start and by the time I got to the rear of these houses they were nowhere in sight. Again, these suspects could not have gotten too far so we continued our search. We started searching house to house, and when I looked under the rear porch of one of these houses, I observed two 17-year-old black males. These two males were curled up against each other and pressed as far as they could get against the wall of this house. I called the other police officers on my walkie talkie and informed them to meet me there, then I told the two males to come out from under the porch with their hands where I could see them. However, they didn't move as if they were not sure I could really see them. I requested that they come out from under this porch several more times but they didn't move. So, I and another officer crawled under the porch and we drug them out by their feet. 1 asked these males what they were doing under this porch and they stated that they were hiding from their mother, smoking a cigarette. I didn't really believe their story because they were all dirty, sweaty and they both had greasy hands. Upon patting these two males down I found several lug nuts in each of their pockets and one of the boys had an Oldsmobile emblem stuck to his pants leg. This emblem was exactly like the one that was now missing from the truck of this stolen car. These two males stated that they didn't know anything about the stolen car or how the lug nuts got in their pocket, how their hands got greasy or where the Oldsmobile emblem came from. The house that these two males were hiding behind was where one of these boys lived. The other boy lived in the house the stolen car was abandoned in front of. The evidence against these boys was overwhelming and the Detectives were later able to get confessions out of both of them.

This was just one of the many cars these boys had stolen, before this incident and after this incident. These boys would sell the car radios, tires and whatever else they could find in the cars, and then abandon them.

69.   Held Hostage With Bear Traps While Guarding House.
I was dispatched one night to a call of a party being held hostage in the inner city. Upon my arrival at this residence, I observed a 19-year-old black male sticking his head out of an upstairs window. this male was talking on the telephone and at the same time yelling to me," heppp mee, heppp mee"(which I determined to mean Help me). I asked this male what was wrong and he stated that the owner of the residence had left him there to watch his house while he was out of town for three days. The owner of this residence however did not really trust this male so he had put bear traps and all kinds of booby traps throughout the downstairs and then he nailed the front and rear doors shut. The owner of this residence had left this male with everything he needed so that this male wouldn't leave the upstairs portion of this residence or steal anything. This male stated that he had been locked up in this residence for three days and now he wanted to go, home, but the owner of the residence had not returned yet. I called my supervisor and the Fire Department, The Fire Department personnel put a ladder up to this upstairs window and as I'm climbing the ladder

I noticed there was a shotgun and shotgun shells laying near the window ledge so I asked the male to just put his hands where I could see them and to come down the ladder. This male came down the latter and he appeared to be very scared, this male stated that he had a shotgun, telephone, food, drink, everything he need but he just could not get out and it was a terrible feeling. This male stated that he had tried to go down stairs but the owner of the residence had apparently removed all the light bulbs so he could not see around. This male stated that he did try to go down stairs once and an arrow had somehow fired at him. We had the Fire Department Personnel pry open the front door of this residence and inside we found three large set bear traps, one right inside the front door, and one in the living room and one at the bottom of the steps. We also found a bow with a hunting arrow in it pointed at the stairwell with a trip wire, as well as an empty bow with a broken trip wire and a hunting arrow stuck in the stairwell wall. This male was right, this resident had put him in this house and set booby traps so he couldn't leave (alive) or steal anything. A warrant was issued by the city for this residents' arrest for endangering the welfare of this male.

70. Stolen Abandoned Van Tracked Back In The Snow.
As I was patrolling my area in the inner city one night, I found what was left of a stolen conversion van. This had been a brand-new van and it had been stolen out of Independence, Missouri several days earlier, stripped and abandoned in our city. Whoever abandoned this van at the location where I found it was not very smart. They had stripped everything off of this van tires, wheels, seats, radio, all the interior, engine transmission the only thing these thefts didn't think about was that they had to drag the van to the location where I found it. It had just recently snowed, so I just followed the trail in the snow where the vehicle had been dragged. This trail led me to a garage about twelve blocks away. I could see into the garage and I observed a new engine on an engine hoist and a new transmission on the floor. This garage was used

by the residents of an apartment building, so myself and a couple of other police officers went into the basement of this apartment building and we located the vans missing seats, seat covers and all the rest of the interior of this van.

The only problem was that this was a large apartment building and any of the residents in this apartment building could have done this. We checked with every resident in this apartment building as well as the owner of the building who lived elsewhere and as always no one seen anything. We were able to recover this van and all its components; however, the case had to be turned over to the Auto Theft Unit Detectives after that.

71. Tracks in the Snow Leading To a Tree, Now 1 Wonder Where He Went.

I was dispatched on an alarm call at a church one evening in the inner city. Upon the arrival of my assisting officer and myself we observed a 25-year-old black male run from the rear of this church. We got into a foot chase with this male suspect and he led us through the yards of several residences. This suspect was fairly easy to follow because he was leaving shoe prints in the fresh snow. However, we did lose him for a few minutes when he went across a busy street an over a couple of fences. This is where this male made another one of his many mistakes, he had gone through a couple more yards across the street leaving his shoe prints and we picked up his trail again. Only this trail of shoe prints led to a tree and stopped. I remember scratching my head and looking at my assisting officer, stating, "Now I wonder where he went". Needless to say, we got this male down from the tree and arrested him. I don't know what he thought that we would think with his shoe prints leading to the tree, unless he thought that we would think that he flew away. Not this time buddy, this male had attempted to break into this church and he had set the alarm off

72.   Kiddy Drug House, Food Stamp Pay Checks.

As a Burglary Detective in the Northeast part of town, I was contacted by a 24-year-old black male one morning by telephone. This male stated that he had broken into a church the previous night, and he felt bad so he wanted me to meet him there. I met this male at the church along with several other police officers. This male stated that he had taken everything he could find from the church and he took it home, then he and his friends traded the property to a drug house for drugs. This male had taken everything, televisions, VCR's, typewriters, everything he could trade for $10 or $15 dollars worth of drugs. This male stated that they had smoked all the drugs (crack cocaine) and when they ran out of the drugs his friends left. This male stated that he and his sister had then gotten into a fight because they both wanted more drugs, so this male traded their radio at the drug house to get some more drugs. This male stated that they had traded almost everything in the house for drugs and smoked it, and then they couldn't get any more drugs. This male stated that he started panicking because he felt so bad for what he had done so he called the police station and told me about it. The funny thing about this was that this male was still high and he wasn't feeling bad because he had burglarized the church but because he had traded all his own property for drugs and he needed to get it back. This male stated that his sister is now mad at him and he really needs to get their property back from the drug house. This male showed me where this drug house was that he traded his property and the churches property to. I then contacted my supervisor who made arrangements for the tactical response team to raid this drug house. The tactical response team really made this interesting; I had never seen them at work like this before. We all pulled up in unmarked vans and the response team jumped out. In seconds surrounded this drug house, got all the people in the front yard down on the ground then they threw flash grenades through one of the front windows. This was really exciting like I was watching television or something.

All the windows in the front of this house popped out and glass was flying over everybody in the front yard. Just as they flash grenade exploded the response team busted down the barricaded front door and they rushed into the house. They found three black male young teenagers in the living room, there was a seventeen-year-old black male in the back bedroom and then there was a black male teenager that ran down the basement steps with a dog. The response team was shoving these males out of the house as fast as they could find them and, into the hands of awaiting police officers. The fifth male that had run into the basement took a few minutes longer because of the dog barking. However, when the response team threw tear gas down the basement steps this male came upstairs rather quickly. Animal control had to be called to get this dog out of the basement even though we later found out that the dog was not vicious only scared. After the response team stated that Ethe house was clear we went into the house and the first thing I had to do was put out a fire on the couch and wall where the flash grenade had landed. We checked the upstairs and found guns hidden under couches and chairs, some crack cocaine in small plastic baggies on a plate by the front door. In one of the bedrooms a window was broken out and one of the response team officers stated that when the officers entered the house a black male had broken this window out and threw out a large plastic bag which contained small baggies of crack cocaine. Under the bed in this bedroom I observed a large roll of money with a rubber band around it. This roll contained about $1600 dollars. In another bedroom I located all the stolen property from the church, and a whole room full of other people's property, such as typewriters, televisions, VCRs, sewing machines, bicycles, Nintendo games, there might have even been a kitchen sink in there, When I went into the basement it was very obvious that a dog had been down there it stunk terrible. However, it was not your normal dog poop here and dog poop there, but apparently when this flash grenade or the tear gas went off this dog became very frightened and started having diarrhea. This dog had pooped all over the basement, the entire basement it was everywhere. Normally I would not have spent much time down there but I had seen something that I thought was unusual. There was an old non-working toilet stool down there and I could see where it appeared as if someone had scooped up some of this dog poop up and thrown it in this toilet stool. It appeared as if someone was trying to hide something in there. However, I was not going to be the one who checked, so because there were no other volunteers, we called one of our K-9 Officers and his drug dog to the scene. The K-9 drug dog sniffed the toilet stool and started barking as if he had the scent of drugs being in that toilet stool. One of the crime scene officers then put on rubber gloves and dug through the diarrhea type dog poop. And sure, enough that was where they had hidden a large plastic bag of crack cocaine, underneath that dog poop. We started questioning these teenagers and we found out that the 17-year-old ran this drug house and he hired these young 14- and 15-year-old kids to stand up by the windows with guns to guard his drug house. These kids were supposed to tell him when he had a customer or if the police were coming. This seventeen-year-old male would usually be in the bedroom with any girl he wanted. These teenagers stated that girls came to the door all the time, from twelve to thirty years old and this seventeen-year-old would have sex with them then give them drugs. This seventeen-year-old also had all kinds of candy and everything else there that a young kid would want, but he didn't share it with the kids that worked for him. The only thing he gave these kids was food stamps for working for him. And if they wanted anything they would have to pay for it with the food stamps. These kids stated that they would usually use the food stamps to buy drugs from him, either for their own use or to give to their families. This seventeen-year-old apparently took in a lot of food stamps in trade for drugs. The kids also stated that this seventeen-year-olds family all operated drug houses, and they all hid their money in a house somewhere that they called the bank. I learned that this drug house was supposed to be abandoned, and that this was the kind of houses these drug dealers were using to do their businesses out of. I thought that this was one heck of a way to use food stamps.

73. Your Husband Was Caught Having Sex With A Female Impersonator. One night I was checking all the locations in my area of the inner city that stolen cars were frequently abandoned at. One of these locations was behind the old Paseo High School.

Usually every time my calls for service died down enough for me to check these areas there would be a stolen car abandoned in at least one of these areas. However, when I usually checked Paseo High School the auto thefts could see me coming and they would run, so I started to have to sneak up on them. On this night I snuck up on a car and it turned out to be a couple of parkers, I thought. What it was however, was a known 21-year-old black male prostitute dressed like a female performing oral sex on another 26-year-old black male. The male that was having oral sex performed on him gave me a pretty hard time when I broke this situation up. I asked this male if he realized that the person performing oral sex on him was a male and he stated," no she isn't, I know for sure", and he just didn't believe me. I couldn't convince this male that the prostitute was a man. I guess it really makes my night when these stupid men get with a female impersonator prostitute and they don't know it, and have to be told. I have had all kinds of reactions from disbelief and nausea, to wanting to kill them. I took this male prostitutes wig off revealing his balding head, and I told this male prostitute that he had better tell this male-the truth or I would put them in the same jail cell together then he would know for sure. This male prostitute then told this male that he was a male and that the only reason he had breasts was because he took hormone shots, then this male prostitute stated to this male," but I was good wasn't I". This male was very angry now and he was still in denial, he just didn't want to believe this, apparently, he had not checked as well as he thought he had. This male was really giving me a hard time, and then he made the mistake of stating, that he wanted me to let him go because he had no way of getting out of jail, and he wasn't about to call his wife and tell her about this. Well, they both went to jail for this indecent act, but I was nice enough to call this guy's wife and tell her where she could pick up her car so that I did not have to tow it. And I might have mentioned to her that he was in jail for letting a male perform oral sex on him in public. I still wonder how well that went over when he got home. Because his wife stated that he had told her that he had a late business meeting to attend.

74. Catching a Bat with Tupperware,
We're always getting strange calls from people such as, their kids won't eat and they want us to come out and do something about it or there is a raccoon out there in the alley or something.

In this particular case one night I was dispatched because there was a bat in this lady's house. Upon my arrival I was contacted by a white female in her late thirties and her three young children. This lady was hysterical and she had her children pretty upset as well. I went into the house and checked where this female had told me to look, and sure enough there was a bat up on a window curtain. I wasn't sure what this lady wanted me to do about this, I guess I could have shot it or hit it with my night stick, but I don't think this lady would have appreciated the mess. As I was trying to decide what to do this bat took off flying around the room a couple of times. I asked this lady if she had a box or something that I could put this bat in. This lady stated that she didn't have any boxes, so I asked her if she had any Tupperware containers that had a lid. This lady was afraid to come back into the house but she did run into her kitchen and she threw me a sandwich sized Tupperware container with a lid, then she ran back out of the house. I walked up to where the bat had landed on a different window curtain and I put the Tupperware container over the bat, then I slid the Tupperware lid under the container and forced the bat inside then I sealed the lid.

I then took the Tupperware container outside and I handed it to this female and I said there you go. I started to leave, when I guess this female realized that the bat was in that container, because she quickly threw it down and yelled, "Oh, No!" you've got to do something, get rid of it! Get rid of it! I ended up letting the bat go outside but when I went to hand the lady her Tupperware container back, this lady didn't even want to touch it. This lady then became angry and she couldn't understand why I had used her good Tupperware container to do this. I wonder what she thought I was going to use it for when I asked for it. Its funny people don't care how you solve their situations, they just want them solved, and then when everything is taken care of, they find fault in what you did. The way I look at it the police should not have been asked to handle this problem anyhow, that is what animal control is for. I thought I was doing this lady a favor by not making her wait two or three hours for animal control.

75. Flashlight Blinding Foot Chase Crash.
I found a good way to catch people I'm in foot chases with at night. One very dark night I was chasing a 27-year-old black male who had jumped out of his car after I had stopped him for a traffic violation. This male took off running across a field and then into a bunch of trees. I shined my very bright flashlight straight towards this male and instead of using my light to see where he was running, he looked back at it to see what I was doing, and then he turned back around and continued running. This male had done just what I had wanted him to do, and I remember getting a big smile on my face when I turned my flashlight off and just waited. My flashlight had taken away this male's night vision so he was temporally blinded. After only a few moments I heard what I wanted to hear, a thump. This male had run right into a tree limb and it knocked him out cold. I think that this is a very beneficial tool and it has worked several more times since then.

76. Nude in Tanning Bed, "IT Just Quit, But I Need Work. And I will Fix It for you".

I was assigned a property damage case which had happened at a tanning salon, while I was working as a Property Detective North of the river. An 18-year-old white female employee of this business had reported that, a 32-year-old white male had walked out of one of the tanning booths nude and he walked that way up to the front counter where she was sitting. This nude male stated to her that the tanning booth he had been in had just quit working. This female stated that she quickly escorted this nude male to another tanning booth and turned that one on so that this male could finish his tanning session. This female stated that she wasn't going to report this because she knew that some people do some really strange things. However, when she checked the tanning booth where this male had been, she noticed that someone had pulled all the wires out of the wall switch causing the switch to need to be replaced, and she would need an electrician to repair it. This female stated that she had been letting people use this tanning booth all morning and it was working fine until this male was in there for 15 minutes. When this male finished his tanning, this female stated that she was scared because she thought that this male was a wake, and because she was there all by herself, she just asked this male to leave and not return. After this male left this female called the police and reported this as property damage, not mentioning that this male had come out of the tanning booth nude because she was too embarrassed to. However later that day this same male called this same female at the tanning salon and he wanted to be hired by her to repair the tanning booth, stating that he was an electrician and he needed the work.

This female stated that she told this male that she had already had the tanning booth fixed and she hung up on this male. This female then contacted me at the police station and informed me of everything that had happened. It was determined that this male had caused this damage himself because the tanning booth had been working before, he went in, and it was apparent that the wires had intentionally been pulled from the switch. This male pervert was just trying to get work for himself. As far as this male walking out of the tanning booth nude, I questioned him about this after this female employee identified him and I had him brought in for questioning. This male admitted to me that he did have a sexual problem; however, he also stated that his sexual problem would come and go. This male stated that on the day of this incident his problem had went away after a while. This male stated that he has these problems because his wife just didn't take care of his sexual problems. This male stated that he always leaves the door open a little bit on the tanning booths because he just sits in the room nude and he likes to be accidentally walked in on. I asked this male if he had had any previous sexually oriented problems with anyone or any previous arrests for this sort of thing. This male stated that he used to be a maintenance man at an apartment complex north of the river. This male stated that after he quit, he had gone back to visit and he had been accused of leaving Polaroid pictures of his penis in single and married women's mailboxes with notes describing sexual things he would like to do to them. This male stated that he had nothing to do with this, but he was very frightened and he definitely didn't want his wife to know anything about this incident or the tanning salon incident. This male was arrested for indecent exposure and property damage. This male also stated that he did damage to the wiring on the tanning booth because, he was unemployed. He was hoping this female would have paid him to fix the tanning booth. I contacted this male's wife and I asked her if her husband had access to a Polaroid camera and she stated that he did where he used to work at this apartment complex. This male's wife was informed of the charges and allegations about her husband and she stated that she knew her husband was stressed out because he did not have a job. She also stated that she knew that her husband did have some sexual perversions but she would have never believed that he would have done any of the things that I had told her about. This male never did get charged in court with these crimes because the female at the tanning salon was too embarrassed to go to court, and she was too frightened to go back to work so she had to quit her job. This male got away with making monthly payments for damages to the owner of this tanning salon, after they settled this between the two of them. I notified the Sex Crimes Unit about this male at that time, and I haven't heard this males name since, thank god.

77. Pro Wrestler, You're too Big to Fight, I'll Shoot You.
I was dispatched with several other police officers on a disturbance at a bar one night. This disturbance involved several very large professional wrestlers who had gotten into a big argument with the mush smaller bar bouncers. Since the bar bouncers could not throw these wrestlers out, they called the police. When we arrived, there was no fighting going on just the bouncers complaining that these wrestlers would not leave and that the wrestlers were causing the other patrons to complain because of their actions. When I took a look at these wrestlers I IQ'1ew that this was one of those situations where you take your gun and put it up to the guy's head and say you're too big to fight I'll have to shoot you if you don't do what I tell you. Basically, they all peacefully left except for one of the biggest wrestlers; this man stated that he had just paid the waitress $100 bucks for a tray filled with shot glasses that were full of whisky. This male stated that he had just bought this whisky for him and his friends and I had made them all leave, and this made him very unhappy. This male them stated, "Well, I guess that now you are going to ask me to leave also, (Runt),"

That's when I pulled out my revolver and stated," yes I do want you to leave or you will be arrested for disturbing the peace to begin with. Since you are too big to fight, I will not mess with you, I will shoot you if you don't cooperate". This male then seemed to understand and calm down, he smiled, then he politely stated, "Do you mind if I quickly drink a couple of these shots I paid for before I leave". This male then started picking up the shot glasses and dumping them down. I didn't have a problem with that part of it at all, he became very polite and did everything I told him after that. This male had drank about 12 of those shots in those few seconds as fast as he could dump them in. When I told him that it was time to go, he let me escort him out of the bar and to a waiting friend vehicle. This male then apologized and said thanks for not shooting him. I was very glad that this male became cooperative after I let him know that I meant business, because I really didn't want to shoot him but I sure would have. I'll also admit that this incident really did make my butt pucker.

78. Prostitute Takes Everyone's Pants.
In the inner city it is a big thing for the black prostitutes to take their tricks (customers) into people's houses. These prostitutes usually rent a room from an older couple who act as if they don't see or hear anything that goes on, as long as they get their money. These prostitutes are sometimes female impersonators and sometimes just regular prostitutes. These prostitutes usually take their trick up to one of these rooms and once they get their tricks pants off, the prostitute would grab their pants and run out of the house with them. The trick then is left with no money, identification or pants, leaving the older people that are renting the room out, to help this person. These older people continue to rent rooms to these prostitutes but they will not give the tricks any of their own personal belongings. However, the prostitutes usually don't take these tricks pants very far, they usually leave them in the yard after they get the wallet out of them. These older people think that this whole thing is funny because they know that these tricks are usually middle-aged white males with money. These tricks will usually will call the police just to try to get there property back, but they do not want to go to court to assist in the prosecution of these prostitutes because they would be embarrassed or their wife might find out. These older people usually will keep a stack of clothing that the tricks have left, and of the pants the prostates dump in their yard for the tricks to ware home. Another thing that

these older people enjoy is the thought of what story this trick is going to make up as to how he came home with different pants on or how he lost his pants and wallet. We have tried many times and we can't get these older people to quit renting rooms out to the prostitutes, they say they need the money and it is entertainment for them. We can't really do anything about this unless we can prove that these older people know what is going on in these rooms, and all they have to do is play dumb. Can you imagine trying to explain to your wife or girlfriend that she needs to come to the inner city and bring you some pants and car keys. When I reached in to pull the gun out of her pants, I released why it had taken this female so long to get this gun out of her pants. What had happened was when she had reached in to pull the gun out, she pulled it up and the hammer had got caught on her panties. I was also having trouble getting this gun out of her pants. I had to take one of my hands and pull her panties up and the other hand to push the gun down so that I could get the hammer loose from her panties. However, while I had both of my hands busy doing this, this female decided that this was a good time to take her hands off of the patty wagon hood. As soon as this female took her hands off of the patty wagon hood, she reached into her coat pocket and attempted to pull a switchblade knife out of it. The part where I got lucky again was when this female flipped the switchblade knife open, it was still in her pocket and she got it caught in there.

Because this female was having so much trouble pulling the knife out of her pocket, I had time to get her arms away from her pocket and get the handcuffs on her. I then was able to get this knife and gun away from her. Needless to say, I left no nook or cranny not patted down on this female, and I had her even more thoroughly searched by a female detention officer at police headquarters. This female was charged with burglary and assault on a police officer. The female was a known prostitute; she had also served time in jail for armed robbery, drug violations and everything else. It was later determined that this female had originally been involved in the disturbance at the bar. She had grabbed her boyfriend's gun from him after she had seen the police coming and she had run out the back door of the bar. This female's boyfriend had fired this gun several times into the ceiling of this bar because he had been angry. This female stated that she was trying to break into these people's residence so that she would have a place to hide from the police.

79. He Abandoned The Gas Station, Because A Prostitute Took His Money And His Pants.

I had been dispatched to check out an inner-city gas station because a customer of the gas station had called the police station stating that the gas pumps were on but there was no clerk there. Apparently, this is what had happened. A 22-year-old black female prostitute had come into the gas station about 4 a.m. that morning when there wasn't much business, and it was raining hard. This prostitute had told the clerk she didn't have enough money to pay for the for the gas he had already pumped into her car, but that she would give him a blow job in exchange. This 23-year-old slightly mentally ill black male had put in $5 worth of gas in the car, and this prostitute told the clerk that she would have sex with him for $20 more dollars. The clerk did not have $20.00 dollars of his own money, but there were several of rolls of quarters there that he was supposed to use for change and this female stated that she would take the change. This prostitute told the clerk, after he had paid her, to get in her car and they would go down to the end of the block to have sex. The clerk did not want to leave the gas station but he figured that she was the first customer he had in hours so it would be all right and she was afraid that if they had sex in the gas station a customer would catch them. This clerk went into the gas station and put all the currency and change in his pants pockets and got into the prostitute's car. The prostitute then drove down the block a little bit to get away from the gas station then she parked her car. The prostitute then helped the clerk take his pants off, after this the prostitute asked the clerk if he needed to go to the bathroom first. The clerk then got out of the car to urinate and the prostitute drives off with his pants and everything. This clerk had put all the gas stations money in his pants pocket so he could protect it. Upon my arrival at this gas station I found that this gas station had been left unattended and the gas pumps were on. I checked the cash register and there was no currency in the register. I contacted the owner of this service station and he stated that this was the first night he had ever left this male to work there by himself and he did not know where his clerk was at. We checked and we couldn't find this clerk so we called his wife and she also had no idea where he was at. We started thinking that the clerk had been shot, robbed, kidnapped or something; we were not sure what happened to him. As I was checking this area for this clerk, the dispatcher contacted me and advised me to return to this gas station for information. Upon my arrival the gas station owner stated that his clerk was ok he was at his preacher's house and his preacher was now on the telephone wanting to talk to me. This clerk's preacher stated that this clerk had walked to his residence and explained to him what he did and the clerk had been praying for forgiveness ever since. We had to make arrangements for this clerk's wife to bring him some pants.

The owner of the gas station did not fire this clerk however he did not let him work along again, and the owner is making this clerk work off the money that was taken. We were never able to identify the prostitute that robbed this clerk.

80. Sprit Festival Slam Dancers, Or Cap Stun Victims.
I work off duty occasionally at the yearly Spirit Festival, and this particular year there was a rock band playing on the stage, and about 40 white males and females in there early twenties slam dancing in front of the stage. Apparently, the private security guards assigned to control this crowd had lost control of them. There were people actually throwing other people up onto the. stage. The people around the stage were running and slamming

into each other. and hitting each other, just a big rowdy muddy mess, fight, or whatever you want to call it.

Apparently one of these security guards had called for assistance. Myself and two other police officers (a black male and a white female) were requested by one of the security guard company supervisors to help get their security officers safely out from in front of the stage. We went into this crowd and made a path for the security guards to get out, however while we were doing so somebody in the crowd tried to punch the female officer. I had not seen this but the male officer next to me pulled out his cap stun (pepper spray) and asked me if I was ready as he was shaking his container up. This crowd was becoming even more violent now that they had seen the police. I know we were all thinking the same thing that these people were going to try to through us onto this stage. Well, we had a different idea and we all three started to spray the people rushing us with cap stun spray. We had only started to spray this cap stun when the wind started blowing it back at us. We then grabbed the security guards and got out of there. This spray really burns your eyes and skin, as well as restricts your breathing. This band never did stop playing until they finished their song, so the people never did stop dancing, at least I think they were dancing I couldn't really tell the difference. I was not sure if some of these people rolling on the ground were in pain or they were still dancing. Apparently, some of this spray also blew up on stage and got on some of the band members. This band was not at all happy about this and we did catch a lot of flak about that, but it was nothing that was not called for.

81. She Hid Her Shoe Laces Where!!!
I had arrested a 22-year-old intoxicated black female in the inner city for trying to start fights with everyone she came into contact with. I had this female transported to police headquarters where she was searched by a female detention officer. This detention officer requested this female to take all her jewelry off and to

take the shoelaces out of her shoes, then lay all of these items on the front counter. This female put her jewelry on the counter but stated that she had to sit down to get her shoelaces out of her shoes. This detention officer had this female sit in a red painted area along the wall with several other male and female arrests waiting to be processed. This detention officer then walked away and I sat down to start writing my reports. A few minutes later I heard this female detention officer yelling at this female trying to get her to stand up, which this female was refusing to do. I assisted this detention officer in convincing this female to stand up, and then the detention officer requested that this female now put her shoelaces on the counter. This female stated that she had already put her shoelaces on the counter. The detention officer checked but when she could not find the shoelaces, she asked this female what she had done with her shoelaces. This female then stated that she had already given her shoelaces to this detention officer, when she had asked for them earlier.

Apparently, this detention officer had been through this routine before because she told this female to quickly come up with the shoelaces or she would be physically searched. The detention officers take these things away from the arrests to keep them from hanging themselves or choking somebody else, as well as for the detention officers and the other arrests safety. This female detention officer patted this female down and she didn't find the shoelaces, so the female detention officer escorted this female into the bathroom. This detention officer came out of the bathroom about five minutes later with rubber gloves on and a pair of shoelaces in her hand. This detention officer stated that this female as well as many others hide stuff in their vaginas, just thinking that they are getting away with something. Why someone would stick shoelaces in their vagina, I don't know why they would want them so bad. I have been in the police headquarters detention area, when other female detention officers have come out of that bathroom with money, drugs and even on one occasion a .25 caliber revolver that females have hidden in their vaginas.

82. Uninvited Guests Covered In Slime.

I was dispatched on a late call, just as I was getting ready to go home one morning while working in the inner city. This call was to investigate prowlers inside of a residence. When my assisting officer and I arrived, we were contacted by a black male in his twenties. This male stated that he and his family had just gotten home from a two-week vacation and when he went to open the front door, he had noticed that it had been forced open. This male stated that he looked inside after opening the front door and he observed two males on the living room floor. My assisting officer and I then went into the open front door and we also observed two black males in their early twenties asleep on the living room floor. We woke the two males up and handcuffed them then had them transported to the police station after this family stated that they had no idea who these males were. This two-story house had been completely ransacked. These males had taken everything they had wanted and had broken everything else. These males had eaten all the food and taken all the blankets off the beds and were using them to sleep on this living room floor. These males had done everything in this residence to make themselves at home except to take baths or showers. It was quite obvious that these males had not seen a bath or a shower for a long time. These males really stunk, and as I was handcuffing one of them, I noticed that he had about a 1/8th inch thick layer of green like slime all over his body, and so did the other one. We had no idea what this stuff was, but it was sickening and we all quickly washed our hands and put rubber gloves on. I've never seen anything like this on a human body or animal, but it was so bad that I washed my hands and handcuffs in gasoline when I got back to the police station, then I poured disinfectant and alcohol on them before I went home. I even undressed in my garage because I wasn't even going to take my uniform into my residence. This was one of the strangest things I've ever seen, I never did find out what it was on them. I don't understand why this man kept fighting these two dogs; it was almost an impossible battle to think you could beat these trained dogs. This male was bit up so bad that he tried to sue this canine security company. However, it back fired on him, and he was sued for kicking the dog. This male was arrested at the scene for fighting in public and resisting arrest.

83. He Was Carrying Her Limp In His Arms.
While working the inner city one night I was dispatched to a disturbance call. Upon my arrival along with an assisting officer we heard what sounded like shots being fired inside this residence. I immediately notified my sergeant and he called for the Tactical Response Unit to respond, which we call an operation 100.

While we were waiting for the Tactical Response Team to relieve us, we surrounded this residence. As I was hurrying to the rear of this residence, I observed through an open bedroom window of this residence, a black male in his early thirties carrying a black female in her late twenties into the bedroom and she was laying limp in his arms (meaning that her arms, legs and head where limp as if she was innocuous or dead.). I relayed what I had observed to my sergeant over my walkie talkie radio and as I was doing so this black male must of heard me talking because he laid this female down and he came to this window and pointed a gun out of the window. The only thing I could quickly hide behind was a 4 x 4 wooden post which was along the side of this residence with bushes growing up around it. I remember thinking to myself, how can I become part of this post. So that this male does not see me. This male was looking out the window but it was dark enough that he apparently couldn't see me. I later learned that there were several people in this residence and that it was reportedly a drug house. It took 45 minutes for the Tactical Response Team to show up and relieve us. During that time a snake had started crawling up my leg, I wanted to scream, jump and everything else, it must have been just a gardener snake or something; I know I grabbed it and threw it as fast as I possibly could. Went the Tactical Responsive team stated talking to the man. As this turned out once we did get these people out of the residence by talking them out. I don't know what she was doing I think she was putting on a show for everybody out there so we would think there really was something going on in that house and it turned out not to be.

84. He Was Having A Vietnam Flashback.
I was dispatched to a suspicious party call in the Westport area. The residents of an apartment building had called and stated that there was a white male that they did not recognize hanging around their apartment swimming pool, and it was the middle of the night. It was a full moon out this night and it is very true, that's when the crazy's come out. Upon my arrival along with a female officer and my sergeant, we observed this 32-year-old white male out fitted in military fatigues. I asked this male what he was doing and he didn't like me bothering him, he seemed to be in his own little world. I told this male to step out to the street with us, to get him away from the apartment building where people were trying to sleep. This male walked out to the street with us then when he reached the street, he started going off on us like he was going to fight for his life. Apparently, this male thought he was back in Vietnam and we were going to take him prisoner. This male started making all these karate and kung Fu motions with his hands and feet. This male stated that we were not going to take him alive and that he would kill every one of us. My sergeant stated that he thought he knew what this guy was going through since he had also been to Vietnam. My sergeant stated for us to just stand back from this male because we didn't know what he's up to. Well, after a few minutes of taking this from this nut case, I got tired of it and so I walked up to this male as he was making all of these motions and I quickly put a neck restraint on him, and with the others help we handcuffed this male with no incident at all. After this male was handcuffed and under control this male

started yelling "Medic, Medic", my sergeant was very quick to respond to this he, informed this male that we were going to have him air lifted out. I had this male taken by patty wagon to the VA Hospital where he was well known, they admitted this male for observation. This sergeant still gives me a hard time about that incident to this day. I guess the only way to describe the way I was feeling that night, it was like in the movie The Raiders of the Lost Ark, when Indiana Jones was confronted by the Arab swordsman all dressed in black and doing all these fancy things with his swords like he is going to cut Indiana Jones up and Indiana Jones stated that he didn't have time for this, and he pulled out a gun and shot the swordsman.

Or I guess you could say it had been a busy night and my patience was really short, I didn't have time for this male's games. This same male I remember, while we were waiting for a patty wagon to take this male to the VA Hospital, he bent over and spit on the female police officers shinny shoes. For some reason this even irritated me more, it wasn't just because the police officer was a female but this male had no business spitting on any police officer's shoes. I then pushed this males head down into the hood of my police car, where he could not spit on anyone else and this female officer then wiped her shoes off on this male's pant leg.

85. Ninja Goofy.
I was dispatched on a disturbance at a residence in the inner city. Upon my arrival a 24-year-old black female contacted me and stated that her 25-year-old black ex-boyfriend had been using drugs and he had been there trying to beat her and her 48-year-old mother up. This female also stated that this ex-boyfriend was dressed as a Ninja and he had just left prior to my arrival. I asked this female if her ex-boyfriend was trained in the martial arts and she stated that she did not know. I informed this female that my assisting officer and I would look around to see if this male was still*close by then we would return to take an assault report. We

looked around for chis male however we could not locate him so I returned to this female's residence to take the assault report. As I was approaching the residence I observed a person in a full black ninja outfit, dressed head to toe, the socks, the hood and even the razor blade silver throwing stars, this male was just coming out of this female's residence. It wasn't even close to Halloween, I confronted this male and I told him that he was under arrest for assaulting his ex-girlfriend and her mother. This male then started making all these squealing noises like you would hear Bruce Lee do when he's fighting someone. This male then started waving his hands, arms and feet around like he was warming up to attack me. Since I did not know if he knew martial arts or not, I was not going to let him get close to me. So I took my gun out and I pointed it at him and I said, "I'm not going to play games with you, I'm going to shoot you if you make another move towards us, just lay face down on the ground and put your hands behind your back". I must have said this convincingly enough, because that's what he did immediately, and then I put handcuffs on him, and took him to jail. It turned out that this male was just messed up on drugs and he had borrowed this Ninja Outfit to go over to his ex-girlfriend's house and try to beat her and her mother up thinking that they would not know who was doing it. I would have killed this male if he had made any further moves as if he was going to attack me, and he didn't even know any kind of martial arts.

86. Radar Officer Needs Help.
I was dispatched on a code one emergency call one early morning north of the river, to check on a possibly injured police officer. This is almost the worse kind of call you can get, it's almost like a family member has been hurt, and you can't get there fast enough. A citizen had called 911 and reported that they had observed a police officer with his head leaning over against the door panel of his police car and his radar gun lying on the ground outside the car. These people believed that this officer had been shot or something. We were really lucky this time, because upon my

approach with my red lights and siren on, this police officer woke up. This officer wanted to know what was going on and I pointed down at the ground where his radar gun was laying and he finally realized what had happened. This officer was really embarrassed, and concerned about the dent, the fall had made in this radar gun. As you can tell I have never let this {now sergeant} forget about this. Sometimes things happen like that when you're on that dog watch shift {mid nights} and it's real quiet.

87. He Was an Adult at Midnight, He Stole At 12:20AM, so 1 sang Happy Birthday to Him.

I had one particular juvenile that was really a thorn in my side. I kept catching this juvenile breaking into and stealing cars, then stealing the car stereos, tires and anything else he could find to steal. As a juvenile there wasn't a lot, I could do with him except send him to the juvenile unit, who would release him back to his parents, (who took no control of him). However, on this particular night I was dispatched on car prowlers in a used car lot. Upon my arrival along with an assisting officer we observed two black male juveniles running out of this used car lot and getting into a vehicle, which started to leave. I stopped this vehicle and had the two juveniles exit the vehicle. Upon checking the vehicle these juveniles were in, I found a couple of car stereos in and several screwdrivers, flashlights and pairs of pliers. I patted these juveniles down and I found several car radio knobs in their pockets along with screwdrivers and pliers. 1 had the dispatcher notify the used car lot owner and have him respond to the scene. Upon the car lot owner's arrival, he checked his used cars and stated that there were 5 car stereos and, some car speakers missing, however the 2 car stereos I had found in these juveniles' vehicle were not from this car lot. We looked around this car lot and we located the stolen car stereos stacked up in a back alley. Upon questioning these juveniles, they both admitted to taking these car stereos and speakers from the vehicles on this car lot. These juveniles both also stated that they were not sure how the other two car stereos had gotten into their vehicle, and that possibly one of their friends had left them there. Both of these juveniles also stated that they were only 16 years old and that I would have to release them to their parents, (which were a common statement) as they laughed, thinking this was funny. However, I got the last laugh, because as I was checking these juveniles' identification, I noticed that it was the birthday of the juvenile that I was always catching breaking into cars. I told this juvenile happy birthday and he stated "No, not yet, it's tomorrow". This juvenile must not have realized that it was after midnight when I was dispatched on this call. That meant that this juvenile had been committing this offense when he was 17 years old, which is the age that he is considered to be an adult. This made me very happy, so I sang happy birthday to him knowing that he'd be charged as an adult in this offense. A juvenile's juvenile record is not accessible so usually a juvenile can start his adult life with nothing on his record, no matter how bad he was as a juvenile. The other juvenile was taken into juvenile custody and later released to his parents. The adult was taken to police headquarters where he was charged with felony stealing, photographed, fingerprinted and held until his court date, because he could not make his bond. This adult was only sentenced to probation, because this was considered his first offense as an adult. However, his criminal life finally came to an end when he was caught at age 22 after stealing a car, then kidnapping a 14-year-old white girl who was waiting for a school bus. This male and a friend kidnapped this girl then raped her several times, tortured her and locked her in the trunk of the stolen car where she died.

88. He Blew Up His Own Butt, To Scare Her Into Coming Back To Him.

I worked the scene of an explosion while a Detective in the Bomb and Arson Unit, in the far south area of town. I had been originally dispatched to The North Kansas City Hospital to receive information from a doctor in reference to a 24-year-old white male who had come into the hospital and It had appeared to the doctor that the male had been involved in an explosion. Upon contacting this male, he advised me that he had just pulled up to his girlfriend's residence in south Kansas City when someone threw some type of bomb through the windshield of his vehicle and it exploded.

This male had large blistering burns on the right side of his face, forehead, right side and three golf ball sized holes full of paper wadding in the right check of his buttocks. I responded to the south Kansas City scene where this explosion occurred and I talked with this male's ex-girlfriend and her family. This male's ex-girlfriend stated that she had broken up with this male and that she didn't want anything to do with him anymore. She also stated that this male had been making harassing telephone calls to her residence at all times of the day and night and leaving threatening notes on her vehicle. This information put a new light on this investigation however it did not explain why someone had threw a bomb into this male's vehicle. I then responded to the private tow lot where this male had his father's vehicle towed, which he was driving at the time of this explosion. My investigation of this male's vehicle changed this story even more. My investigation revealed that that this explosion actually occurred inside this vehicle causing the vehicles windshield to blow outward. This was contradictory to the male's statement that the explosive devise had been thrown through this windshield which would have caused the glass windshield to have broken inward. This devise that had exploded had to have landed or was sitting between the bucket seats of this vehicle when it exploded. About one week after this male was released from the hospital I requested that he come into my office so that I could get some more information about his explosion. This male asked me if I would speak loudly, because he was having hearing problems since the explosion, as I asked him questions like could he describe the person who threw the object at his vehicle. This male gave me some off the wall description which I could tell he was making up as he went along. I asked this male if he would assist in the prosecution of anyone involved in this explosion, and he stated yes that he would because it was his father's vehicle that had been blown up. I then decided that he had had enough fun making up stories so I confronted this male with the facts. The device had not been thrown through the windshield, he had been having problems with this girlfriend, he had this girlfriend take him home instead of to the hospital, then he later went to a hospital way up north when there were many hospitals closer to his home, and the fact that he had arranged for a private tow to get his vehicle out of sight as well as the fact that the police were never called, and that this devise could not have landed under his buttocks. This male then broke down crying and he stated I'll tell you what really happened just don't tell my dad what I did to his car. This male then was read his rights and he stated the following. This male had gone to his ex-girlfriend's residence to scare his girlfriend into feeling sorry enough for him to come back to him because they had broken up and she didn't want anything to do with him anymore. This male had taken an assortment of fireworks and put them in a paper sack along with a large fireworks ball (mortar shell), then he dumped some pop it's (things children throw down hard in the street and they make a popping sound), in the paper sack. These pop- it's contained flash powder, and there is almost always loose flash powder all around them. This male might have been ok if it wasn't for the flash powder which ended up all over the paper sack and on this male. This male had the 10-inch fuse of this mortar shell sticking out of this paper bag and the top of the bag twisted around it. This male had then sat the paper sack down beside himself between the front seats. This male's intention was to light this fuse and then throw the sack out of the window so that it would blow up in his girlfriend's driveway so it would scare her. However, because of the flash powder being all over the inside and outside of this paper sack as well as all over this male himself, when he lit the fuse the flash powder ignited there was a big flash then the explosion. This male didn't even have time to pick the bag up off the floor to through it out the window. This explosion had pushed the roof of this car up about 1 1/2 feet, tore out the dash broke all the windows, pushed the side doors outward and tore off half of the driver's seat.

Well, needless to say this male did not get his girlfriend back, he infuriated his father especially with court costs, after I got him charged with the felony of making and exploding an explosive devise as well as making false police report/ hindering and interfering by lying causing me extra time to investigate this offense, and all the pain and suffering he must have gone through with all his injuries. I sure hope he asked himself if it was worth it, or was it very stupid, and of course he concluded that it was the stupid part.

89. They Shit All Over The School Nurse's Office.

I was dispatched about 2 a.m. one morning on an alarm call at a grade school up north of the river. As my assisting officer and I pulled up to the school we could hear the loud outside alarm going off. I drove around to the rear of this school and my assisting officer went to the front. As I was driving around to the rear of the school, I could see two flashlight beams quickly moving down an inside hallway heading towards a rear door. I informed my assisting officer of this and we both headed for this rear door. Just as I arrived at the rear door two white male 13 and 14 year old juveniles ran out of the rear door dressed in Halloween like costumes, one had camouflage make-up on and he was dressed in military fatigues, the other one had black and white makeup on and was wearing all black as if to resemble the rock stars in the rock band "KISS". Both of these juveniles ran right in front of my police car and were heading for a wooded area behind the school. I jumped out of my police car and started chasing the juvenile in the 'KISS" makeup as the two juveniles split up as they entered the woods. This juvenile was running through the woods without his flashlight on and I realized that my flashlight beam was lighting his way for him so I turned it off for a second and then I turned its back on. When I turned my flashlight back on this juvenile was looking back at me so I shinned my flashlight beam right into his eyes then I turned it off again. I just stopped and waited then, I knew it would only be a few moments until I would hear what I wanted to hear and sure enough, THUD then OHHH, as this juvenile ran right into a tree branch because he had been blinded by my flashlight beam. I turned my flashlight back on and went over to where this juvenile was lying on the ground with a bloody nose and mouth, and I took him into custody. My assisting officer was not able to get around to the rear of the school fast enough to see where the other juvenile had gone into the wood so the other juvenile temporally got away. I asked this juvenile who the other juvenile was and he stated that it was his cousin and he told me where this cousin lived. I informed the dispatcher of this and she dispatched police cars to that address. The police officers who went to this address woke up the people at this residence and they stated that their son was in bed asleep and that his cousin was spending the night with him. However, upon checking they discovered that both juveniles had snuck out. We searched the area for a while but we could not locate this other juvenile, even though it made no difference because we already knew who he was. Upon checking the inside of the school, I found that a bunch of the school lockers had been broken into and gone through. The principal's office had been ransacked as well as the nurse's office, things had been thrown all over. I noticed a foul odor and on the nurse's bed someone had shit like they had diarrhea. As I was checking to see what other room these juveniles had gotten into, I again smelt this same odor and sure enough one of these juveniles had shit in the hallway. I have no idea what causes this, but it is very con-mon for people when they are scared or nervous for them to get diarrhea, which apparently happened to these juveniles. I had noticed when I patted down this juvenile that I had caught that the only things that he had in his pockets were pencils, paper clips, erasers, etc... When I checked the area where these juveniles had run out the rear door at, I found a lot of the same type items all over the ground outside where these boys must have tried to empty their pockets as they were running.

90. **He Was Okay Until 1 Woke Him, Then He Had To Go To The Hospital.**

I was patrolling the Westport area one early morning about 4 a.m. when I observed a 25-year-old white male laying on top of a narrow retaining wall which was about 4 feet tall. 1 stopped to see if this male was okay, I shook him several times trying to wake him up but he had apparently passed out from being intoxicated. I broke an ammonia capsule under this male's nose and he started rolling around, waking up slowly and I said, are you okay. This male started mumbling something I couldn't understand; it was very obvious that he was intoxicated. I informed this male that he needed to find another place to sleep, then I started to walk away. I guess this male didn't realize where he was at because he rolled over and fell off the wall hitting his head on the sidewalk. This male now had a large gash on his forehead and it was bleeding very heavily. I gave him first aid an ordered an ambulance for him, he then had to go to the hospital for stitches. As the ambulance started to take this male away, he looked at me and stated." I was okay until you woke me up." Whoops, Ohhh Wellll.

91. **Women Can't Run With Their Pants Down Either.**

I was patrolling the Westport area one warm dark night when I observed someone take off running on the sidewalk ahead of me. I wasn't sure what is was but I also observed something on the sidewalk in the area this person had started running from. I spotlighted the object on the. sidewalk and it turned out to be an attractive white female in her early twenties squatting down with her pants around her ankles urinating on the sidewalk. This female had apparently come from one of the bars and was intoxicated, when I shined the spotlight on her she tried to take off running with her pants down around her ankles and she wasn't doing a very good job. I could hear someone laughing loudly at the end other sidewalk so I shinned my spotlight to that location and another attractive white female in her early twenties was standing there laughing at her friend as she was trying to run with her pants around her ankles. Apparently, this friend had seen me coming and took off running leaving her friend to be embarrassed, which she really was. I did not embarrass this girl any further but I did tell her friend to advise her to find a restroom next time. To think back on this, it was really a pretty comical situation seeing this woman trying to run with her pants down around her ankles.

92. Drunk Female, Kisses Kids That Stole Her Purse.

I was dispatched to an accident in a very dangerous part of the inner city about 2 a.m. one morning. Upon my arrival in this all-black neighborhood, I observed a very attractive 22-year-old very intoxicated white female who had hit a telephone pole with her convertible and had spun around in the street making her car not drivable. After the accident a couple 9- or 10-year-old black males came up to she and she asked to use their telephone to call for some help. The boys showed her where a pay telephone was and while she was using the telephone to call the police these two black males stole her purse. This female didn't realize that the boys had stolen her purse because she was still pretty upset about the accident and she was very intoxicated. When I arrived, this female was giving both of these little black boys a kiss and she thanked them for all their help, then they took off running as I approached. I requested that this female let me see her driver's license because it was very obvious that she was intoxicated, however when she went to get her purse it was gone and the two little black boys were the only ones that had been around there.

Quite obviously they had stolen her purse, her identification, her money, apartment keys, and everything, and she even kissed them for doing it. That was a pretty good trick on their part but sometimes you never know who you can trust. Even though children that are out at 2 a.m. in the morning, in a dangerous neighborhood would not be my first choice to trust. This female stated that she was new in town working in a night club temporally while waiting to be sent to china with several other models to do cosmetic ads for several months. This female stated that this was her night off and she had been bored while sitting alone in her apartment and so she went out to find something more to drink and then she had gotten lost and into the accident.

93. **Her Blood And Hair Were On The Driver's Side Of The Windshield.**

I was dispatched on a car accident in the Plaza area about 2 a.m. one morning. Upon my arrival I observed that a car had hit a tree and there was a 40-year-old intoxicated white female walking out in the street away from this car and nobody else around. I contacted this female and I asked her if she had been in this car accident. She stated no, and that she did not know whose car it was, it was there when she walked by. I then noticed that this female had a fresh cut that was bleeding on her forehead. I asked this female how she got this cut and she then admitted that she had been in this car but that she was not driving. This female stated that a guy she had met at the bar was driving and he had run off when he hit the tree. This female stated that she did not even know this guy's name or where he lived. I examined this female's car and when I looked up at the windshield right above the steering wheel, I could see long blond hair and blood on the steering wheel. I thought that this was really quite funny because this female also had long blond hair and a cut in the middle of her forehead. Well, even though she did insist several times that she was not driving that car and that an unknown male was driving, she was charged with drunk driving and being involved in the accident.

94. **Vice President Quayle.**

One of my Detective partners and I were eating lunch one day, at a BBQ restaurant in the eastern part of town. All of the sudden several Secret Service people started coming in. They all had their radios and they were all wearing suits, and of course as Detectives we were wearing suits and we had our radios with us too. The only difference was that the Secret Service people had small lapel pins. As we were waiting for our order a couple of the Secret Service people came and sat down by us. They informed us that Vice President Quayle was coming into the restaurant with his wife and several others. When Quayle came in, he went around shaking all the customer's and employee's hands, however since this other Detective and I looked so much like the Secret Service people he shook everybody's hand but ours. I think he thought we were some of his Secret Service people. They were only there for a few moments long enough to get their food and they got back on the bus. I was really kind of disappointed that the only reason I did not get to shake his hand was because he thought we worked for him.

95.　Sophisticated Flasher.
I have worked off duty at almost all the Plaza Lighting Ceremonies that they have had since I became a Police Officer. This is a big event usually over the Thanksgiving weekend in the downtown/Plaza. I have been assigned different jobs every year sometimes out in the cold and sometimes inside one of the big hotels where it is warm. On one occasion I was assigned to the area outside off the elevator on the top level outside of a very fancy bar/restaurant.

My job was to watch the elevator and keep the sightseers out, since this was an expensive high-class thing going on there. I remember being very bored and tired after working all day and then all night not to mention listening to so many fake and snobbish appearing people. All the sudden this very elegant looking apparently slightly intoxicated white woman in her late forties walked up to me and she commented that I looked pretty tired and bored. I informed her that I was trying not to look that way, but that I would have really rather have been partying with them than working. This woman was wearing this real pretty sparkling green long wrap around dress which was really clinging to her shapely body. This lady just looked at me then looked around to see who was looking. She then grabbed the fold on her dress and unwrapped it, until one of her braless breasts was completely visible. She then put it back and stated, I hope that livened up your evening and will keep you going the rest of the night, then she walked away. It did, it really did! One year I was assigned to a rear parking lot of one of these big hotels, because there was a lot of construction going on back there and they wanted the parking lot controlled. It was very cold so I was sitting in my van(which has dark tinted windows) about 20 feet from an overhead street light watching for people trying to come into this parking lot. There is a lot of vehicle traffic on these nights however there are thousands of people walking everywhere. These people are all drinking and celebrating and this causing them to have the need to use the restroom. Since there are so many people the businesses usually will only let their customers use their restrooms, so the non-customers have to find other places. Because of all the construction in this back parking lot, I guess people thought that this would be a good place out of the way to privately use the restroom outdoors. They however all seemed to be picking the spot near this street light right in front of my van. I did not pay much attention at first then after about 30 men, women and children had used this spot it started to get old. I became bored, so if it was a man, child or ugly woman I would scare them off by turning my headlights on before they got started. This became a very game, it kept me and my relief officer amused for most of the night.

96. He Even Stole Their Pots And Pans.

As A Property Detective in the northeast area of town I worked a lot of aluminum, and other metal thefts. It was such a big problem because the price of brass, copper and aluminum was way up at the recycling plants. My partner and I worked one particular group that traveled together stealing metals and we spent 13 hours straight with just one 26-year-old black male suspect who was driving for this group. We brought this male lunch and everything else while he continued to direct us around to all the places where he and his friends had stolen items from. This male and his group would take the storm windows off your house. They would take your screen door, the aluminum siding off your house. They stole aluminum ladders, boats anything that was not tied down. We caught one of this group standing outside a recycling plant at noon waiting for the owner to come back from lunch. This male had a box full of pots and pans he had stolen from a house. Aluminum ladders, we would go out to the recycling plant and there would be stacks of brand new and good used aluminum ladders waiting to be melted down. This group would also steal all the copper tubing from old homes and new homes under construction. There was one particular aluminum fishing boat that the recycling plant refused to take because it looked to new so the suspect put a hole in the boat with an ax then they bought it. This boat even had a license sticker on it. The license was good for 5 years; the license had just been purchased. I traced that license back to the owner of the boat and found out where the boat had been stolen from.

This group had stolen hundreds of feet of copper drainage spouts one of the downtown historical buildings had to keep having to have specially made to keep the building on a historical registrar. There was nothing safe from these guys, nothing whatsoever. These guys used the money they got from these metals to buy drugs, (crack cocaine) of course. Another case that happened with this same group of people was this 43-year-old black male went up and kicked the front door in on a house. He did not knock or anything he just went up and kicked the door and walked in. The residents of this home, a black couple in their mid-twenties and their two young daughters were just sitting there watching television. This male kicked the door open and he just walked up and unplugged the television set without saying a word. This male then picked the television set up and carried it out of the house as if no one were even around even though this family was yelling at him. The male resident followed this male as his wife called for the police. This male walked straight to a drug house where he sold the television set for crack cocaine while the victim was standing there yelling. The victim was yelling to the people in the drug house, that the television set was stolen, they also just ignored him and took the television set and went inside. The male that had broken into the house and stole the television set walked right by the victim as the victim was yelling at him. He acted like the victim was not even there; like he never even saw him and that this was not a big deal. By the time we got this sorted out and got to the drug house with a search warrant there was no television set to be found. There was not a lot we could do about this thing we had no idea who the suspect was at that time.

97. The Sergeant, Got Up On the Bar Table, and Blew His Whistle. We had several bars in the southern part of the inner city that were mostly all black bars and it was very common to have fights and shootings there nightly. They usually had their own security but it was hard to tell what side they were on many times. Usually these bars handled the problems themselves and we knew when they called the police their problems had to be already out of control. We would go in these bars in groups of four with our shotguns out. We would rack a shell in the chamber as we walked into these bars. Usually this distinct noise would quiet everyone down because they knew it meant trouble. The reason we did this, is because most of these bar disturbances were caused because of alcohol, and most of the people in these bars had guns. On this occasion we entered one of these bars our normal way, however the music was so loud that no one even paid any attention to us. We could not even locate the disturbance we were called there to handle. While we were in there trying to get the place quieted down and to locate the disturbance we had been called there to handle, nobody was paying any attention to us at all. Then all of the sudden to all of our surprise the sergeant that had come inside with us got up on a bar table and he starts blowing his police traffic whistle. None of us expected that, it was the last thing we expected anyone to

do, we were really surprised when nobody turned around and shot him. Everybody did quiet down although I think they cursed at him pretty bad saying how stupid and dangerous it was to do that. I think it was so stupid and unexpected that it worked. It was one of those times that you got away with it, but I highly do not recommend doing that at all.

98. The Ironing Board That Attacked Me.
     As a new police officer, I had been dispatched to a dinner theater in the southern part of our city, on an alarm call. Upon my arrival I located an unlocked door. This could mean that someone is inside the business that is or is not supposed to be there, or that that the door was just left unlocked. You have to have an open mind but you also have to be ready for anything.

My assisting officer and I checked the interior of this building. We had our guns out as we normally do, because we never know who is in there or what they might have in their hands. As I was checking the very dark stage area, I opened what I thought was a closet on stage and I shinned my flashlight in to see if anyone could be hiding in there. When I opened the closet door out popped what I thought was a person jumping out at me, I only got a glimpse at it when my flashlight beam hit it. I remember thinking I was prepared for anything to happen but I know now that I was not, it scared the shit out of me and I almost shot it. I mean it almost made me go home and change my pants. What they had done was attach a fully dressed male mannequin to one of these ironing boards. It was one of those ironing boards that come down when you open the closet door. It was a prop in one of the plays being put on there. It definitely was a hair rising experience on that dark stage up there. I almost shot that ironing board, but at least I did not. It was just a beginning lesson that I will always remember, because similar things like this happen all the time. They have happened to me many times since.

99. He Calmly stated, if You Don't Stop, You'll Break My Wrists.

I was dispatched to a liquor store one night in the inner city. I had been dispatched to assist a female police officer who wanted assistance removing an intoxicated 45-year-old white male from the business. Upon my arrival there I observed this intoxicated male passed out on the floor right by the front counter. The store owner stated that this male had walked up to the counter and he wanted to buy some more liquor. The store owner did not believe this male even had any money to pay for it, so he refused to get it for him. The store owner stated when he told the male to leave, the male started to turn to leave but he fell over passed out. I took a couple of ammonia capsules and put them up in his nostrils and broke them in an effort to wake him up. This normally works on the best of them but it did not even phase him. The store owner asked us if at least we could drag him out of his business. I had checked this male's identification and he was living at a shelter a few blocks away so we were going to take him home. I grabbed this male by the wrist and put on a wrist restraint, which means to bend the hand backwards until it hurts. This usually brings people to their feet very quickly. The female officer also but a hand restraint on this male's other hand. We were both starting to apply pressure to these males' wrists, which should have begun to hurt badly. This male did not budge, he just looked up at us and calmly stated, "If you do not stop bending my wrist, you're going to break it." This male was just as calm as he could be. I do not know how he could stand all that pain, but I really do not think he was even feeling anything. This male was awake, but he just remained like a wet noodle, so we had an ambulance come and get him. We had him taken to an area hospital, so he could be checked out.

100. My Pain Loving Instructor.

I had an instructor in the police academy that was a pain loving instructor. He loved to dish out pain and he loved to dish it out to the people who showed the pain the most. I guess I must have been one of those people who showed the pain because he used me as a guinea pig every time, he wanted to demonstrate a new technique, it seemed like anyhow. I left the academy many nights black and blue. I try to think positive, so I say he did it for a good reason. He just wanted us to know what it felt like, so when we applied it to somebody else, we would know what it felt like and we would know that they would not like it. He also wanted to give us confidence in what we were doing and show us that this stuff really worked and it did quite often. I will admit that I have still got a lot of respect for that instructor, and I still can feel the pain every time I think of him.

101. My Flaming Flares, Were Sticking Out Of The Hood Of His Car.
I was involved in an incident near the Royals Stadium one time when I was sent there to assist in directing traffic because of a traffic accident. Since there is always so much traffic in that area, we were putting out flares. We were using the old-style flares that had a nail sticking out of the end of them, so that we could stick them in the pavement and the dirt. I had just lit two of them up and was getting ready to stick them in the ground when this car came by and clipped me on the butt and hip with its front fender. The impact swung me around, I used both of my hands to catch myself, when I hit the hood of his car. I hit the hood of this car with those two flares, the nails pointing down. Both flares stuck in the hood of his car. It was quite a sight, two flaming flares sticking out of the hood of this car. It was like; I had just put the sword in a bull during a bull fight. (Ho-Lay). He was not really happy about this, but he did not have a lot to complain about after striking me with his car. We got it worked out, I was not hurt and he had some minor body work to do.

102. Dumbo, Hammer, and the Predator.
I worked an off-duty security job at a large downtown hotel. This security job was to keep outsiders from interrupting this $100 dollar a plate dinner. This dinner was a 45th year celebration for Kansas City's first black radio station. The entertainment consisted

of greats such as Hammer, The Whispers, Perry White, The Gap band, and several others. At one point during this dinner one of the organizers requested that I go to the front of the stage area. He wanted me to keep the crowd away from M.C. Hammer as he was performing. I responded to the stage area and I was only there a few moments when a woman stepped into the {forbidden zone} to take a picture of Hammer. In doing what I was requested to do, I politely asked the woman to please step back. Hammer must have seen me do this because he stopped performing, he walked over to the edge of the stage where I was, he leaned over and into the microphone he stated,Officer either you leave or I will. Needless to say, I was quickly advised to leave the stage area by the person who sent me there. My instructions upon arrival at this dinner were to not let anyone into the dining room area that did not have a suit and tie or was not formally dressed. The first person I observed that I was going to ask to leave turned out to be Perry White, who was wearing a multicolored shirt. I did not know who Perry White was, but he was surrounded by beautiful women, so I guessed that he must be somebody important so I left him alone. The next person I was going to ask to leave was a black male that appeared to be high on something. He was dancing around, going upstairs, downstairs, then in and out of the dining room. This male was wearing jeans and a shirt; he also had long dreadlocks {which I can only describe as looking like someone had a black floor mop on their head}. Since this male was coming and going into the dining room through another door where another police officer was posted, I asked this police officer why he was letting this male into the dining room. This police officer informed me that this male claimed to be with a band called The Gap Band who was performing there that night. Well, I had never heard of this Gap Band or anyone else there that night, except the guy who used to call himself M.C. Hammer. Randy Miller just does not play those bands on Young Country Q104, the radio station I listen to. Well, I did not get to bother that guy either. I thought I had seen my next target, when this hippie looking guy with a back pack, came over very quickly and opened the dining room doors. This male then quickly backed out of the dining room stating, "I do not think I belong in there." I wanted to tell him that he had that right, and to be on his way, however, he ruined my fun by politely introducing himself as Jimi Macon, a guitar player for The Gap Band. You could just imagine my impression of this Gap Band now; I did not know what to think.

To my surprise this Jimi guy was really down to earth, even if he did resemble the rapper ICE- T, people say, but I think he looks more like Sinbad. We ended up exchanging addresses, so I could send him this book and he could send me photographs of himself. He stated that he was going to send me photographs of him, playing guitar with other groups such as James Brown, Taste of Honey, Natalie Cole, and Johnny Taylor. Jimi stated that he had been around for a long time, and he has played guitar for so many of the greats that he could not remember all of them. Another thing I thought was really cool about Jimi, was that he said that he had been almost everywhere on this planet. He said that he had been married three times, and now he just wanted to stay close to home with his present wife of many years. Jimi stated that his friends call him "DUMBO," because he has such good ears for music, and he can play about anything after he hears it once. While I was talking with Jimi, the guy with the dreadlocks came hurrying through. I asked Jimi if this guy was also in the band and he stated that he was. Jimi then introduced me to The Gap Bands keyboard player Terry Scott, better known as the "PREDATOR." Because with those dreadlocks he closely resembles the predator creature in the movie. I had thought that Terry was high on drugs, but he was just high on life and he was hurrying around because he was looking for a friend. Terry seemed to be a great guy; I have never seen a smile as big as his. Jimi had left to get ready to perform and when he returned, I did not even recognize him, he had changed from a hippie to a cowboy, hat, and boots an all. Jimi was really decked out, he really had me confused now, on what kind of music his band played. When they did start playing, I was amazed, it was like a mixture of Hammer, acid rock, rap and oldies. No country music, except when one of the band members tried to yodel. I did not know if it was because I had met Dumbo and the Predator or not, but they really stuck out in this band. They really knew how to get down on the guitar and keyboard. This night was a very good reminder to me that you should not make judgments about people until you know.

CHAPTER 2

JUST EVERYDAY LIFE

1. No Accident, No Marijuana, It Didn't Even Happen, You Weren't Even There.
2. Rubber Glove in the Vaseline Jar.
3. Engineer Lesbians Fighting.
4. Contempt of Court.
5. Hitting the FBI Agent.
6. The Accident I Don 't Remember.
7. The Hospital Personnel Just Stood There and Watched, While I Was Fighting Him.
8. Deer Suicide on the Plaza.
9. He/She Prostitute, Patty Wagon Accident.
10. He Shot Me with A Fire Hose, Because Of A Traffic Ticket.
11. I Looked in The Broken Window, Into A Gun Barrel.
12. He Just Laughed, When I Said, I Almost Shot You Twice.
13. Asleep in His Car with a Gun under His Leg, Money, and Drugs Next to Him.
14. I Might Have A Shotgun in That Cooler, Pointed at You.
15. Standing There with His Attack Dog, He Stated, Do You Remember Arresting Me.
16. Okay, How Could He Resist Arrest, With Only One Arm.?
17. You Watched Them Steal My Car.
18. Someone Threw A Brick Through My Patrol Car Window.
19. They Should Not Have Done It, In Front of Me.
20. The Suspect Who They Said Was Not There, I Found Hiding in The Basement.

21. The $10,000.00 Dollar Newspaper Burglary, I Stumbled Upon.
22. Trucking Company Employee Arsonists, On Video Tape.
23. They Hid the Shotgun in The Woods, Let Me Show You Where.
24. Their Kid's Wrote in the Cement, but it's Not Their Kid's Fault.
25. No Crime to Steal My Signs, but a Crime for Me to Steal Someone Else's.
26. The Homeless and Bridge People.
27. I Found A Gun Like That, So I Threw It in The River.
28. Responsible Teens, Need Love To.
29. But It Looked Like You Were Hurting Him, For No Reason.
30. Why Was the Female Officer Going to Shoot Me, What Was She Thinking?
31. Tattooed at Three Years Old, Now Stealing from Cars.
32. Cattle Rustlers.
33. I Should Have Anticipated the Injury, And Went Around the Fence.
34. Frozen, And Pinned Down.
35. He Said, Let Me Feed the Baby, Then He Dumped Cereal on the Floor by The Baby.
36. Peter Fonda, At the Vietnam Veterans Memorial.
37. Prisoner Escape, But that's Not My Son.
38. Her Daughter's Boyfriends, Threw Knives in Her Floor, And Stole Her Jewelry.
39. He Played at Their House at Night, And He Stole from Their House by Day.
40. He Got Him to Do the Burglary, and then He Called the Police on Him,
41. Fox Guarding the Chicken Coop.
42. Security Guard Stealing for Years, He Even Took the Christmas tree.
43. Just Because His Finger Prints Were Found in the House, Doesn't Mean He Did It.
44. House Explosion.
45. Italian Club Explosion.
46. Snow Covered Cripple.

47. Robbery Suspect Hits My Police Car in Get-A-Way.
48. Gas All Around the House, But The Matches Won't Light.
49. He Was So Low, That He Even Stole From the Dream Factory.
50. We Herded Cattle On The Plaza For Hours.
51. Teacher Stole Kindergarten Kids Money, To Buy Drugs.
52. Kids Stole His Gun, Shot It, And Then Sold lt.
53. Michael Jackson in Concert.
54. Michael Jackson at His Hotel.

1. No Accident, No Marijuana, It Didn't Happen, I Wasn't Even There.

    Christmas Eve a few years ago it was and had been snowing very hard. I was dispatched on a hit and run accident/assault, near Swope Park. Upon my arrival I observed a tow truck and a vehicle with its hood up, at this location. I contacted the tow truck driver and he stated that he had been trying to help this victim get his car started. When a big white Lincoln pulled up to the corner, then backed around the corner striking the car the tow truck driver was working on. The tow truck driver stated he yelled "Hey, what are you doing? The 34-year-old black male driver of this Lincoln then pulled up to the corner and got out. This male then pulled out a knife and walked over to the tow truck driver and stated, "What do you mean, what am I doing." The tow truck driver put his hands up .in the air and said. "Nothing, no problem here." As this was happening, a female passenger got out of the Lincoln, and hurriedly jumped in the driver's seat and begun to take off. The black male noticed this and he ran and jumped in the Lincoln as it was pulling away. The tow truck driver gave me the license number of the Lincoln and I responded to the address listed for the owner of this Lincoln. Upon my arrival I observed the Lincoln sitting out front of the owner's address running; it was occupied by several black males and one black female. I requested an assisting officer to back me up on this car check, and upon his arrival we checked the occupants of the Lincoln. Inside I found a tall black male in the driver's seat that matched the description of the black male who threatened the tow truck driver. I requested all the occupants of the Lincoln to exit the vehicle. As I interviewed them, I learned that the man in the driver's seat was the person driving the car earlier when it ran into the car the tow truck driver had been working on. I handcuffed the black male, and patted him down checking for weapons, at which time I located four plastic baggies of marijuana in his overcoat pocket. I then informed this black male that he was under arrest, for the possession of marijuana, and the fact that he was quite obviously intoxicated. This black male then became very angry and belligerent, stating that I could not arrest him "It was Christmas Eve." I called for a paddy wagon to come and take the black male away but it took a few minutes for the paddy wagon to arrive because it was quite a distance away. As we were waiting for the patty wagon to arrive, a large group of what appeared to be this black males' relatives (they were as huge as he was), emerged from the house. They started yelling "You are not taking him to jail its Christmas Eve!" The people that had been in the Lincoln then started yelling the same thing. It was apparent that this situation was quickly escalating. I grabbed the black male I had arrested by the handcuffs, which were behind his back and the neck. I started running dragging my arrest up the street toward the patty wagon, which was just then coming down the street. My assisting officer had taken his baton out, put it up to chest level and began running backwards behind me. He was attempting to fend this group off until we could get the arrest in the patty wagon. The patty wagon driver seen this happening and he jumped out of the patty wagon. He opened the rear patty wagon door; at which time we literally threw my arrest in the back of the patty wagon. We then hurriedly got into our police vehicles and headed for the police station. We returned moments later and towed this Lincoln, for evidence in this hit and run accident. When this case came to court, the judge asked me, this black male, the witness (tow truck driver) and the victim of the accident, to come up to the bench, and tell him what had happened. Unfortunately, the witness, the tow truck driver, and the victim, whom I had not spoken to since the night this, happened, failed to show up in court. I am sure the tow truck driver wanted to testify against this black male. They must have been threatened or paid off not to come to court. All I know was something was fishy about this case it was not even continued until the tow truck driver and the victim could be located as they normally are. The judge stated, "We need that victim and witness here," and since they are not here the case is being dismissed.

The judge then looked at me and stated that without a victim or witness, the accident never happened, I was never there, and thus nothing after the accident, had ever happened. Including the finding of the drugs, and having to defend ourselves against this black males' relatives. None of that ever happened. Just to top it off, the black male that I arrested had said to me that Christmas Eve night, "I hope you and your family have the worst Christmas ever, cause all my Christmas presents were in the trunk of that car you towed off. Like this whole thing was my entire fault.

2. Rubber Glove in the Vaseline Jar.

One spring night I was dispatched on a disturbance in the inner city, as I was driving up the street, I noticed a white person running down the street toward me. I assumed the person was a female because it was wearing a feminine-looking pink robe, that it was modestly trying to hold shut while running. Because this person was running like a woman with her hands in the air, but when I got closer, I knew immediately that it was a male who was quite obviously gay. Upon questioning this 20-year-old man, he stated that he had called the police, because his lover had beaten him up. This male then gave me the following account of what had happened. He stated that his lover is married, and his lover's wife was a prostitute. The three of them lived together and had different sexual needs at different times. They could take care of their needs in different ways as needed, as well as the fact that his lover had not yet came out of the closet. His lovers' parents thought their son was a straight married man. This night there was been a candle-lighting ceremony at Liberty Memorial for people who had died of aids, and this man's lover and his wife had gone there, leaving this man home alone. This male stated that he had become bored so he had called four of his gay white male friends over to party with him. When this party turned to sex, all five of them went into the master bedroom. This is where they were when this man's lover and his wife came home. This man's lover was very angry catching him in bed with these other lovers, so he grabbed him from the bed, slapped him on the face and told him to leave the house. This male stated that he grabbed a pair of shorts and his robe, and then ran outside crying, and that was when I arrived. My assisting officer and I then went to the victim's residence to contact the victim's lover. The first thing we noticed upon entering the house was a large, king-sized waterbed with a giant, economy-sized jar of Vaseline on the headboard that had a rubber glove sticking out of it. The victim's lover stated that he did slap the victim and ask him to leave the residence, because he was angry at the victim for having sex with these beautiful men without waiting for him. The victim stated that he did not wish to make a complaint against his lover; however, he would stay somewhere else for the night to teach his lover not to hit him.

3. Engineer Lesbians Fighting.
I had an incident one summer evening near the Plaza, an area gay bar, that's a known hangout for lesbians. About a block away from this gay bar, there was a disturbance reported and upon our arrival we observed two white females in their middle twenties, ripping each other's clothes off in a cat fight. We separated these girls but they would not quit screaming at each other. They were just screaming at the top of their lungs and trying to get away from us so they could continue fighting. We were having a lot of trouble holding them apart, and trying to get control of the situation. We had to handcuff both females and take one of them down almost a half a block away just to keep her from screaming at the other. Nothing we did was calming these girls down, so we could talk to them to find out what their problem was. As a final resort, with an open hand I slapped the girl I was restraining on the face.

It was like a miracle, she calmed right down as if she snapped out of a trace or something. After getting her attention, I learned that she and her girlfriend had had a fight at the gay bar. It all started because her girlfriend had danced with another girl, so they left the bar, but pulled over one block away, after they started hitting each other in the car. Both girls were extremely intoxicated and we. decided to take them both home and tow their car away. Upon checking their car, prior to towing it, we located two golden cigarette cases filled with rolled marijuana joints. That was a new one on me, that's really class isn't it. Both of these females also stated that they were train engineers for a local large railway company. That reminded me of the two male homosexuals who had gotten into a fight and one of them stated to me. "He hit me with his purse."

4. Contempt Of Court.
    I have often said that going to city court is one of the worst parts of this job. It seems that many times the criminals have more rights than the Police Officers, victims, or witnesses. I remember one-particular incident with a new middle-aged white female judge. She was in front of the court room handling a case when the prosecutor came over and started talking to me with his back to the judge. All of the sudden I both heard, "Officer, Officer!!!!" I looked around the prosecutor to the judge who was motioning with her finger for me to approach the bench. I went up to talk to her and she said, "Officer, if you say another word in my court, I will hold you in contempt." I knew better than argue with her so I just sat back down. Meanwhile the prosecutor, who realized that he had been the one talking, put his tail between his legs and sat down, not saying anything.

5. Hitting the FBI Agent.
    I remember the first time I ever used my night stick. I was just off break-in. I had gotten a call to a disturbance in a vehicle in the area of 40th and Main, a known prostitution area. I had been assigned to drive the paddy wagon that night. When I arrived at the scene of this disturbance. I observed a 47-year-old white male and a 20-year-old black female moving around quickly in the front seat of a vehicle, as if they were struggling. As I was waiting for my assisting officer, they observed me and the male pushed the

females head down under the dashboard, as if he was hiding her from me. I informed my assisting officer of the situation, and told him that I needed him to get there as soon as possible. However, the male in this vehicle. Was not going to wait and he got out of the car and started coming towards me. Since I was just getting off my break-in period as a new Police Officer, I knew that I should not try to handle this person by myself. I knew that I would have to wait for my assisting officer. I yelled at the man approaching me, and told him to stay where he was. I told him that I would be with him in just a minute. He appeared to be very intoxicated and was very loud and belligerent. I repeated several times for the man to stay where he was. However, he kept coming toward me. I stepped back to the paddy wagon, and grabbed my night stick. I then held it in front of me in a defensive manner, and again yelled for him to stay back! This male became even louder and came rushing at me as if I was bothering him. When this male got within reach, I lunged at him with the point of my night stick. I struck him in the chest, and then I was getting ready to hit him in the head with the other end of my night stick, (as we were trained to do at that time). All of the sudden an arm came around his neck and an officer from another zone pulled him back out of my reach. My adrenaline was really flowing by then. I was especially nervous because I was new out on the streets, and this was a whole new experience.

After this officer and I got this man settled down, I told him that I wanted to see his driver's license. This man opened his wallet and pulled out an FBI identification card. He then stated, "I work for the FBI." I took the card from his hand and threw it down on the ground and said, I did not ask you where you worked, I asked to see your driver's license. (Why I did that, I do not know, you never know how you will react under stress, until you have been there a few times.) As it turned out this man did work for the FBI. However, he was still intoxicated, and had been involved in a disturbance with a prostitute. He did however finally become embarrassed and he realized how stupid he was acting. He then became very apologetic, and I had someone take him home. I then informed the prostitute to get off the streets. This incident was documented; however, I never heard any more about it.

6. The Accident I Don't Remember.

I was working the dog watch shift (1 pm to 7am) in the Westport/ Plaza area, the day Reagan was elected President. We had just gotten brand new blue uniforms, previously we wore brown uniforms. This was my first night wearing my new blue-uniform. I had just finished eating breakfast on the Plaza when I was dispatched on an alarm call at Paseo High School. I remember driving north bound on Broadway, when this call came out so I pulled over at a bus stop at Westport and Broadway to write the call down on my activity sheet. The most direct route to Paseo High School from there would have been for me to take a right turn onto Westport, or go straight on Broadway to 39th street then turn right. Instead, the last thing I remember is pulling over to write down the call. The next thing I knew was that I was somehow involved in an accident. I woke up to see the car radio microphone flying up in the air, and my Police Car wrapped around a wooden post on the north side of Westport Road. I must have passed out a couple of times. I do remember trying to use the microphone, but it would not work, so I grabbed my walkie-talkie and informed the dispatcher that I had been involved in an accident. I am not really sure what happened next, but I do remember someone cutting my new uniform pants off. When I got to the hospital a Police Accident Investigator I recognized was there with a man in civilian clothing and they started asking me what had happened. I told them that I only remembered pulling over to the curb, while driving north on Broadway at Westport, to write down the call. That was all I remembered, other than the car radio microphone flying up in the air. I was sore all over, I had a concussion, I broke my hand and I cut the bridge of my nose on the rear-view mirror. The accident had knocked the emergency light bar off the top of the Police Car and sent it flying about 100 feet across the road. I later found out that there was another vehicle involved in this accident. It was an older white lady who they said I had hit her car and knocked it into a glass building causing her to break her leg. I was also later informed that I had ordered an ambulance for this lady. I do not even remember seeing any other car, or calling an ambulance for anyone. To this day I do not have any idea what happened. However according to the accident investigator, they said I had to have been going eastbound on Westport, which is impossible in my mind. I was told that the accident was my fault, that I hit the lady's car when I ran a flashing red light. My sergeant was very irritated with me; he could not believe that only after one day of wearing my new uniform pants I had to have them cut off.

7. The Hospital Personnel Just Stood There and Watched, While 1 Was Fighting Him.
I had taken a 28-year-old white male drunk driver to an inner-city hospital one evening.

He had suffered minor injuries in an accident, but was now passed out in the hospital hallway, laying down on and handcuffed to a hospital gurney waiting for treatment. I was sitting in a chair writing my reports at the head of this gurney. I was not paying much attention to him, thinking that he was at least quite while he was passed out. He must of woke up and seen that I was busy writing my reports, so he grabbed a fire extinguisher from where it was hanging on the wall next to him. The first thing I noticed was this male swinging the fire extinguisher at me. I was however able to block it with my arm, and I stood up and jumped back quickly. He kept swinging the fire extinguisher at me with one hand. He was able to strike me several times on different areas of my body. Even with his other hand handcuffed to the gurney. I yelled someone for someone to come help me get this guy under control. At which time five or six doctors and nurses came out into the hallway. They just watched, as I was attempting to get the guy under control, but having trouble, because he was still swinging the fire extinguisher at me. I was finally able to knock the fire extinguisher from his hand, at which time he grabbed the other gurney rail, picked up the gurney and started striking me with it. No one was doing anything to help me, they had not moved, they were just watching. I finally pointed to one male doctor in front of the group and told him to call 911 or something. Finally, a Police Officer showed up to help me. We were able to get the man pinned against the wall with the gurney, and were able to get him under control. This was a situation where the Medical personnel think they know more about these belligerent people than we do. A lot of times the medical staff will go into the room with the person we had just been fighting and tell us that the person does not need handcuffs on. Then they tell us that they do not need the police officer in the room with him. The next thing you know the medical staff is being punched or beat up and we have to go in the room and rescue them, causing us to have to fight them one more time. Sometimes we do know best about handling belligerent people; after all we do it almost on a nightly basis.

8.   Deer Suicide on the Plaza.
I was dispatched to the Plaza area one night to check out the report of a dead deer in the street. Upon my arrival I observed a six-point buck lying in the street dead. The deer was just below a three-story Plaza parking garage. It was obvious that the deer had fallen, because all four of its legs were spread out. I determined that the deer had to have somehow gotten up to the third level of this Plaza parking garage, because this was the only area the deer could have come off of. The deer must have become scared, panicked and jumped off. It was the first deer suicide I had ever worked.

9.   He/She Prostitute, Paddy Wagon Accident.
One night in the area of 40th and Troost, I arrested a 25-year-old black male/female impersonator, which we refer to as a "he/she." He was a known street prostitute and these prostitutes usually

carried syringes to exchange sex for drugs. I arrested this he/she after I observed him trying to flag down traffic in the middle of the street. I had called for a paddy wagon, I put the he/she in the back of the patty wagon and it headed for the Police station. However halfway to the station, I heard other officers get a call over the police radio to an armed robbery at a local Quik Trip. At about the same time the patty wagon driver all of the sudden turned around and activated the patty wagon's red lights and siren and took off in the opposite direction. I had no idea what the patty wagon driver was doing, but I did know that the patty wagon does not normally make emergency calls. I followed the patty wagon at a normal speed, just to stay with my prisoner. When the patty wagon got to the intersection of 47th Street and Troost the patty wagon driver attempted to drive through a flashing red light.

However, a station wagon was going thought the same intersection and could not stop in time for the emergency vehicle so there was an accident. The patty wagon ended up on a twelve-inch-high curb. I called for an ambulance, and then I checked the patty driver and she had some leg injuries and she was shaken up, but was otherwise all right. I then checked the he/she whose hands were behind his back in handcuffs. He was uninjured, even though he was thrown around in the back of the patty wagon, because he had nothing to hold on too. He was however very upset, which you cannot blame him for being. He stated he only wanted only to get out of the patty wagon and go home. The ambulance took the officer to the hospital and I took the he/she in my police car to the station, where he got his wish. The he/she was quickly released on a signature bond at the station. As it turned out the patty wagon driver had been at the Quik Trip that was being robbed just prior to my call for her assistance. She had seen the possible suspects at the time. She had wanted to get back to the Quik trip to try to stop the robbery or at least give information on possible suspects, and that was why she turned around in such a hurry. However, things did not turn out the way she planned.

10 He Shot Me With A Fire Hose, Because Of A Traffic Ticket.
During the 1 and 1/2 years I was in the Bomb and Arson unit one fire in particular stands out in my memory. This apartment fire was almost under control and one of the fire trucks had parked in front of a neighboring residence. The resident of this residence the fire truck had parked in front of must of came home sometime during the fire and parked his vehicle behind the fire truck where it could not be seen. When the fire truck backed up to leave the fire scene the fire truck driver backed into this resident's vehicle causing damage. The law does specifically state that no vehicles should park within 100 feet of a fire truck. The police were called to investigate the accident, and the traffic officer wrote a ticket to the driver of the fire truck for causing damage to the car. Technically, the traffic officer should not have written the ticket, but that was to be determined later. As it turned out the fire truck driver was only driving on this shift because a driver makes more money than the other crews. This firefighter was having financial troubles, so they were letting him drive. This incident had gotten back to some of the firefighters inside the building that had burning. Many times, I went into a fire with the fire inspector while a fire was still burning. In this case, part of the building was still burning. I was wearing a fire helmet that said "Bomb and Arson Unit and Police" along with my other fire gear. One firefighter inside the burning building had apparently heard about what the police had done to one of his buddies outside. When he saw it said police on my helmet he waited until I walked past him then he turned the fire hose on me striking me in the back. The force of the water knocked me across the room and against the outer wall. There were several firefighters with hoses when I got up and turned around, so it was not obvious who had done it, but it was obvious that it was done intentionally. I was not injured, I was just surprised, and I was just going to caulk this incident up to experience. However, the fire inspector I was with knew who had done this and he apparently informed the fire chief what had happened. It should be noted that as a member of the Bomb and

Arson Unit, you almost work more with the fire department then the police department. It was like the fire inspectors and us were on the same team. Even though the Police Department and the Fire Department do not always get along because of past strikes that happened even before I came onto the police department. The Chief of the Fire Department personally called and apologized to me for the incident. The firefighter who had turned the hose on me also called and apologized. He said that he was angry that the police officer who had written his buddy the ticket and he took it out on me. I of course accepted their unnecessary apologies. I was just at the wrong place at the wrong time.

11. I Looked In The Broken Window, Into A Gun Barrel.
     I got a call on a burglary in progress, at a residence in the Northland area. The residents had been inside asleep when they heard the rear bedroom window get broken out. Upon our arrival my assisting officer went to knock on the front door. As I went to check out the back of the house, at which time I observed the broken bedroom window in the back. As I approached this broken window the barrel of a gun poked out of the window and was pointed right at my face. I did not know if it was the burglar, the victim, or who. So, I drew my gun and dropped down, luckily, no shots were fired. I then pointed my gun at the window and said, "Drop the gun!" The resident of the house then said it was ok he lived there. The resident stated that he had gotten his gun because he thought that I was the prowler out back.

12. He Just Laughed When I Said, I Almost Shot You Twice.
     One early morning I went to assist the Plaza Patrol on the Plaza. The Plaza Patrol had reported that they were chasing a black male suspect who had run from them after being involved in some kind of disturbance. This male was running in between some apartment buildings in my area north of the Plaza, and he was eluding them. I was in my police car driving around looking between the apartment buildings hoping to see the suspect, when

all of the sudden the suspect ran in front of my Police car. I slammed on my brakes, got out of the police car, pulled my gun, and identified myself as a police officer, then I told him to stop or I would shoot. The suspect stopped for just a second and just looked at me, and then he jumped up onto a 3-foot retaining wall then ran a few feet into a yard. The suspect then stopped and quickly turned around toward me. He started to bring his out stretched arm in which he held something shiny, which I taught was a gun, toward me in a swinging motion. It looked as if he was going to point this object at me. So, I began squeezing the trigger of my gun, while yelling stop or I will shoot. The male suddenly stopped his motion before he pointed it at me, then he put his arm up in the air, then down at his side and he turned around and continued to run. I notified the other officers of this situation over my walkie talkie, and then I continued the chase, telling the other officer's where we were. I chased the suspect around a couple of houses and down an alley, with my gun out. This suspect ran around one of the houses and by the time I got to the corner of the house the suspect was waiting for me. He started to once again swing his arm around towards me with the shiny object in his hand. I staffed to again pull the trigger of my gun with the intention of shooting him before he shot me. He however again, all of a sudden, he stopped his motion and raised both arms in the air. He then started running with both arms in the air, shouting don't shoot. I then somehow lost sight of him. The Plaza Patrol however had gone into the area the suspect was running towards and they caught him a few blocks away. I responded to that area, to check this suspect out. He was a 6'1 " tall, 180-pound, 16-year-old kid. When I had been face-to-face with him with my finger on the trigger of my gun, he appeared to be at least 21 years old, an adult. It really bothered me the thought that I had come very close to possibly killing this kid twice. I told the kid that I had almost shot him and he had almost died twice, the kid just turned and looked at me and he just laughed. As it turned out the suspect only been in a disturbance with his girlfriend on the Plaza and this running from the Plaza patrol and me was just for fun. Also, the shiny object in the suspect's hand turned out to be a wraparound watch band. It had come unlatched and the suspect had been making the swinging motion to keep it on his arm. This juvenile was turned over to the youth unit where he was most likely just released to his parents.

13. Asleep In His Car, With a Gun under His Leg, Money, and Drugs Next To Him.

I was dispatched to a call of a white male armed with a gun, passed out in his car in a bar parking lot north of the River. Upon my arrival I observed that the engine of the car in question was running and a 28-year-old white male was passed out behind the steering wheel of it. I could see a brown wooden hand grip and the chrome barrel of a handgun sticking out from under this male's leg. The doors on this car were locked and the windows were rolled up, so I could not get into the car. On the seat beside this male appeared to be several hundred dollars in currency, and a large quantity of miscellaneous drugs. Myself and other officers got into position, one officer on each side of the car with our guns drawn and ready. At the same time our sergeant pulled-up in his police vehicle and parked in front of this male's car. However, the sergeant did not get out of his vehicle he just sat there, because as we found out later it was muddy outside and he did not want to get his boots dirty. I then knocked on the car window, until the male in the car woke up. The first thing this male did was grab for his gun. We were ready to shoot into the car if he pointed the gun at us. Instead, he pushed the gun under his leg farther as if to hide it. I then requested that he unlock the car door which he did, at which time we jerked him out of the car. This male was extremely intoxicated, high on drug's etc...; several syringes, money, drugs and the handgun were located next to where this male had been sitting on the car seat. Upon inventorying this car so that it could be towed to the tow lot after we took the male to jail. We found numerous small bags of white powder, razor blades, marijuana, capsules, syringes, tablets, the gun, and a lot of cash. Apparently, the male was selling the drugs out of his car in parking lot of this bar, which is a common occurrence. I had all the substances found in the car tested and they all turned out to be illegal drugs. This male was found to be on federal probation out of the Ozarks, for the sell and manufacture of drugs. This male of course had just bought himself a ticket back to prison.

14. I Might Have A Shotgun In That Cooler Pointed At You.
I got a call one night to a tavern up north of the river. Someone had called and reported that there were drugs being sold out of a tavern, in the office and the kitchen area. Upon my arrival at this tavern, my assisting officer and I went in the front door and as we did, we noticed that the back door opened and people started rushing outside. This tavern was having a 25th anniversary party and the place was packed wall to wall. I also noticed that a lot of men were rushing into the restroom. I checked the restroom and it was full of the three-piece suit type men.

Which I thought was very unusual because this was a nice tavern but not really a high-class place. The tavern owner all of the sudden jumped in front of me. He could tell that I was heading to the back of the tavern, to check the kitchen and office area. The tavern owner stood in front of me and asked me to leave the tavern because I was ruining his party. I tried to explain to him that we had gotten a call to the tavern about drugs being sold out of his office and kitchen and we were there to check it out. This bar owner was very intoxicated and he stated to me," you're not checking my place." Well, as he knows the police have a right to check any business during any reasonable hours or anytime it's open for business. I informed the tavern owner that he could not prevent me from checking his business. The tavern owner continued to stand in my way as I walked so I kind of had to push him out of the way, at which time he became very belligerent. A sober relative of this owner then grabbed the tavern owner and told him he needed to straighten out and calm down. This apparently made the tavern owner very embarrassed and even more irritated. The tavern owner then stated, "Ok, I will show you my office and the kitchen, let's go."

However, when we got to the kitchen cooler, I asked the owner to open the cooler because I wanted to check in there, it was a large walk-in cooler. This set the owner off again and he stated," what if I got somebody in there with a shotgun and as soon as I open that door, he's going to blow your ass off." Normally we would have taken the tavern owner into custody at this time, because he was trying to prevent us from doing our job. As well as the fact that he was intoxicated, and he had been serving liquor behind the bar, which is also illegal. Not to mention the fact that he was making threats to a police officer. This night we were so busy with so many different calls and an armed robbery was being reported just down the street at the same time. I found no evidence of drugs or anything at the time we were there. However, as I said, the back door flew open when we came in a lot of people went out, and a lot of people went into the bathroom. This probably speaks for itself.

15. Standing There With His Attack Dog, He Stated, Do You Remember Arresting Me.

I had an incident a few years ago when my son was about (5) years old and I had him up on my shoulders at the Lion Creek Park looking at the buffalo and the deer: This 28-year-old white male came up to me and my son with his large growling attack dog and he said do you remember me? I said no I don't, and he stated, "You are the cop who arrested me for drunk driving, and I didn't appreciate it, there was no way you should have arrested me for that". It was obvious that all this male had to do was let his growling dog go and my son and I would have been in a world of hurt. It was one of those situations where you wonder what do you do, I had my son on my shoulders and there was no way I could fight this dog not to mention the male. This male had me in a very frightening situation. If my son had not been there, I am not sure how I would have reacted, I had to act like a father not a Police Officer. I remember wishing I had a gun or something and I would have taken care of that dog right there. However, I knew I had to think fast and use my head to talk my way out of this one. Luckily, I was able to get this guy calmed down by asking him to remind me of the incident where I arrested him. He described an incident where he was drunk driving and he ran off the road. When I remembered the incident, I told him that I was only doing my job. I stated, if I did not do my job, I would not get paid. I informed him that my job was just like anyone else's job, and that It was nothing personal against him. Well, again luckily, he was satisfied with that and he left. Since that time, I have always carried a weapon on and off duty, because you never know what is going to happen.

16. Okay, How Could He Resist Arrest, With Only One Arm.?
I was dispatched on prowlers one night up north of the river. Upon my arrival at this residence the resident pointed to a 28-year-old white male asleep on the enclosed front porch of this residence. This resident stated that he did not know this male and that this male had been with another white male and they were both very intoxicated. The resident stated that both males had broken into the locked screened in front porch of his residence and went to sleep in chairs on the front porch. The resident stated that he had heard a noise, then nothing, so he just laid in bed awhile. After a few moments, he decided to get dressed and check the noise out. The resident stated that when he came out to the front porch, he saw two males asleep there. He stated that, he yelled at them, at which time one of them got up and took off running. The other one just laid there passed out. I checked the area surrounding this residence. Just over a fence in a neighboring field, I found a 25-year-old white male lying on the ground passed out. It appeared that this male had been running through the field in the dark and he hit his head on a low tree branch knocking him out.

I tried to wake this male up but it was pretty tough to do, even with ammonia capsules. When this male finally woke up, he was found to be quite obviously intoxicated. This male was very surprised when I awoke him; he wanted to know what I was doing to him. This male stated that he did not know what happened or how he got there, but that his head hurt. I asked this male for some identification and all the sudden he just started kicking me. This male had only one normal arm and then he had a dwarfed arm. Normally you would not have thought he would be a big problem to arrest, but he just started kicking me. My assisting officer and another officer then came over to help get the male under control. Even the three of us were having problems trying to get close enough to grab him, without being kicked. It was obvious that he knew what he was doing with his feet. I found out later that he was a kick boxer. We all three eventually rushed him and tackled him but even then, he was really hard to hold down. We did put some handcuffs on him however we could not get him to hold still long enough for us to double lock the handcuffs to keep them from tightening up. I can double lock the handcuffs so they do not tighten, but he would not give me a chance to do that. So, he had one handcuff on this little deformed wrist and then one on his normal wrist, and they just kept tightening up all the time he was resisting us. We had to hold this male down and wait approximately (15) minutes for a patty wagon. This male was very belligerent and all this time he is non-stop trying to get away from us. Finally, when the patty wagon driver arrived, we were able to get some shackles to put on this males' feet. He still continued to try to kick us, so we just put him in the back of the patty wagon. When we, got this male to police headquarters we took him out of the patty wagon and he was complaining that the handcuffs were cutting his wrists. I took the handcuffs off but they had gotten pretty tight. I do believe it did bruise this male dwarfed wrist a little bit however he never did stop fighting long enough for us to do anything about it. This male made a citizen's complaint against me for abusing him by hurting his dwarfed wrist. This male had been uncontrollable. I was sure that I would be in trouble now, because all the review board would see would be a one-armed man. They would not think anything about him using his feet and being able to take on three Police Officers. However, when the review panel tried to get this male's side of the story, he was so belligerent to them that they dismissed the case against me. This male was charged with burglary and resisting arrest.

17. You Watched Them Steal My Car.
One Halloween night I was working off duty at a haunted house in the inner city. I was watching, a block long line of people, waiting to get into this haunted house. I observed a vehicle going down a one-way street the wrong way and turning onto the street the haunted house was on and pulling in front of a vehicle already traveling on that street. It appeared as if the 27-year-old blackmail in the second vehicle that had been pulled in front of was angry with this. He got out of his car, leaving it in the middle of the intersection with the door open and the engine still running. This male runs up to the first car opens the car door and tries grabbing the 24-year-old heavy set black intoxicated female driver out of the driver's seat. This male jumped in the front seat and starts wrestling with this large black female. As they were wrestling, this female's vehicle swerved over and almost hit the crowd of people standing in line. I then rushed over and got this vehicle stopped and I pulled the male out of the vehicle. I then held this male's hand behind his back and I asked him what he thought he was doing as I leaned him against a parked vehicle at that location. This male stated that this female was his sister-in-law and she had just stolen his wife's car. This male was very belligerent and I was having trouble trying to get him to calm down so I could really understand his story. At this time an off-duty firefighter asked me if he could be of help.

I asked the firefighter to watch this male as I tried to find Out what the female had to say. As I approached the female's vehicle she started to drive away. I reached into the vehicle put it in park and I took the keys out of the ignition. This female was extremely intoxicated, so I called for some on duty police officers. When the other officers arrived, this male asked them if he could go get his vehicle out of the street. However, upon looking where he left his vehicle was gone. This male made a citizen's complaint against me stating that I watched as someone stole his vehicle. I did not see anybody take his car at all. The last time I saw his vehicle, it was where he left it out in the middle of the street. There was nothing I could do about it. Apparently, both of these vehicles belonged to this male and his wife. His sister-in-law, who was in the first vehicle, had taken the car from his wife, without her permission. He was out trying to stop her. This male's complaint against me was also unfounded.

18. Someone Threw A Brick Through My Patrol Car Window.
     I had an incident in the inner city where I was dispatched code one, on an emergency call an armed robbery where the victim of this robbery was injured and inside a bar. I was the first one on the scene and a bar patron came outside and informed me that the suspect had already left but the victim needed my help. The victim was a black male older street person and he had been hit in the head with a gun, after which the suspect took a bottle of wine from the victim and ran away. I gave this man first aid for a large gash in this head until the ambulance arrived. I obtained my information for my report then I went back out to my patrol car. I immediately noticed that the rear window of my police car was shattered and there was a brick in the back seat. I checked the area and I did not see anyone suspicious in the area. I then notified my sergeant who immediately came over. The sergeant wanted me to do an area canvas and start knocking on doors to see if someone seen who did this. The sergeant then asked me why I had not been watching my police car. None of what the sergeant was asking made any sense, because it was about 3:00 a.m. in the morning and nobody was outside except for the bar employees as

well as it happened while I was inside giving first aid the injured person. It's not like I could be in there giving first aid to the victim and watching my police car at the same time. Another one of those awkward situations, where you cannot ever do anything right.

19.   They Should Not Have Done It In Front OF Me.
I was patrolling one early morning up north of the river when I observed a car with its headlights off driving around in a hotel parking lot. A few moments later this same car went across the street an into another hotel parking lot, so I just sat across the street with my patrol car's headlights off and I watched this car. It was about 2 a.m. in the morning and very dark outside so I could not really tell what the occupants of this car were doing but, I did see them get in and out of this car several times. I waited until this car left the hotel parking lot a few minutes later, and then I followed it. I requested a backup car through the dispatcher and I followed this car at a distance until my back up car arrived, then I pulled the car over. When I checked this car, I found that it was occupied by two white males in their early twenties. I also observed several car radios, radar detectors, checkbooks, and a little bit of everything. These two males had been breaking into the cars in these two hotel parking lots, just as I suspected. These two males immediately confessed to what they had been doing. With the help of the two suspects, I was able to return a little over $1,000 worth of property to its rightful owners, and put two thieves in

20.   The Suspect Who They Said Was Not There, 1 Found Hiding In Their Basement.
As a Detective North of the River, I had been looking for an 18-year-old white male. He was wanted by numerous Detective Units throughout the city for armed robberies, burglaries, stealing, assault, all kinds of offenses. This male had run away from home and he had been hiding in different friend's houses where nobody could find him. On this particular morning, there had been (2) dirt bike style motorcycles stolen. They were taken from a residence

a few blocks away from another residence, where a neighbor stated that they had seen kids riding the dirt bikes that morning. I went over to the residence where the kids were seen riding the dirt bikes, and police officers were already there. However, the police officers were unable to get anybody to let them in the residence to look around because they did not like the police. It should be noted that this residence appeared to be a safe haven for young male and female runaways. The only adult in this residence was an intoxicated 27-year-old white male, the boyfriend of the adult female resident who was now at work. Upon my arrival at this residence, I got the same story that without a search warrant no one was searching this residence. About six young smart mouthed teenagers were now out on the front porch of this residence giving the officers a hard time and telling them to get off their property. A police sergeant stated he had had enough of their smart mouths and he had the officers run each of these juvenile's names in the computer. Two of the teenage females were found to be runaways and were taken home. As the officers were checking the teenagers, I looked over a chain link fence and observed a dirt bike partially covered up in the back yard. I asked the teenagers whose dirt bike was hidden in the back yard. Several of them stated that this 18-year-old male everyone was looking for, had put it there then left that morning. I requested that the adult male let me look at this dirt bike at which time he voluntarily showed it to me. This was one of the stolen dirt bikes and we recovered it. I explained to this adult male that we did find a stolen motorcycle in the backyard. I also informed him that I would like to look in his residence for the other motorcycle, and for possible suspects since no one outside knew anything more about it. They were all blaming it on the 1 8-year-old male I had been looking for. This adult male stated that he could not let me into the residence to search because his girlfriend the owner of the residence had asked him not to. I then asked this male if I could talk to his girlfriend over the telephone. He then called his girlfriend at work and let me talk to her. I explained to this female that we had found a stolen motorcycle in her backyard and that the teenagers there were saying it was this 1 8-year-old male who had put it there. This female stated that this 18-year-old male was at her residence this morning riding this motorcycle when she left for work but she had told him to leave. I was finally able to convince this female that I wanted to look in her residence only for this 1 8-year-old and the other stolen motorcycle. Apparently, this female was scared that I wanted to go into her residence and I would be going through all her drawers' closets etc..., possibly she had something to hide. When I convinced this female that I would not look in anyplace smaller then where a teenager or a motorcycle could not be hidden. This female finally told her boyfriend to sign consent for me to search this residence only for hiding people and the stolen motorcycle. Also, with the stipulation that he was always with me, and that I was the only one to go inside. This adult male then asked the teenagers to tell him if anyone was hiding inside and they all stated no that there was not. This residence looked hardly livable, it stunk, it was filthy, and there was dirty clothes and rotting food laying everywhere. In one of the upstairs bedrooms, I did find 3 sleeping infants. Upon checking the basement, I did find the 18-year-old male I had been looking for hiding behind a couch in the basement.

I arrested this 1 8-year-old male and he admitted to taking the motorcycles along with another teenager at the residence but he would not say which one. This 18-year-old male also admitted to the armed robbery, the burglaries and all the rest of the offenses. It seemed that what had happened here was that the officers who initially arrived on the scene were treating these people like they deserved to be treated, and the way they were being treated. That was why they would not let them in the residence to search. When I got there, I treated them nice, (good guy bad guy routine always works) I handled it with kid gloves. These kids did deserve to be treated rough but we were getting nowhere, so sometimes you can get more with sugar than with salt, and this was one of those cases.

The sergeant then reported this residence to family services who made them clean it up and have been closely monitoring it since.

21. The $10,000.00 Dollar Newspaper Burglary, I Stumbled Upon. I arrived at work one morning as a Detective in the center part of the city. I was immediately informed by some police officers that they had been dispatched on car prowlers at a local apartment complex. When they arrived, they observed a newspaper company maintenance pickup truck parked in the parking lot. The driver's door of this pickup was open and a black male standing at the door with a bucket of tools. There was a second black male sitting inside the pickup. Upon the black males seeing the police officers, one dropped the bucket of tools and they both ran. Because the police officers did not know the area as well as the males did, the males got away. These police officers then picked up the bucket of tools and put them in the truck and locked it up, after being unable to contact the driver of the truck. These police officers were thinking that no offense had occurred since nothing was stolen. About 10 minutes after the police officers told me about this incident. The manager of that same apartment building called me. He stated that he had been seeing somebody moving stuff from that newspaper truck into the apartment building all night long. This apartment manager also stated that he had never seen this newspaper truck in the parking lot before. He showed me the apartment that the items from the newspaper truck had been moved into. I went over to this apartment and knocked on the front door. A black female opened the apartment door and invited me in, just inside the door in the living room I observed it to be packed full of greasy tools, tires and equipment. I asked this 28-year-old black female if she knew where all these tools came from and she stated that she did not. She stated that, all she knew was that they were not there when she came home at 3 a.m. I asked the dispatcher to have a police car go to this Newspaper Company and check to see if they had a burglary in their maintenance building. Sure, enough the tool's etc... Had been taken from a local newspaper maintenance building as well

as the truck out in the parking lot was also stolen. The female I had contacted at this apartment, and her boyfriend, whom we found asleep in a back bedroom were arrested. Representatives of the newspaper maintenance building responded and positively identified this property as having come from their newspaper maintenance building. The stolen property was released back to the newspaper employees. It was determined that approximately 10,000.00 dollars worth of property and the truck had been stolen and now were recovered. The black female and the 21-year-old black male were taken to the police station where I interrogated them. It was determined after interrogating these two that the female had picked the male up in a bar that night. They had come back to this friend's apartment where they were having sex in a back bedroom. They both said they had heard some noises as if someone was moving something early this morning but they were not concerned because they had other things on their minds. These two did not even know each other's first names. This female appeared to be quite a party person however the black male was very frightened and he appeared to be a goody two shoes.

I asked this female where the residents were that lived in this apartment and she stated the last she knew they were in bed when she and this male came to the apartment. I returned to this apartment after letting the male and female go. The 36-year-old black female resident was now home. I explained to her what had happened earlier that morning and she stated that she knew she had been out walking when she returned all the police were there so she watched until we left. This female stated that her boyfriend that lives there with her and his friend had brought this stuff to her apartment early this morning. She stated they made so much noise because they were drunk that they woke her up. This female stated that she knew that they had to have stolen this stuff but her boyfriend stated that he was getting paid to store it for someone so she went back to bed. This female stated that when she woke up this morning her boyfriend and his friend were both gone

22. Trucking Company Employee Arsonists, On Video Tape.

I had an incident when I was working as a Bomb and Arson Detective. I had been called to a local trucking company in the northeast area after they had a fire in their restroom. Nobody at the trucking company had any idea who set this fire. The fire had been set in the men's restroom inside a paper towel dispenser. The fire only burnt the paper towels and the dispenser; however, it caused a lot of smoke damage inside and outside the restroom. I had really nothing to work with, so since this fire was started during working hours, I started asking employees around the restroom area if they had seen anything. No one had seen anything suspicious about men coming and going from the restroom. I did get lucky because to get to this men's restroom you had to go past the counter where the truck drivers had to check in and out. I noticed that there was a video camera pointed at the counter at all times recording. I asked to view the video tape, and upon watching the video tape. I was able to watch men come and go past this counter on their way to this restroom. I watched this tape until I started noticing smoke coming into the picture. I then rewound the video tape and there they were two white males in their early thirties had gone into the restroom stayed a while then came out. The smoke then started coming into the picture a few minutes later and no one else had been into this restroom. The next thing I observed on the video tape was other employees noticing the smoke and going into the restroom to put the fire out. Upon letting one of the trucking company dock supervisors look at this video tape, he was able to name these two men. I had uniformed police officers then respond to the trucking company and arrest these two men who on the trucking company dock working. I interrogated both of these males and they both admitted to staffing this and several other small fires, (nothing fires they called them). These males thought that it was funny to see all the dock fire alarms and sprinklers go off. They also liked watching fire trucks responding to the scene each time because it was such a large business. Both of these males had families, this was a union job, that paid very well, the company treated their employees great, and they provided great benefits. One of these males had 9 years and the other male had 11 years on this job. These males did get off easier than they really should have. They were given the option by the company president to resign and keep their pension, or be fired, loose their pension and go to jail. At least they were smart enough to resign, but think of all they gave up, just to have some stupid fun.

23. They Hid The Shotgun Somewhere In The Woods, Let Me Show You Where.

I investigated a burglary in the northland area involving some juvenile boys that the victim suspected of doing his burglary. I went up to a couple of these juveniles' residences, trying to contact their parents and to talk to them, but I was having no luck. However, I did see a 14-year-old white male juvenile on the street and I asked him if he knew where juveniles I was looking for were. This juvenile wanted to know why I wanted to know, and why was I looking for them, so I explained to him about the burglary. This juvenile then asked me if this case had anything to do with a shotgun. I knew that there had been a shotgun taken in this burglary, but I was wondering how this juvenile knew about it... So, I asked this juvenile what about a shotgun. The juvenile then stated the one that's hidden in the woods out there. I then told this juvenile that this was my only purpose of trying to find these juveniles, was to get the shotgun off the streets. I then asked this juvenile if he would help me find this hidden shotgun.

This juvenile was very excited now because he was going to help the police out. This juvenile then started into the woods as if he knew where he was going so, I asked him if he knew where the shotgun was. This juvenile then stated that one of the males I was looking for told him only that he had hidden a shotgun in the woods. This juvenile led me up into the woods to a large tree about 25 feet off the road. Then he started digging. There was no way this juvenile could not have been there when this shotgun was hidden, because it was hidden underneath tree branches, underneath leaves, underneath dirt and wrapped in a towel. Upon digging this up, I grabbed it from him and unwrapped it revealing a shotgun whose handles had been recently sawed off as well as the barrel. The shotgun was even loaded, I recovered this shotgun, and then I went to locate the two juvenile male suspects. Upon finally locating these other two juveniles, both 14-year-old white males, who immediately informed their parents that they did this burglary. I learned that the shotgun had been sawed off in the basement of the juvenile's residence that showed me where the shotgun was. I wanted to confirm this story, so I got permission from this juvenile's mother to check the basement. I did find the sawed-off parts of this shotgun, along with several knives and several other pieces of property that had come from the victim's house. It turned out that the victim (a 43-year-old white male), is one of these people who buy beer for these juveniles. He let them party at his residence, just to be cool for his 14-year-old son. However, these kids just thought that he was weird, and they just turned on him in this particular incident. You never know who you can trust. There are times when a parent can be a friend however when It comes to setting an example you need to act like a responsible adult. It was later learned that all of these juveniles, and a couple of others, had been skipping school. They had been doing burglaries, stealing from cars, etc... One of these juveniles stated that they stole the shotgun and sawed it off because his cousin had had his residence shot up in a drive by shooting. This juvenile stated that he was going to give this shotgun to his cousin so his cousin could get back at whoever shot up his residence.

24. Their Kid's Wrote In the Cement, but it's Not Their Kid's Fault. I investigated a much-publicized incident one time that I really wished I would not have been involved in, regarding kids writing in fresh cement sidewalks north of the river. I had gotten a call from a contractor stating that this had happened several times, so I went there to check it out The contractor was putting a new

cement walkway in this park. However, every time he finished a section and he would leave to let it dry overnight, the next day it would be written in and he would have to repair it. It was obviously kid's writing in the new cement because of their drawings etc...

Some of the kids had even written down their first names, their last names, birth dates or their ages. I wrote down as many of the names and identifiers as I could make out, then I went to a grade school directly across the street. Upon checking at the grade school, I learned the identities of quite a few of these kid's, their addresses and their parent's names. I also found out that there was a school teacher that had observed some kids doing something by the cement while walking home from school, but she was not sure what they were doing. I started contacting the parents of these kids, because the contractor wanted this damage to stop. However, while contacting parents, I learned that one parent had loaded his pickup truck full of kids, took them to this fresh cement. He had given them each a nail and encouraged the kids to write in the fresh cement. This new sidewalk was. Being put in this city park, and us tax payers were paying for it, as well as my time there. The contractor stated that if this had been just a few kids writing their names in the cement he would have over looked it. However, the kids were just tearing the cement up to the point that you could not hardly walk on it because it was too rough, and they were writing everywhere on it. The contractor stated that, that was just one section of the cement and then another section was damaged the next night, and then the next. I checked with our Police Juvenile Unit and the juvenile unit supervisor requested that all of the juveniles involved be identified so that they could later be brought to the juvenile unit. All I had to do for the juvenile unit was to furnish them with the juveniles' names and birth dates and I would have been done with this case. Well, that was easier said, then done, because as I started calling these juveniles' parents most of them were very cooperative. Originally stating, that if their kids were involved in this they were going to be punished, there is no way they should get away with this, (parents from the old school that teaches responsibility). Then I contacted a set of parents who stated that this was not the kid's fault, the contractor should have had guards there to protect the fresh cement. The cement was right across the street from the grade school and these kids were too young to know any better than to do this. While doing this investigation I was also contacted by a police officer who also lives across the street from this new sidewalk. This police officer informed me that he observed a female (most likely the mother) in a car stop and let two little girls out. The little girls went directly over to the fresh cement wrote in it then ran back to this waiting car and it drove off. I feel that this is pretty ridiculous when parents do this sort of thing. What kind of example is this, it makes the parent just as bad as the kids, (Or worse)? The next step on this case, because this last set of parents refused to cooperate and give me their child's birth date. I contacted the County Juvenile Officers, they informed me that they would need birth dates on these kids and if I was not able to get the information they needed for this criminal case. Then I should take the juvenile into custody and have the parents respond to the County Juvenile Office and pick them up, at which time the parents would have to furnish this information. I again reluctantly contacted these uncooperative parents, by telephone and informed them of my new orders. I also advised these parents that this was getting ridiculous, and that I really should not have even been involved in this. I advised them that this was something they should be settling with the contractor, not the police. These parents again refused to give their child's birth date, and stated send the police over here and come pick up my child right now, and I will have the news crews waiting for you. I called the County Juvenile Office back and I explained the dilemma I was in. The County Juvenile Officer decided I should temporarily stop my investigation right there, because these parents were blowing this whole thing out of proportion. In the meantime, even after I let everything drop, this family apparently notified the newspapers, and the television stations. That night this story was on television and the next day it was on the front page of the newspaper. The articles and the news casts informed the public about this incident, and how I had threatened to arrest all the area children.

The media made it sound as if I handcuffed and interrogated these children, the truth be known, I never even saw one of these children including the ones who spoke on television with their parents. I heard about the children on television talking about this incident, with their parents, and how scared the children were that I was coming to arrest them, but I did not see it. I had talked to some teachers, and I talked to some parents on the telephone, that was the closest I got to this incident. The city then decided to step in because this situation was getting too political. The Police Chief had been contacted the mayor, the contracting company etc... This case was dismissed and all we tax payers paid for all the damage the children did and some of the parents encouraged. I even had one parent tell me that his neighborhood had lobbied hard to get this jogging trail in the park. He also stated that the kids writing in this fresh cement was like a memorial, after all, their parents had to fight so hard to get this jogging trail. The contractor the city hired to do this work, was advised to repair the damages at the city's expense, however if this were to happen again the city would pursue prosecution.

25. No Crime to Steal My Signs, But a Crime for Me to Steal Someone Else's.

It is really strange how when politics become involved in things, they are done so much faster and so much differently. In this particular case campaign signs had been stolen. These campaign signs were taken by a person who had run for an office and lost. However, the person who took the signs was observed taking some of the signs by a person who put the signs up for the candidates. Upon these two people confronting each other, the person taking the signs gave the other person a hard time and refused to put the signs back. I had been assigned to investigate this case as a stealing case, after the person who put the signs out gave me a description of the other person, his vehicle and his license plate number. I was able to track this person down, and he stated that all his signs had been stolen on a previous election. This person stated that he had gone to make a police report at the sheriff's department, but they would not take a report. The sheriff's department had advised him that there was no offense, because it had been after the election and his signs were not taken off private property but off the side of the road. So, this person decided that this time it would be ok for him to take someone else's signs, since it was after the election and the signs were not on private property. I guess where the real difference was, was the fact that the campaign signs this person took belonged to 5 different candidates for different offices. This incident got around to many politicians very quickly and they were not really happy, since these campaign signs were very expensive. I tried very hard to head this thing off before it became blown even further out of proportion. I requested this person bring all the signs back, with the understanding that the person who put the signs out, would be happy and he would not be prosecuted. However, after this person returned the signs and I thought this case was closed. I was contacted by the county prosecutor who stated that the signs taken did not all belong to the person who put them out, but some of the signs belonged to the 5 candidates. The county prosecutor stated that he wanted me to put a case file together so he could file charges against the person who took the signs. This put me in an embarrassing position after I had told this person that everything would be over when he brought the signs back (which was my understanding). This person ended up being charged with stealing and he had to post a $20,000 bond. In many cases a lot of more serious crimes happen and you are unable to get the person charged, even if you do the bond would only be around $5000.

26. The Homeless and Bridge People.
     There are many people living underneath the bridges in Kansas City and around the railroad tracks in the western part of the city,

along the river. A couple of summers and winters I took my video camera with me underneath these bridges and along the river. I taped some of these people and their surroundings because it would help me find out what kind of crimes, they were committing to stay alive. Most of the time I would find the plastic or rubber coating that had been stripped off wire. This was a big thing with these people stealing wire and stripping it then selling the wire to recycling places. They would get this wire from overhead cables or wherever they could get their hands on. Sometimes they would even steal large spools of wire off the trains. Another popular item I would find down there was women's purses. I would always find a lot of junk the kind of thing's people would leave in their cars. One time I even found a gavel like a judge would use. These people would make their homes out of plastic, cardboard, tarps or whatever they could find. Then they would fill them with stuff (junk) they collected. There is one particular home where two white males in their late forties live. This home has couches, chairs, cabinets, beds and it is even divided into separate rooms. These men have actually made a house under the bridge, and they put up signs all around it making it look almost like a business. Some of these people would move on by the time I would return each time, however there were also many of these people who have lived here for years. One of the most interesting ones is the cat man, He never wears shoes and he keeps a lot of cats for pets. This man is very, very intelligent. I mean he reads all these really sophisticated books and he sounds almost like he is a college professor or something. He never wears shoes, winter or summer, and he has lived up there in this same canvas tent, he says for 10 years. He just loves it up there; he is a white male in his early fifties I would guess. He has real long hair, a long beard, he is a dirty looking guy but very intelligent and cats are his only company apparently. There are lots and lots of cats everywhere around this man. I had one 47-year-old white male that I would frequently visit with, because he lived in the district that I patrolled. The man lived underneath a business driveway that the dirt had washed away from underneath one section of it. This man lived underneath there and he had three sleeping bags, this man would rent the sleeping bags out to people living on the streets. A lot of the inter city street people are just drunks however this man did not even drink. This man was just a really nice guy and he told me that he used to be a truck driver, and he had a really nice family. However, he did not like the everyday pressures, so one day he decided to give up all his responsibilities, and he just up and dropped out of what I call a reasonable life style. He lived underneath this driveway and rented out his sleeping bags. This man did go to the bank occasionally on the Plaza if he really needed money. Because he had relatives that would deposit $25 dollars a week just for emergencies. This man stated that he has no contact with any of his family or relatives. He stated that the only reason there is a bank account is because one of the shelters arranged it for the relatives. This man along with most of the street people would go out only at night or early morning to collect cans to sell. Some mornings when it was snowing and slow on the streets, I would take him some hot chocolate and we would sit there and talk, we had some good conversations. These people are really interesting people and why they drop out, it's for all different reasons, but if they do not want help, and they are not hurting anyone I figure it is their business. It is quite obvious however that a lot of these people living under the bridges by the railroad tracks are Hispanics that are catching a ride on the trains. Most of these Hispanics I would imagine are illegal because they cannot speak English. These people leave all kinds of signs that they are Hispanic, their comic books from Mexico, newspapers and even the makers of their clothing are all in Spanish. As well as all the graffiti they write on the bridges. I think Kansas City is just a stop-off between places for them.

27.   1 Found A Gun Like That, so 1 Threw It In The River.
Up north of the river I was having a lot of problems with a group of juvenile males. They were always breaking into houses and cars. Harassing kids on the school bus and at school, sexually and

otherwise. I had one case where a county juvenile officer, who was there to check on these boys, was approached by three of these boys as they came out of the woods. These boys were carrying a blanket with something long covered up it. The boys told this juvenile officer that they were going to make a tent. It was later determined that these boys had walked up to this juvenile officer carrying loaded shotguns, rifles, and handguns covered up in that blanket they were carrying. These boys had just burglarized a residence and they were taking these guns out into the woods to hide them. Another case that involved this same group of juveniles. I approached one of the parents of these juveniles, after a witness to a burglary stated that the juvenile suspect was observed going to his residence. I informed the father of this juvenile, that a handgun had been taken in this burglary. I also informed him that an antique car, the victim was restoring, someone had spray painted all over it, and they had urinated on the seats of it. The juvenile suspects had gone into this residence when everybody was asleep and taken several things out of the house including a handgun from a car that was parked in the garage. I explained this to this father, and I informed him, that I believed that his son and this group of juveniles were involved in this burglary. This father stated that he agreed that this residence that had been burglarized was really close to his residence but his son was at home watching television with him and his wife. I knew right away that this father was lying for his son because I had not even told this man when this burglary occurred, and he had already given me an alibi. Upon asking this man some other questions, he stated that one day the previous week he did find an automatic handgun, that matched the description of the gun taken in this burglary the previous week. He said he found it lying in his backyard. This man stated however he threw the gun in the river because he did not want his family to have anything to do with a handgun. I again explained to this father that the boys were seen running to his residence, and he had found the stolen gun in his backyard. I told him that this led me to believe that his son was involved in this burglary.

This father stated that if no one seen his son do this burglary, then his son was not involved in it. This father also stated that no one could be sure that the gun he had found was the stolen gun, and even if it was anyone could have thrown it in his fenced back yard. This father stated that the police, lawyers, juvenile authorities, and teachers were all out to get his son and the group he hangs around with. The father then stated, "you all make stuff up just to get these boys, and that is why I hate all of you, your all crooked."

28. Responsible Teens Need Love To.

I was dispatched on a disturbance at a residence in the inner city one night. This disturbance involved a 14-year-old black male and his 36-year-old mother. These two were screaming at each other and the male would not do a thing that the mother asked him to do. My assisting officer and I separated these two. As the male was being taken by the other officer into another room, I asked the mother what was going on. This female stated that she had been divorced for five years. Also, that her ex-husband could not be located so she has not gotten a penny from him since. This female stated that she works 3 jobs just to support her four children. This woman had 14, and 7-year-old sons and 8 and 6-year-old daughters. This woman stated that for the last 5 years she has depended on her oldest son to take care of his brother and sisters while she was at work. She stated this was necessary because she could not afford a baby-sitter. This woman stated that this had been working out fine until the last couple of days.

Then her son stated that he wanted to run away, because he did not want to take care of the kids any more. This woman stated that she really could not understand what the problem was with her oldest son, and she was not able to be home long enough between jobs to deal with this new problem. I then went into the other room and talked to her 14-year-old son. He was crying and he stated that his mother made him do everything. He stated that he did not have time to be a kid. He also stated that when he did the kids at school made   of him, because he had a weight problem. This male stated that he loves his mother but all she wanted from him was for him to be the man around the house. This mother apparently had taken this boy for granted and she never even stopped to think about her son being a growing teenager with needs to. I brought them to of them together and I explained what both of them had said to me and they were both surprised. The woman's son really wanted to help as much as possible. He had given all he had to give, and he had reached his breaking point. I suggested that the mother make some time for this son. I suggested that she get a baby sitter, so she could spend some time alone with her oldest son," go to a movie, out to eat, for a walk or something." I must have said the right thing, because the mother and son then both started crying hugging each other, stating that they loved each other. The officer I had made this call with was a new police officer. I did not know until afterwards, that he had previously been a juvenile counselor. This officer stated that he was impressed by the way I handled that situation. He stated that he had gone to school for years to learn how to handle these situations, and he would have handled it the same way. I thought it was just common sense. This officer also wrote a letter to my supervisor about this incident, which is still in my records today. My supervisor stated that he waited one week after this incident happened and he called this woman to see how things were going. This woman informed my supervisor that thing had never been better. This woman also on her own contacted this same supervisor about a year later and stated that things between her and her son were still great.

29. But It looked Like You Were Hurting Him, For No Reason.
I had another incident in the inner city. I had pulled up to an intersection a couple blocks from the police station, where I observed (4) bicycles lying on the street corner. I stopped to see what was going on, at which time I observed some male juveniles running away down the side walk. I called for an assisting officer and we checked the house on that corner. It looked as if somebody

had tried to get in this house there were pry marks on the front door. I then walked down the sidewalk in the direction these juveniles ran. I was able to find 3 of the juveniles in the front yard of another residence where these boys were acting as if they had been there playing. I recognized 2 of the juveniles by their clothing, which I had noticed when they ran. I asked the boys what they were doing, and if those were their bicycles on the street corner. It should be noted that, the officer that was assisting me on this incident had just completed his break-in period. He was not real familiar with the way we did things on the street yet. The boys stated that the bicycles on the street corner were theirs. I then asked the boys what they were doing by that residence, and why did they run when they saw me. One of the boys stated that they were not messing with the house, and they did not know why they ran. I then took the boys back up to where their bicycles were, and I had them put their hands on the back of my police car. My assisting officer was standing behind and to the side of me watching my back, while I patted these juveniles down to make sure they did not have any weapons. I had no problems at all with the first juvenile. I was going to pat down the rear pocket of the second juvenile, when he reached back and tried to pull out a screwdriver. This screwdriver had a piece welded on top of it making it a T-handle.

As I observed this action, I shoved this juvenile's face down into the trunk of my police car. I then grabbed the screwdriver out of his hand and I was going to handcuff him. However, all my assisting officer had seen was me slamming this juvenile down on the trunk of my police car. This officer could not believe what he had seen, so he said, "Hartman, what are you doing." He was thinking I was hurting this juvenile for no reason; he had not seen the weapon. In the meantime, while this officer is just standing there amazed, the first juvenile I had patted down grabbed my arm. This first juvenile tried to pull me away from the juvenile I had slammed on the trunk. Then to make things worse, the mother of one of the juveniles comes running towards me very angrily screaming," what are you doing to my boys." My assisting officer was still standing there saying," Hartman, what are you doing." Well, thank god another veteran Police Officer pulled up on the scene at that time. Upon this other Officer seeing what was happening, he jumped out of his police car and helped me get this situation under control. These 3 juveniles were taken to the juvenile unit and then later released back to their parents. As it turned out, this new officer having previously been a juvenile counselor, he could not make up his mind what to do, help the juvenile or me. Well, in police work no matter what is going on, you get things under control and then you ask questions. This officer was still acting as a civilian would; if they saw somebody hurting someone else, they would wonder why they are hurting them. There was really no hurting going on, it was just the fact that the juvenile was thrown against the car because he was going for this weapon, which my assisting officer never saw. I have to say that this assisting officer has turned out to be a great police officer, with a lot of experience under his belt now.

30. Why Was The Female Officer Going To Shoot Me, What Was She Thinking?

I had been dispatched to a burglary in progress and upon my arrival along with a couple of other police cars we surrounded this residence. Upon searching this residence, we located a suspect who we found hiding in a part of the residence that was being remodeled. After getting the suspect into custody, I started checking the outside of this residence to see if there were any other suspects and to find out how this suspect had gotten into the residence. I had been walking around the side of this residence wearing my uniform, looking around using my flashlight, and being lit up by a street light. I thought that I was very visible and I had noticed that there was a sergeant sitting in his patrol car just a few feet from where I was walking. We had been at this scene for about 5 minutes, when all of the sudden a female police officer came squealing around the corner in her police car. I had looked up and noticed that it was a police car so I had gone back to my search, thinking that this police officer should not have been driving like that because there was a police sergeant sitting there. I heard this police car park at the curb, but I didn't expect what happened next at all. I heard a female voice yelling," drop it or I'll shoot, drop it", at which time I looked up and observed this same female officer running towards me with her revolver pointed at me. Luckily that sergeant was watching this happen and he yelled, "don't shoot it's a police officer". She was still looking and running right towards me, so I looked behind and around myself to see what she was trying to protect me from. However, there was no one else there, for some reason this female officer thought that I was a suspect and my flashlight was a gun. I was in full uniform including a police service cap, under a streetlight and shinning a flashlight. Thanks to that sergeant paying attention to this female officer and that he spoke up, I think that saved me from getting shot. I really have no idea what she was thinking, you just never know.

31. Tattooed At Three Years Old, Now Stealing From Cars.
I investigated a case up North of the river where a citizen had observed a vehicle stop and a couple of white males get out of the vehicle. These males then went into a used car lot and took some car radios and hubcaps from two Cadillac's on the car lot. This citizen was a white female in her early thirties, when she seen this happening, she contacted the owner of this car lot. The 45-year-old white male owner of this car lot responded in time to see the vehicle the suspects had arrived in leaving the area so he followed it. This used car lot owner waited until he seen which residence these males went into then he confronted the parents of one of these males. This owner advised this males parents that he had followed the vehicle which was parked out front of their residence from his business and he had observed two males exit this vehicle and go into this residence. These parents stated that their boys had nothing to do with this theft, even if it they had been in this

vehicle that this male had followed. The parents of one of these juveniles had their son and another male who their son had just came home with in that vehicle, come to the door so that this male could see them. This owner had not seen the boys steal anything or even see who was in the vehicle; all he did was follow the vehicle that this witness had described to him. This lot owner then had the police respond to take a stealing report then he contacted me. When I got involved in this case, I first got a statement from this witness, which consisted of the same information she had told the lot owner. Then I interrogated these two males, one of the boys stated that he and the other male were involved with a group of teenage kids. This male stated that the kids in this group were all 14 and 15 years old. This male stated that he was 17 years old and his friend was 19 years old and married. This male stated that the two of them were running around with a group of younger white girls 14 and 15-year-old. This male stated that all of these girls wanted to have sex with them so they were changing partners. This male stated that all the girls in this group were all very over weight, and that there having sex with them was just a game they were playing between all of them. This male also stated that the reason that they go out and steal stuff is just for fun. This same male stated that his father was currently in the penitentiary and his mothers' location was unknown to him. This male stated that he had just been staying at different friend's houses and sometimes at some of his aunt's houses. This male then showed me a small circle tattoo on his hand. This male stated that his father gave him this tattoo when he was three years old, and his father told him that it meant that he hated "nigers". Well, it's no wonder these boys turn out like this when their parents do things like that at that young of an age. These males were convicted of these thefts as well as several others in that same area. The older other male had informed me that they had stolen the Cadillac radios, and hub caps, but when they see this female watching them, they dropped the stolen items in a ditch and ran. This male was very proud of this because he stated that even thought he was married he was with his girlfriend at the time they were doing this, she was driving the car and no one had even seen her. The 17-year-old boy was sent to a group home in Kansas at one of his aunts' requests and the 19-year-old was put on a supervised probation. I informed these males that they were asking for trouble having sex with under aged females. I also contacted the younger girls' parents that these boys were having sex with and they none of the parents appeared to really believe me or maybe they just didn't care. Well, I feel I did my part and hopefully these kids straightened out when they went their different ways.

32. Cattle Rustlers.
I assisted Detective Bob Arnold investigate a case where two white males in their late thirties were stealing cattle up north of the river.

These males also stole a large horse trailer to haul the cattle. We suspected that it was the same people stealing the cattle on each offense because we found the same tire tracks each time. These males would actually set up a portable pen in the pasture and lure the cattle into the pen with a special brand of a sweet cattle feed, then they would herd the cattle into the horse trailer. The tire tracks we found at each scene appeared to be that of a large trailer being pulled by a semi-tractor. We had gotten an anonymous tip one day, stating that somebody had cattle behind a business in the north east part of the city and they were possibly in a stolen horse trailer. This caller stated that they believed that the horse trailer was stolen because there was a white male peeling all the decals off of this brand-new looking trailer. My sergeant and I responded to the location this caller had advised us of and we did find an empty horse trailer behind a business at that location. This trailer matched a trailer that was reported stolen near one of the locations where some cattle were stolen. I then started checking with the businesses in this area to see if they knew who had parked the trailer. Upon talking to some employees of one of these businesses I learned that a white male whose father owned a business on that block had parked that trailer there, these employees also gave me this males and his father's name. These same employees stated that a couple of days earlier this same male had cattle in this trailer and they had asked him to move them because they stunk so badly. These same employees also stated that this male used a semi tractor parked in front of the business to haul this horse trailer. I checked out front of this business and parked on the street was an old semi-tractor. I checked the tires on this semi-tractor and they appeared to be very similar to the tire tracks left at each of these cattle theft scenes. My sergeant and I then went up to the business where this male suspect's father reportedly owned. Upon approaching this business an older white male hurriedly walked up and locked the front door of the business from inside. We identified ourselves and showed this male our identification, then I requested this male to unlock this door and let us in. I asked this male if the male whose name the business employees had given me was there and he stated no. I then asked this male for some identification and he produced it revealing that he was the 60-year-old father of the male I was looking for. I asked this male where his son was a he stated that he didn't have any idea. I then asked this male if he knew anything about the cattle or the trailers behind his business and he stated that he didn't know anything about them. I then asked this male if there was anyone else in the business, and he stated no that there wasn't. Just to make sure because I already knew this male was lying to me, I checked this business. I found a white male in his thirties hiding in the kitchen area of this business, and this male gave me a false name. I believed that this was the male I was looking for so I asked this male to show me some identification and sure enough it was the male I was looking for. I asked this male if he knew anything about the trailers, behind the business or the semi-tractor parked out front. This male stated that he didn't know anything about the trailers but the semi-tractor was his. I asked this male if he knew anything about some cattle being in the trailers behind this business and he stated yes and they sure stunk. I looked into the window of this semi-tractor and I observed a sack of the same special sweet cattle feed, the same kind of feed that had been found at the scenes of each of these cattle thefts. I had this male and his father taken to our police station for questioning and I had this semi-tractor and horse trailer towed to our city tow lot. Det. Bob Arnold interrogated these males and eventually Det. Arnold did get this male to admit that he was involved in these thefts with another person. This male stated that they were taking the stolen cattle to sale barn auctions in Kansas and selling the cattle. Det. Arnold had to call the manufacture of this horse trailer to see if it had any identifying numbers on it, so that we could prove that this was the trailer stolen from our victim. We learned that a number was welded on the underside of these trailers and this manufacture even told us what the number of this victim's trailer was. I went to the tow lot and found this number and it matched the victim's number perfectly.

Detective Bob Arnold got the privilege of going with the Highway Patrol Investigators in an airplane to these cattle auctions in Kansas, in an attempt to locate these cattle. Det. Arnold found out that the stolen cattle had been already sold, so he then went to the feed lots that the cattle had been sold to. Det. Arnold stated that the first feed lot he went to had 75,000 head of cattle on it; however, he also stated that the 5 stolen cows that were sold to this feed lot were easy to locate because they had been raised together since birth and they were all together in a separate group. While Det. Arnold was having all the fun in Kansas the suspect that the first suspect stated he was involved in this case with, was arrested and I interrogated him. This second suspect stated that he did not know the first suspect however he did buy some cattle at an auction in Kansas from a man he didn't know. The funny thing about this story was that the Highway patrol had stopped the first suspect and this second suspect on a traffic violation just outside of the town where this cattle auction was, so this second suspect was also lying. Both of these suspects were arrested and charged with cattle theft. The First suspect's father was also charged for aiding the other two suspects. The first suspect also made the statement that when he gets out of prison, he was going to retire from the cattle theft business. This case had involved the Kansas City, Missouri Police Department, The FBI Kansas Highway Patrol, and the Kansas local law enforcement agencies. Det. Arnold did such a good job on this case that the Clay County Prosecutors now call him "Bessie the Moo Cow Detective".

33. I Should Have Anticipated the Injury and Went Around the Fence. I was dispatched to the scene of a disturbance in the inner city with another police officer. Upon our arrival a 17-year-old black female pointed to a 19-year-old black male that was walking away from her residence. This female stated that this male had a knife and he had threatened her with it. Myself and the other officer started after this male at which time this male started running. We chased this male through some woods and across some yards, then over some fences. Myself and the other officer both jumped over one of these fences at the same time and when we came down, for some reason we both twisted one of our ankles. We both continued to chase this male and we were able to catch and arrest him. I reported my injury to my sergeant because it was required and an injury report needed to be made in case the injury was worse than I thought. The police officer who assisted me and also sprained his ankle did not report his injury. We both limped a little bit and both of our ankles healed after about a week and a half.

The major difference between me reporting my injury and the other police officer not reporting his injury was that when my sergeant wrote up an injury report, he wrote in the area marked how this injury could have been prevented, that I should have anticipated injury and went around the fence. Now if you think about this, and you anticipate injury at any time I'd never go to work, I would just stay in bed.

34. Frozen and Pinned Down.
I was dispatched to assist several other officers who were responding to an inner city call of shots being fired from an apartment building.

Upon my arrival two officers had already started up the back-outer stairway of this apartment building, towards the apartment that the shots were supposed to be coming from. As these police officers were going up the steps a 28-year-old black male started firing shots at them from an upstairs window. These two police officers were now stuck on this stairway. If they went up the stairs, they would have been right in front of the apartment door, if they went down the stairs, they would be right in this male's line of fire. The only thing myself and the other police officers could do was take up positions surrounding this apartment building, and if this male comes out of his apartment door with a gun or leans out the window again to shoot at these police officers, we would have to kill him. My sergeant also showed up on this call with us, and he ordered us to all hold our positions and not to take our eyes off of this window and door way. The sergeant then ordered the Tactical Response Unit for an operation 100. It was winter outside the wind was blowing snow and the temperature was around zero. Myself and another police officer were both-leaning over the trunk and hood of my police car, the other officer was watching the window and I was watching the door. We knew that we could not let out guard down for a second or our fellow police officers pinned down on these steps could be shot. We were standing there with our guns pointing at this window and door waiting for the Tactical Response Unit to relieve us. This black male every once in a while, would stick his head out of this window to look at the police officers on the stairs, however he would have his hands where we could see that he did not have a weapon in them, so we could not shoot. This situation went on for about 45 minutes and I had been continuously changing my gun from hand to hand because my fingers were getting so frozen that I didn't think that I could have pulled the trigger and I knew that It could mean these officers lives if I could not do my job. While we were standing there a female police officer came up and took a position at the rear of my car. We had already been out there for about 45 minutes changing hands because our hands were freezing and the female officer comes out and she is only out there with me for about 25 minutes, when she was relieved by the Tactical Response Unit even before we were. The Tactical Response Unit provided cover for the two officers who were pinned down on this stair and they were able to get them out safely. The next day this same female policer officer took off work for the next 3 days, complaining of a back was sore because-she stood-there with her arm extended pointing her gun at the window for 25 minutes. There were a lot of other officers out there long before this female officer arrived however none of us took off work because we were sore. The Tactical Response Unit eventually talked this male and five other women and children out of this apartment. It was later learned that the male that had been shooting out of the window, had been shot at from a passing car and when the police officers were coming up his stairs, he thought that they were the people who had shot at him earlier. When this male realized that this was the Police, he had been shooting at he became scared and didn't know what to do. This male stated that he was too scared to give up because he was afraid that we would have shot him and his family.

35. He said, Let Me Feed The Baby, Then He Dumped Cereal On The Floor By The Baby.

As a Burglary Detective in the northeast area of the city, I went to a northeast residence to contact the victim of a previous burglary because they did not have a telephone. Upon arriving at the residence, I immediately noticed that there were no adults in or around this residence. A 10-year-old white male answered the door and let me into the residence, without even asking who I was. This 10-year-old male was taking care of his 7-year-old and his 5-year-old sisters as well as his 4-year-old and 2-year-old brothers. I asked this 10-year-old where his parents were and he stated that their mom was over at the bar, but he didn't know the name of the bar. I asked him where his father was and he stated," That you police put him in prison, but he's going to get out and get you back". I asked the 10-year-old what he would do if there was an emergency, a fire or something and he said we don't have a telephone but we're supposed to walk down the street and go to the next block. He said then we walk until we see two old people on the front porch and that's our grandparents and they'll help us. I remember thinking to myself that these old people better always be on that porch or these kids are in trouble, because if they were not there these kids would not know what to do. This 10-year-old asked me if I could wait a minute because his 2-year-old brother was crying and he wanted to feed him to make him be quiet. He picked the 2-year-old up off the kitchen floor and put him on the living room floor which had the door way blocked so that the baby could not get out. This 10-year-old then took a box of cereal and dumped some of it on the floor next to the baby. The atmosphere these children lived in was ridiculous, there was also four dogs running around the house and there was dog food everywhere on the floor. There was one area of the kitchen that had newspapers spread out on it where the dogs went to the bathroom; it really stunk in that house. The dogs seemed to have plenty to eat but the kids had hardly anything. The refrigerator had nothing but moldy bread in it, there was some crackers and peanut butter on the table as well as the box of cereal, that's all the food I could find. I notified the youth unit who sent some people out to pick these children up and take them to a safe clean place.

I then started contacting neighbors trying to find out where the children's mother was and I learned that these kids usually wake up and their mother will be gone to a local bar, so the ten-year-old takes care of the young children sometimes even till late in the evening. The neighbors stated that the children never complain and that they occasionally go over there to see if the children need anything but their mother gets mad when they try to help her. They also stated that the mother is always gone drinking, or home sleeping. The local bars were checked for the mother but she could not be, located and the area was canvassed for 2 old people sitting on their porch also with negative results.

36. Peter Fonda at the Vietnam Veterans Memorial.
    This job does have its benefits, I worked an off-duty job as security for Peter Fonda when he was in town during the Vietnam Veterans Memorial Dedication. This was a very interesting time for me, I was able to shoot the bull for about two hours with Peter Fonda since it was snowing outside and only a very few people were coming by for this Dedication of the Vietnam Veterans Memorial. I talked to Peter Fonda about all his friends, which included Crosby, Stills and Nash, who he was getting ready to go on a sailboat trip with. I was very interested in his Easy Rider days, and at one point I joined him in singing (Get your motor running, head it down the highway) from the movie Easy Rider, he was really a pretty interesting person to talk to. 1 was even fortunate enough to get my picture (as young police officer), with Peter Fonda.

37. Prisoner Escape, But That's Not My Son.
    Before I became a commissioned Police Officer, I was a civilian volunteer for a little over a year, at the old East Patrol Station at 27th and Van Brunt in the Northeast area of Kansas City. One of the nights after I got off of my shift, working the front desk, taking reports, and bonding prisoners, I was going to ride along with one of the East Patrol police officers which I often did. I was waiting in the lobby for the police officer I was going to ride with to get out of his role call. A black gentleman was at the front desk in the lobby bailing his son out of jail. While this gentleman was waiting for the clerk to complete the paper work, I was making small talk with him. This gentleman explained to me that his son was really a good kid; however, he had not paid his parking tickets and was caught and taken to jail. While we were talking the desk, clerk clicked the detention door release, (an area where nonviolent arrests are held only temporary until their bond is made, then the lock is released on the door and the bonded-out person is released into the lobby area) to let this gentleman's son out of the detention area. However, when the detention door came open a 17-year-old

white male came out of the door running underneath a young black males' arm as the black male was coming out of this door. This white male ran out of the detention door and was headed for the outside door. I had just talked to this black gentleman and I knew that it was supposed to be his son coming out of the detention door, and so when this white kid came out going underneath the arm of the black male, I knew something had to be wrong. So, I grabbed this white male around the neck, putting him in a neck restraint that one of the police officers I had ridden with had taught me, and then I took him down to the floor and held him.

In the meantime, the desk clerk when she seen this white male run out of the detention door, she ran into the back-office area of the station and informed the desk sergeant of the escape. The desk sergeant put a bulletin over the intercom that a prisoner had just escaped. Since there was a roll call in session there were quite a few police officers and sergeants in the station at the time, and they all ran outside to look for the escaped prisoner. Since the clerk had run into the other office when this white male ran out of the detention door, she did not know that I had already caught this male. I was holding this white male down on the floor, while yelling for someone to come and help me. Finally, one of the sergeants who had run outside came into the front door of the station to ask for a description of the white male that had escaped. When this sergeant observed me holding this white male down on the floor he quickly helped me, then he took this white male and put him in a regular jail cell and charged him with attempted escape. This sergeant then informed the other police officers that the suspect was in custody. This incident really surprised me, the sergeants, the officers and even the desk clerk who didn't even know I was holding the escaped prisoner on the floor. I feel that this incident is one of the reasons that I am now a police officer; I was congratulated by everyone clear up to the station commander who requested that I apply to become a police officer. The sergeant that me with this escaped white male requested that I accompany him to court on this white male's court date on the escape charge. By the time that the court date came around I was in the Police Academy.

38. Her Daughter's Boyfriends Threw Knives In Her Floor And Stole Her Jewelry.

As a Property Detective up north of the river I was assigned to investigate a case which involved the teenage boyfriend of one of the victim's two teenage daughters stealing the victim's jewelry and damaging the victim's residence, along with two friends. One of the victim's daughters had an unauthorized party at the residence while the parents had gone away for a weekend. While this daughter was in another room with a girlfriend this daughter's boyfriend and two of his friends took steak knives out of the kitchen drawer and started throwing them and making them stick in the victim's kitchen and hallway linoleum floor, making approximately 50 holes in the floor. While this was happening the female in her twenties that the victim had hired to stay with her daughters while they were out of town, was out driving around with the victim's other daughter in the victim's sports car which no one was even allowed to touch. During my interview with this victim, she stated that ever since her daughter started dating this boyfriend, that she and her other daughter have started to notice jewelry missing each time after he leaves. This victim stated that she has let this boyfriend come over many times; he has even had dinner with them on several occasions. The victim stated that at one point after she became suspicious of this boyfriend for taking their jewelry, she confronted this boyfriend about it and he acted very hurt, and swore up and down that he had nothing to with these thefts. This also hurt the victim for accusing him, so she apologized and they gave each other a big hug and she had not suspected him since, even though jewelry continued to disappear. However, after this party when the victim was out of town there was a large amount of jewelry taken, not only from the victim but her husband and both daughters. The victim stated that with the very expensive jewelry that was taken on this last incident the value of their losses was now around $10,000 dollars. I then had the victim bring her daughter in and I questioned her. The victim's daughter stated that some of the jewelry that came up missing was her jewelry which because she was having this party, she put it in a can and hid it prior to the party. This daughter also stated that no one knew where she hid her jewelry however while she was hiding her jewelry, she thought she heard someone in the hallway, but when she checked no one was there.

This daughter further stated that the only one in the residence with her when she hid her jewelry was her boyfriend who she thought was in the other room watching television at the time. I then had this daughter bring in her girlfriend who had been with her at this party. This girlfriend stated that she had went to the bedroom of this daughter to get something on one occasion during this party and she had seen this daughter's boyfriend and his friends going through this daughter's dresser drawers. This friend stated that when she asked the boys what they were doing they stated that they were just goofing around and she forgot all about it until she heard that the victims were missing property. I had the three juvenile male teenagers brought in and they confessed to damaging the victim's kitchen floor however they all stated that they knew nothing about the missing jewelry. I started receiving telephone calls from this victims' daughters' friends after this almost on a daily basis with information that they had seen or heard about this daughter's boyfriend and his friend's stealing jewelry from other friend's parents as well as bragging about taking this victims jewelry. I was at a stalemate at this point until the victim on her own started checking pawn shops and found some of her jewelry on display for sale. Upon checking with the pawn shop and the victim giving identifying information on this jewelry it was learned who pawned this jewelry a 21-year-old male who   brought in for questioning. This male stated that he got this jewelry from this daughter's boyfriend to pawn for him. This daughter's boyfriend had also been having this male and others pawn items her was stealing from his friends' parents' homes while he was visiting them. This goes to show you; you can't trust anyone.

39.   He Played At Their House At Night, And He Stole From Their House By Day.

I was assigned a burglary case to investigate while working as a burglary detective up north of the river. This case was a residence that had been burglarized three times in the two previous months, and each time a VCR and a camera were taken. The burglar was somehow getting into the residence without leaving any clues as to how he did it. I originally had no clues to work with, and then I received notification that one of the VCR's that had been stolen from this residence had been sold to an inner-city pawn shop. I was able to go to this pawn shop and recover this VCR and find out who had sold it there. The person who had sold this VCR at this pawn shop was a 17-year-old black male. I had this male picked up and brought in for questioning. This male stated that he was asked to sell this VCR for a friend at this pawn shop because this friend said that he didn't have any identification. I then went to the victims of these burglary's and I asked them if they knew the male who sold their VCR or the male that this male had said gave him the VCR to sell. The victims stated that they did not know the male who sold their VCR, however the male that this male stated gave him the VCR was a very good friend of their son. The victims stated that this male had quit school and his parents had kicked him out of the house, so they let him come over almost every night and play basketball with their son and have supper with them. This friend of this white family's son was a 20-year-old black male. I had this black male arrested and brought in for questioning and he confessed to all three burglaries in which he had several other friends sell or pawn the VCR's and cameras for him. The victims were very upset at this male, because they had been feeding him and having him in their home every night, almost like a member of their own family. Since this male had been kicked out of his parent's residence, he would wait until his 16-year-old white girlfriends' mother would go to sleep at night, and then his girlfriend would sneak him into her house where he would sleep in a car in their garage. Upon checking with the mother of this white female she stated that she had told her daughter that this male was not welcome in her house.

This female's mother was also informed of several other items that this male had his friends sell at pawn shops, such as a lap top computer. This female's mother then checked her basement where her son who was overseas in the military had his personal belongings stored and she discovered that some of his personal belongings were missing including this lap top computer. This female told her mother that she knew that this male had pawned her brothers lap top computer, but that when he got a job, he would get it back out of pawn and that the only reason that he did this was because he was hungry. This female also stated that the only reason that this male stole from his friend's family was also because he was hungry and that he really wasn't a bad guy. It was really hard to see what this intelligent, cute little white female that worked hard every day, saw in this older, non-working, smoking, strange looking, high school dropout, thieving, black male that she was supporting. However, I figured that it was none of my business and I worked off-duty at a mall where this female worked and I see them together very often. This male was charged with the three burglaries of his friend's residence and this female's mother wanted to have this male charged with trespassing and stealing, however she later decided not to assist in this male's prosecution. This male was given a year's probation for these crimes and I really believed he was trying to straighten out his life by getting back in good with his parents and trying to find a job. He was very friendly to me when he seen me at the mall after that and when his probation officer called me and asked what I thought about this male, I told her that it appeared that this male had just been stealing because he was hungry and that it looked as if he was going the right direction now. Boy, was I wrong, about one year later we were having a rash of 1st degree burglary's (where the suspect enters a residence while there are people in the residence), as well as auto thefts? This same males' fingerprints started showing up on items left at the scenes of these burglary's and in some of the stolen auto's, such as on beer bottles etc... When this male was finally caught after being seen driving one of the cars stolen in one of these burglaries, he confessed to about 14 other burglaries and auto thefts. Some of the burglaries and auto thefts that this male admitted to we didn't even know about or the victims did not even report. This male also blamed another of his friends for doing some of these burglaries, auto thefts and putting him up to them as well. This male even bragged on how he and his friend would enter people's apartments while they were asleep through the sliding glass doors which they would find unlocked or that were easily shaken open. This male stated that in almost every instance they would find the car and house keys, a female's purse or male's wallet on the kitchen table, the counter or by the door. This male even stated that a few times they went into people's apartments and would only find the car keys so they would just take the car for a joy ride then about 5 a.m. they would return the car then throw the car keys back into the apartment and leave. This male stated that they did this because they knew that when the residents woke up, they would think that this was strange but that they would not report it. I am happy to say that this male is now locked up and he should be staying that way for quite some time to come. When I arrested this male at his girlfriend's residence asleep in a car in the garage, his girlfriend had no idea that he had been doing these thefts and she really was angry at him for deceiving her. This female stated that this male was supposed to start a new job that day. I asked this female if her mother now let this male stay there with her permission and she stated that her mother said that she does not want him there however even though she knows that he does stay there, she acts as if she doesn't.

40. **He Got Him To Do The Burglary, And then He Called Police On Him.**
As a property detective I investigated a church burglary north of the river where two suspects were in custody.

The police officer at the scene called me at home and informed me that they had arrested two white males, one 17-year-old and one 15-year-old. This officer informed me that the 911 call taker had gotten a call from an unknown male who stated that he was standing by as this burglary was taking place. This officer stated that upon his arrival at the scene he was contacted by this 1 7-year-old male and informed that the 15-year-old was inside the church at that time. This officer stated that they arrested the 15-year-old as he was coming out of a recreation building behind the church and they had also arrested the 17-year-old because the 15-year-old informed them that the 17-year-old had set him up, and had helped him commit this burglary. I responded to this church and I found that not only was the church broken into but a recreation hall in the rear of the church had also been broken into. Both buildings had broken windows and were ransacked, however nothing was taken other than some food eaten and some small change taken from some desks. I interrogated the 17-year-old and he stated that he was very surprised that I had him arrested; he stated that he was only trying to help the police out because he wanted to become a police officer. This 17-year-old stated that he suspected that this 15-year-old was doing burglary's because he was always bragging about doing them. This 17-year-old stated that he

*asked this 15-year-old if he wanted to do a burglary with him of this church and the 15-year-old agreed to. The 17-year-old stated that he met up with the 15-year-old at the church and he stated that the 15-year-old would not go into the church unless the

17-year-old broke out the window. The 17-year-old stated that he figured that there would be no way that the police could catch this 15-year-old if he could not get him in the church so the 1 7-year-old broke out the window and the 15-year-old went inside the church. After the 15-year-old went into the church the 17-year-old went to a telephone and called 911 and informed the call taker of the burglary, also stating that he would wait there until the police arrived to make sure the suspect did not get away. This 17-year-old stated that when the police arrived, they could not find the 15-year-old in the church, however while they were there the 15-year-old came out of a recreation building behind the church which the 17-year-old did not know the 15-year-old was going to break into. This 15-year-old was interrogated in the presence of his mother and a juvenile officer, he stated that he had been doing burglaries because his friends thought it was cool and they liked it when he gave them some of the stuff he got from the burglaries. This 15-year-old stated that the 17-year-old had contacted him at school and asked him to help do this burglary. He stated that because he wanted to make another friend, he said that he would help him. The 15-year-old stated that after the 17-year-old broke out the church window and he went inside of the church the 1 7-year-old disappeared. The 15-year-old stated that he could only find food and small change in the church so he went outside looking for the 17-year-old. The 15-year-old stated that when he could not find the 17-year-old, he went to the recreation hall and broke into it hoping to find something to give the 17-year-old to make him like him. Basically, it was one of those set-ups deals although I think it's pretty below the belt. We did catch this burglar and he had been burglarizing other residences in his neighborhood and we recovered some of their property as well. This 15-year-old quite obviously had mental problems, he really seemed like a nice kid and it was easy to see how he could be convinced to do some of these things for attention and to make friends. The 15-year-old was put on probation and ordered to get counseling. The 17-year-old was just put on probation, however this 17-year-old had what we call the security guard syndrome, when someone wants to make themselves look good in front of their peers, and in this case the police because he wanted to become a police officer. It should be noted that even to most police officers a person that would set some one up or do a friend dirty, does not set well with most of us either, even if it does help solve crime. Another story about this 17-year-old (Fox guarding the chicken coop).

41. Fox Guarding The Chicken Coop.
While working as a Detective up north of the river I was contacted by the owner of a northland security company. This owner informed me that he suspected one of his employees of stealing from the businesses he was supposed to be guarding at night. This owner stated that he wasn't having any thefts from his other businesses only the one where this 17-year-old white male security guard worked. This owner stated that at first there was just small things taken, that weren't even reported to the police by the businesses, then when car stereos started coming up missing, he knew he had to do something. This owner confronted this security guard about these thefts and this security guard confessed that another one of this same owner's security guards would come to this security guard and ask him to steal things with him. I questioned this first security guard and he stated that at first, he didn't want anything to do with these thefts; however, the other security guard would go into the service area of this new car dealership and go through the customer's cars getting all kinds of money and stuff. The customers would not even report it and he was getting away with it, (however the customers had been reporting the thefts to the dealership, the dealership was reimbursing the customers for their losses and not even notifying the security company because they could not tell if the losses were occurring during the night or day). This security guard stated that the other security guard had new wheels, tires, a car stereo, and several other new parts on his personal vehicle that he had stolen from cars on this dealer's new car lot. This first security guard stated that he had never

taken anything except on two occasions, once when he went with the other security guard through the cars in the service area and once when he and the other security guard took a car stereo from one of the new cars. This first security guard was charged with a felony, given probation and he can never work as a security guard in Kansas City, Missouri again. The first security guard also returned a couple of pockets and the car radio he had taken. This second security guard was the same white male who had got one of his friends to do a burglary then he called the police on him, in one of my other stories. However now this second security guard was 20 years old and he had become a security guard because he could no longer become a police officer because of his previous burglary conviction. I had this second security guard brought in for questioning and he stated that he knew nothing about the thefts of property from the car dealership where this first security guard was working. I informed this second security guard that I thought that he was lying because on his car were new tires, wheels, a stock car stereo that was now being put in the new cars that this car dealership sold, and the same type that was being stolen. This second security guard stated that he had stopped to visit this other security guard on one occasion to see how it was to work at this dealership, and the other security guard sold him this new equipment. I asked this second security guard to explain the similarity between the fingerprints I recovered on the car stereo the first security guard returned and his fingerprints. This second security guard then quickly stated that the first security guard asked him for his help to unscrew this car stereo from the dash of one of the new cars, but that was all that he did. I then asked this security guard how the first security guard was getting into the new cars and he stated that he must be using a slim gym, (a tool for unlocking car doors). I asked this second security guard if you would have to but your hand on the car window or door to use this slim-gym and he stated that he was not sure, but it was possible. I then asked this second security guard to explain how his fingerprints got on the car door that was opened on the new car that had the car stereo taken from it. This second security guard stated that the first security guard asked him to show him how to open a car door using a slim-gym because he didn't know how, (it should be noted that I had not even seen the car stereo or the new car at this time, and I sure didn't know if there were fingerprints on them, this was all a bluff that worked).

This second security guard stated that when he had the car door open, he was going to close and lock it again however the first security guard wanted to steal the car stereo from this new car. This case was almost just like the incident this second security guard had been in when he had the other boy commit the burglary.

This second security guard picked on young not so smart kids and would get them to do things for him. This second security guard was also responsible for guarding other new car lots; however, nothing was ever reported missing at those locations, most likely because he would have no one else to blame. This second security guard not only was charged with this stealing offense but he also violated his probation for the previous burglary he helped commit. This second security guard will also never be a security guard in Kansas City, Missouri again. I am not sure what sentence this second security guard got but it was not long enough. One year later I worked another case in which a 15 and 17-year-old white male high school dropouts, stated that this same male had told them that he had been watching this trading card shop and that it was an easy target to burglarize. This male told them how to break in and what to take. However, this male was not charged with this burglary, because I could not prove that he participated in it. Thankfully the last I heard male he had moved out of state, with his corporate lawyer father and social worker mother.

42   Security Guard Stealing For Years, He Even Took the Christmas tree. I investigated another incident where a local college had the fox guarding the chicken coup. In this incident this 27-year-old white

male, had been a security guard with this college for five years and before that maintenance man for 2 years. This college had noticed small items coming up missing for years that they were unable to explain. Then they started missing things like computers, software, telephones, typewriters and larger items. The college could not figure how someone was getting by their security, and why whoever was taking these items would only take one of them at a time when many times there were many other items available. The college had hired a private investigator without the knowledge of their own school security. This investigator installed surveillance cameras in several locations where this theft was frequenting. At first, they had no luck and things were still coming up missing, even the college indoor Christmas tree. The college cafeteria snack bar manager informed the college security that she had frequently been losing small amounts of money, which was being taken from a very well-hidden place that no one except her knew about she thought. Vending machines had also been randomly broken into in various parts of the college however it was determined that these machines had to have been being broken into after the college was locked up at night and only maintenance and security would be in the building. When this was realized the vice president of the college contacted me and requested that all of the college maintenance and security personnel take a lie detector test. As I was preparing to have these tests administered, the private investigator contacted the college vice principle and myself and showed us a video tape from one of his surveillance cameras. This video tape showed one of the college security guards breaking into some vending machines taking money and candy. This video tape had been taken the previous evening and this same security guard had been dispatched to take the report on this break in. I asked the vice principle if I could see what this security guard wrote on his report about this incident. This security guards report said that this was a false report, and that he was unable to locate any damaged machines at that location. I then asked to be shown where these machines that had been broken into as shown on the video tape were located. According to the video tape one of the smaller gum ball machines was the only thing that was actually visibly damaged by this security guard, however now this gum ball machine was nowhere in sight.

The private investigator then removed the current video tape from his surveillance camera and we all watched it and observed the same security guard that was sent to take the report and the one videotaped breaking into these vending machines, now taking the broken gumball machine into a maintenance storage area and coming out without it. This security guard was called into a private office where I interrogated this security guard in the presence of the private investigator. This security guard was really a nice personable guy and he originally denied any knowledge of their thefts other than what he had heard or the reports he took. I asked this security guard why it was that these thefts usually occurred only on nights when he was working, (bluff) even thought I really didn't know that for sure. This security guard then broke down crying and stated that he did take a television and a computer a long time back and that he had them at home and he would return them. I asked this security guard if he had ever broken into any school vending machines and he stated no but he had chased some black males out of the building the week before without reporting it. As I was continuing to interrogate this security guard, the private investigator and a couple of police officers went to this security guard's residence, with a list of missing items and their serial numbers. I informed this security guard that I had seen him on video tape breaking into the vending machines and then hiding the machine the next day. You should have seen his face when I said this, his mouth dropped to the floor, and he stated," you put up surveillance cameras didn't you, I never even thought of that, where did you hide them. I had brought a stack of police reports of losses the college had reported for the last 5 years and the vice principle gave me copies of losses the college had not reported to the police department over the last 5 years. This security guard then stated that he had been having trouble sleeping for the past 5 years because he had been stealing from the college, however he felt that as hard as he worked, he should be getting more money. I asked this security guard if he knew anything about the money missing from the college snack bar and he stated yes and that he was also very ashamed of that also. He stated that the manager of the snack bar had been really nice to him and when she would close up at night, she would give him free food. He stated that on one of these occasions while this manager was closing, he seen her hiding her money and so he would go and take a little bit of the money every now and then, not really believing that she was even noticing it missing. While I was doing this interrogation, I was interrupted by the vice principle who stated that the private investigator was on the telephone and that he needed to talk to me right away. This private investigator stated that the security guard's wife was home and she had let them in, where they found most of the missing property and a lot of property that they did not know was missing. This investigator further stated that this security guard even had an extremely large Christmas tree in his front room. I informed the police officers at the scene to recover any property that was believed to have come from the college. The police officers informed me that this security guards' wife and two young children were very upset, about them taking all these items because this security guard (husband/father) had •been giving these items for birthdays, holidays, and special occasions over the last 5 years. This security guard's wife informed the officers that she wondered how her husband could afford the nicest stereo's, televisions, camera's, computer's etc. But he would always tell her that they were gifts from the college or that they sold them to him at a very low price. I asked the security guard if this was the colleges Christmas tree in his front room and he stated that it also belonged to the college. This security guard was very upset now because he did not realize that I had sent the police to his residence, he thought that I was just going to let him go and bring the stuff back, so that he would not have to tell his wife about this.

I asked this security guard how he had been getting into the locked classrooms and the locked vending machines without damaging the locks. The security guard stated that he just kept his set of keys he had when he was working with the maintenance staff, and he knew the maintenance people's locations in the building at all times.

He stated that he would always help the vending machine venders stock the machines and when the vender was shutting the doors to the machines, he would make sure the door of the one he had stocked did not get all the way shut. This security guard had the latest in almost all electronic equipment and software, he had televisions, VCR's, Nintendo's etc... Even in his children's rooms. This security guard stated that he was really sorry but that he was only doing this for his family, he had never given anything away or sold it. There were so many thefts this security guard had committed that they all could not even be found. These security guards' cases were taken to the Grand Jury; however, I am not sure what sentence he received, but I do know that he will never be a security guard again. This security guard had stolen around $10,000 dollar's worth of property, but he lost he long time job, future, future good jobs, wife and kids trust and respect, as well as possibly them, was it worth it.

43. Just Because His Finger Prints Were Found In The House Doesn't Mean He Did It.

I was dispatched to the scene of a burglary in the inner city where an elderly white woman said that somebody broke her-front plate glass window and reached inside and took her grandchildren's Christmas presents from under a Christmas tree, which was sitting by the window. This elderly lady stated that she was very scared of black people because even though most of her neighborhood was now black, every time she would try to be nice, they would hurt or steal from her. This woman stated that her deceased husband had built this same house 50 years earlier after they were first married, and she was going to say in this house no matter what until she dies. I processed the scene and I recovered some finger prints on a glass coffee table just inside of the broken window where the suspect had to have moved items away to get to the presents under the Christmas tree. I asked all this woman's neighbors if they had seen anything and they were very cooperative. The neighbors stated that they had seen a 27-year-old black male by the victim's residence earlier in the day, and they gave me his name. I found out that the police department had this black males' fingerprints on file and I had his fingerprints compared to the fingerprints I recovered from the lady's coffee table and they matched. I asked this elderly woman if this black male had ever been inside of her house, and she leaned over and whispered, " no there has never been a black person in this house ever, I'm scared of them". This woman stated that she even tells the service companies to send a white repairman because she would not let a black one in. This black man was arrested but he denied doing this burglary and he stated that he did not know how his fingerprints got on this woman's coffee table, unless he touched it when he walked by after seeing the broken window. I thought that this case would be open and shut, however when it came to the county prosecutor, he said anybody could have stuck their hand inside this broken window and left their fingerprints on this glass table but it did not mean that they did this burglary. This male was released, but I think that there should have been no doubt that this was the person who committed this crime. Sometimes the courts work in mysterious ways.

44. House Explosion.
While I was working as a Detective in the Bomb and Arson Unit, I was requested to respond to the scene of a house explosion in the northeast part of town, by the Fire Department.

Upon my arrival I observed that all four walls of this one story 2-bedroom house had been ripped away from the foundation. One wall was lying out in the street to the north, one out in the street to the west, one against a neighbor's house to the south and one against the back fence to the west.

All four walls had been blown away but were still intact; the window glass hadn't even broken out or cracked. The roof had fallen straight down on top of the basement floor. Upon investigation I determined that this had been a natural gas explosion, because the gas had built up to the point that there had been a lot of pressure built up in this house causing the walls to come apart at their weakest point, the corners. It was also obvious that the explosion had occurred by the basement water heater because, that was what we call (ground zero) or where the explosion went off at, the center of the explosion. It appeared as if a coupling connecting the natural gas to the water heater had gone bad and started to leak, because the coupling was split wide open. Pretty interesting sight but I'm sure glad it wasn't my house, and no one was home at the time.

45. Italian Club Explosion.
While in the Bomb and Arson Unit I was requested by the Fire Department to investigate an explosion in an Italian Men's Club in the north eastern part of the city. Upon my arrival I observed that the fire department had a very small fire put out, and this 3-story building had all the windows broken out of it, as well as some of the doors having been blown outward. Some of the window glass and debris had blown up to half a block away. My investigation of this explosion revealed that this club had been closed at the time and the explosion had taken place in the middle of the floor in a basement lounge area. This explosion caused a hole in the concrete floor approximately 12' in diameter and 8" deep. There was a mark on the floor which revealed that someone had used a very long fuse, which burnt into the floor tile. It could not be determined at that time what was used to make this explosion however it was very obvious that this was an intentional act. The front concrete steps of this old brick building were pushed upward and cracked because they were immediately above where the explosion had

gone off. Almost every floor had a lot of damage from broken doors, windows, furniture, things hanging on the wall, kitchen appliances etc... During my investigation of this explosion, I could not get any information from neighbors even though there was a large party across the street, still going on during my investigation. One of the ladies at this party stated that she went outside after she heard the explosion but because it was dark, she could not see anything so she went back inside. I contacted the maintainers of this building and they had no idea who would want to do anything to this club. I then obtained a list of the members of this club and it read like an Italian Who's Who in Kansas City. • I contacted all the members on this list and most of them stated that they knew nothing and had no idea who would want to damage the club. However anonymous calls started to come into my office shortly after this, stating that this explosion was a just a warning for certain members of this Italian Men's Club to vote and support the right candidate in the upcoming election. Since apparently some of the members of this club were supporting a candidate that the other Italian organizations did not want them to support. As this investigation got deeper it had to be turned over to the FBI because it involved things a lot deeper then I was ready for or could handle. I did learn however that it was possible for elderly people in nursing homes to vote absentee ballots, even though they were incapacitated, just by someone using their name and having registered them to vote. This was a major explosion in this place and apparently it was all because some Club Members were supporting the wrong candidate. I was never advised if any of the above information turned out to be true after I turned the investigation over to the FBI, however, I did find out that several threatening letters were sent by the groups involved to each other.

46. Snow Covered Cripple.

About 4 a.m. 'one cold snowy morning as I was patrolling the downtown area where a lot of the street people hang out, I observed a pair of crutches lying next to the side of a building and I looked down and there was a man lying on the ground and he was almost completely covered with snow. This man was a 45-year-old white male who looked 65 years old. The only part of this man that was visible was his hat and his hands which he had covering his face. I stopped to check this poor guy out; after all, living on the streets had to be hard enough without having to deal with the snow and the broken leg. I figured I would be a nice guy and take this guy to jail where he could sleep off his drunken condition and have a warm place to sleep and a meal. Back then we called it sacking a drunk, getting them off the street for the night, and then letting them go in the morning when they sobered up. I tried waking this male up and it was hard to do but once I did, he became very angry. I informed this male that I was just going to take him to jail for the night and he could leave in the morning. This male started cussing me out and said," I was just fine until you woke me up, it took a long time for me to drink myself asleep". He did not want to be disturbed so I left.

47. Robbery Suspect Hits My Police Car, In Get-A-Way.
I was taking my 10-year-old son and his friend home from football practice one evening and I decided to stop at the grocery store on our way. I was driving my unmarked police vehicle because I was on call for the North Burglary Unit. As I pulled in front of the grocery store, we observed a 30-year-old Hispanic male run out of the grocery store pushing a grocery cart which appeared to be full of meat products. There were two store clerks chasing him and it looked like they were trying to stop him. I had to stop my police car immediately because all this was happening right in front of us. The two grocery clerks were scuffling with this man in front of my car so I put it in park and had the kids lock the doors as I got out to help the store clerks. Just as I closed my car door however another vehicle with 3 Hispanic males in their thirties pulls up and the male that was fighting got away and jumped in this car. The car that had picked this male up was now blocked in because traffic was still moving in the parking lot. I ran up to the window of the suspect vehicle and I showed my badge and gun at which time

the suspect vehicle started ramming the vehicles around it front and back in an effort to get away. I then ran back to my police car but before I could unlock the door this suspect vehicle rammed into my police car and moved it far enough to get out and away. The kids in the car were fine but very scared because they had no idea what was going on. I got on the police radio and informed the dispatcher of this robbery and my police car being rammed, as well as a car and suspect license number and descriptions, the dispatcher put out an alert to the surrounding agencies as well. I was contacted the store clerks to find out what happened inside the store and they stated that the male just came into the store got a grocery cart loaded it full of large hams and other meats and started to go out of the store without paying for it. The clerks stated that several of them told this male to stop but he just started to run and two of them chased him. One of these clerks handed me a shoe and stated that it belonged to the male they had been chasing he had lost it in the parking lot during the scuffle. A few minutes later the Riverside police called our dispatcher and stated that they had the suspect vehicle and suspects in custody. The Riverside Police officers stated that they had stopped this suspicious vehicle after they followed it down a dead-end street.

They stated that they had four Hispanic males in the car and one of them only had one shoe on. We had our patty wagon go to the Riverside Police Department and pickup these suspects and bring them to our location for positive identification.

The store clerks all positively identified the Hispanic male they seen and I also positively identified him and gave him his matching shoe back. I was also able to identify the driver of this vehicle even though he stated that he had not been driving. This was classified as a strong-arm robbery and this male had over $200 dollar's worth of meat in the grocery cart he had pushed out of the store. The male who had taken the meat out of the store was charged in city court with stealing, and assault, the driver of the get-a-way car was charged with stealing, assault, and hit and run-in city court.

48. Gas All Around The House, But The Matches Won't Light.
     While working with the Bomb and Arson Unit I was dispatched to
     meet officers on a prowler call at a residence in the inner city one
     night. The 5 children and 3 adult residents of this residence been
     repeatedly harassed and threatened by an ex-boyfriend of a family
     member. The residents stated that they had all been in bed when
     they heard noises outside and started to smell a gas like smell, so
     they called the police. I checked the exterior of the residence and
     I located an empty gas can, it appeared as if somebody had taken
     gas and poured it all the way around the outside of this residence.
     I also observed an empty match book on the ground and a lot of
     matches that had been torn out of this match book but apparently
     didn't light. If one of those matches would have lit it most likely
     would have put the whole residence up in flames, and blocked all
     exits causing everyone inside of this residence to die or be badly
     burnt. God must have really been looking after these people.

49. He Was So Low, He Even Stole from the Dream factory.
     There have been many times in my career where I have volunteered
     my free time in uniform to help with handicap children's Christmas
     parties, charity events etc... One of these situations was working
     with the Dream Factory on their Las Vegas night. The Dream
     Factory is a great organization making last wishes come true for
     many terminally ill children. On this particular night several of us
     police officers had volunteered our time. The Dream factory had
     also hired some private security guards as well. One of these security
     guards was assigned to guard the money coupons that were being
     purchased for cash. The money coupons were what we're being won
     and lost at the gambling tables and then they could be exchanged
     for donated gifts. This security guard in charge of guarding the
     coupons was helping himself to the coupons and on each break, he
     got he was purchasing the big dollar items that had been donated to
     the Dream Factory. This security guard was not very smart he was
     doing this in front of everyone even the people who were working
     the coupon booth that he was supposed to be guarding. We stopped

this security guard and the Dream factory Personnel did not wish to prosecute him but they did ask this paid security guard that steals from charity to leave and we notified his supervisor.

50.   we Herded Cattle On The Plaza For Hours.

I was dispatched to the Plaza area one early morning to check out a report of cattle in the street. Upon my arrival I observed 6 calves running up the street. Upon checking the area, I located a horse trailer that the rear gate was found to be open. I checked with the resident of the residence that this horse trailer was parked in front of. I learned that a judge lived there and he had gotten home late the night before so he had left the calves in the trailer out in front of his residence.

The judge stated that it was his intentions to take the calves to a butcher shop but he had gotten home to late. Somehow during the night, the calves had kicked the rear gate open and got out, and now we had these six calves running down Ward Parkway. It was not easy with our lack of experience to herd these calves; it was not anything like they show you on television or the movies. We chased these calves through yards, we tried getting ropes around them, and we tried everything it was just an impossibility because these cattle were so scared of all the traffic. We finally had to call some people who actually did this for a living. They came out and herded up these calves for us but it was approximately 4 or 5 hours that these calves were out running in the traffic. That was just another interesting thing for police officers to have to do; you never know what will be next.

51.   Teacher Stole Kindergarten Kids Money, To Buy Drugs.

I investigated a stealing case at an inner-city school. This case involved a 58-year-old white female school teacher and her 35-year-old black female substitute school teacher. The school teacher had called me and stated that when she came back to school after having a day off. She found that all of her kindergartner kid's money was missing from their field trip fund, as well as their milk money. Each student had been collecting a few pennies at a time and a dollar here and there and putting it aside to take a field trip. Somebody had taken this money and this teacher did not think there was much she could do about it; however, she suspected the substitute teacher who was also assisting her this day as well. This teacher stated that she suspected this substitute teacher because; when this teacher checked her purse during the noon hour, she found that $50.00 dollars was missing from her purse. This teacher stated that the only people with access to her purse would have been the children and the substitute teacher. This teacher stated that she felt very comfortable that the children would not know what to do with this much money. This teacher also stated that the substitute teacher had had an older black male visitor interrupt the class that morning. She noticed that the substitute teacher had tried to secretly give this male something, and then he quickly left. Upon questioning the substitute teacher, she admitted that she did take all the children's money and the teacher's money. She stated that she gave it to this boyfriend when he came to the school, so he could buy drugs with the money. This substitute teacher was charged with stealing and she is no longer a school teacher in the Kansas City Public School District.

52. Kids Stole His Gun, Shot It, And Then Sold It.
I guess this is one of those stories where it does not pay off to be nice, however you never know who you can trust and I would hate for people to quit being nice. This incident happened up north of the river at a mom-and-pop hardware store. The store owner, a real great guy who he knew everybody in the neighborhood, when kids came by, he would even have candy out for them. This business did not have a public restroom in the store because it was just a small business. The store owner would let the kids use his private restroom when they needed to. He just liked kids and treated them really good. This store owner suspected that a couple of the boys that frequented his store might be shoplifting but he hated

to accuse them falsely so he never said anything about it to them. This store owner continued to trust the boys and he was trying to be nice hoping to be a good example for them. However, one day another of the neighborhood children came into the store and informed the store owner that the boys that he had suspected of shoplifting, had taken an old handgun. It was an old handgun that he had hidden in his bathroom. This juvenile stated that the boys were out shooting the handgun.

This really shocked this store owner that these boys not only betrayed his trust but that they were now in danger playing with a handgun. The store owner had forgotten that he had hidden two of his old weapons in that bathroom because he did not want them lying around his residence. The store owner stated that he had hidden the guns really well and he had even been putting stuff on top and around the guns. He stated that the boys really must have had to search hard to find the guns. Apparently, the boys would ask to use the restroom then they would search around to see what was in there and they found the guns. Because store owner did not want to see these boys get into bad trouble, but he did want to get his handgun away from them he called me and asked for my help. I contacted the parents of the boys that where reportedly supposed to have this handgun and I learned from the boys that. One day they had taken this gun out of the store and they went out and shot it in the woods then brought it back. A few days later the boys figured that it had been so easy to take the handgun out of the store that they would take it out again which they did. However, this time they became too scared to take the handgun back so they sold it to another older neighbor boy who was always in trouble. I then responded to this older boy's residence and contacted his father and informed the father of the accusation. This boy denied he bought the gun or that he knew anything about it. However, when his father did not believe him, the boy confessed and went and retrieved the handgun from where he had it hidden under his bed. I returned this handgun to the store owner. He did not wish to have the boys prosecuted; he was hoping that the parents of these boys could handle this the old fashion way, without involving the police. He wanted the parents to take care of this as it was done years ago and, in my day, of course. This store owner decided that he would work out probation of his own for these boys with their parent's assistance. He wanted to have the boys work community service• with their parent's guidance; I believe it was for 20 hours. He also wanted the boys to bring their parents to the store and apologize in front of them for doing this, as well as do things for their parents so that they would never forget this incident. This punishment sounded like it was really fair for the younger boys. I could not do anything to the older boy because he did not have anything to do with the theft of this handgun. I was hoping that his father would take care of this matter himself. Everything seemed to be working out fine, until one of the neighbors of these young boys heard about this incident. This neighbor notified the juvenile authorities who contacted me and wanted to know why this case was not brought in front of them. The juvenile authorities had more power than the store owner, myself or the parents had. This case did end up in front of them, and the dispositions I do not know at this time. I thought this was really great on the store owner's part to bring things back to the parents and the parents were very happy as well to let them handle this themselves. I felt these boys' parents were very caring people and they were doing a good job turning these curious but not really bad boys around.

53. Michael Jackson in Concert.
One of the benefits of this job is getting to work the concerts, shows, etc... I remember working the Michael Jackson concert when he came to town a few years ago. My job originally was just to keep the peace on the exterior of the stadium and then later I was assigned to the area right in front of the stage. I was also able to go into Michael Jackson's dressing room and few other areas most people do not get to go into before the concert. He had several of the fancy jackets he wore at that time thrown all over the floor as

if he could not decide which one, he wanted to wear. He had a real formal setting of vegetarian food, china, glassware. It really did not make a lot of since unless he was just spoiled, this fancy setup and all his jackets and stuff thrown all over on the floor. While he was performing on stage, he had a laser light show and it was a really neat show of course.

So, us police officers assigned to the front of the stage were watching the crowd, and at the same time looking over our shoulders trying to see some of the show. Apparently during the show Michael Jackson observed several of us officers looking up towards him. He had one of his private security people inform out supervisor that Michael did not want the police officers to look up at him. This made him uncomfortable because we were carrying guns. We were asked to keep our eyes focused straight ahead on the crowd and not to glance at what he was doing on the stage. I thought that was a little paranoid but what you can say, with the money he has gotten, he can do whatever he wants.

54. Michael Jackson at His Hotel.
In Michael Jackson's show he also had his brothers with him and they were all staying at a Plaza Hotel. We had the sidewalks roped off and we had to direct traffic because there were so many people out there trying to get a look at Michael Jackson. Everything was O.K. until the Jackson brothers came out on the balcony and all these people started screaming at them and pushing to get closer to them and we had to hold them back. The brothers would finally go inside, then Michael would come out then go back in, then a couple of the brothers would come out again, back and forth. There were teenage girls on the balconies surrounding the Jackson's rooms and they would come out and flash their breasts at the crowd and us, whenever the Jackson's were not out there. It was a lot of work trying to control this crowd; it was like something new was happening every minute. We were just really happy when the Jackson's finally went in and went to bed, at which time the crowd left.

CHAPTER 3

WARNING...THESE STORIES CONTAIN VERY GRAPHIC VIOLENCE

<u>VIOLENCE</u>

1. He Used A Pick Axe To Get The Devil Out Of Himself.
2. He Slashed Me With A Butcher Knife.
3. He Shot Him 30 Times, And then Said, "Get My Guitar".
4. 1 Like My New Teeth
5. Whoops! His Toe Was Caught In The Patty Wagon Door.
6. He Was Shot In the Leg, But It's Not Who We Thought Did lt.
7. 1 Heard My Hand Break When I Hit His Bald Head.
8. Rape...Same PJ's My Son Was Wearing.
9. Shoot Me, Shoot Me.
10. Animal Tranquilizer Death.
11. Foot Chase, Dog Bite In Swope Park.
12. His Intestines Were Hanging Out, But He Wouldn't Stop Fighting.
13. Mentally Ill Arsonist Dressed Like A Mummy.
14. Stranded Motorist I Shot And Killed.
15. Mentally Ill Nude Man in His Basement with a Knife.
16. Shoe String Murders.
17. He Raped Her While She Protected Her Baby.
18. He Died Foaming At The Mouth.
19. Rape...injured Vietnam Veteran.
20. He Put Her Panties Over Her Head, And then He Raped Her.
21. Rape on the Basement Mattress.
22. Strip Search for a Ring.

23. "1 Won't Call the Police", She Said. He said, "Why Not".
24. Rape...Please Leave Now. I Can't, My Bus Doesn't Come Until 12:10.
25. Purse Snatch. She Hold Him That It Was Not Going To Happen, But It Did.
26. She Said, "My Husband's due Home now." She Said, "Shut Up And Fuck Me Now."
27. She Was so Drunk That He Threw Her Out Of The Window.
28. You Better Kill Me in My Sleep, Or You're dead.
29. Husband's Girlfriend Takes Wife's Side in This Assault.
30. The Stolen Car Went Over The Chouteau Bridge Railing During The Car Chase.
31. I Broke My Toe Chasing A Window Peeper/Burglar.
32. She Said That He Was Sending Messages To Her Over Her Car Radio.
33. He Was Bleeding, But He Wouldn't Let Us Treat Him Until His Lover Arrived.
34. We Got A Standing Ovation After The Spirit Festival Tackles.
35. He Had $10,000 in His Socks and His Cheek Was Slashed Open.
36. The Cyclops Accident.
37. Trash Bag Harley, Life flighted.
38. She Had A Gun And A Knife. She Tried To Use Both On Me. Thank You, Lord!
39. Good Identification on Murder Victim, "Daaaaaad".
40. He Kicked The Dog In The Mouth And Got Bit, Many Times.
41. Full Blown Aides Carrier, Burn Victim/Burglar.
42. Let Me see if this Railing Will Hold Me. It Didn't.
43. Followed One Mile Of Blood Trail In The Snow.
44. They Just Dumped Her Off. She Could Have Died.
45. It Didn't Happen In This Bar!
46. My Kids Were Watching As I Fought This Drug Crazed Man.
47. 14-Year-Old Killed Him Because He Thought That He Was a Cop.
48. Two Children Die in Lawnmower Fire.
49. Attempt Suicide in Car.
50. Gang Style Assassination.
51. Bag Lady Fire.
52. School Talent Show Shoot-Out.

1. He Used A Pick Axe To Get The Devil Out Of Himself.

   One summer evening I was dispatched on a "party injured" call in the midtown area. Upon my arrival I found a 20-year-old white male, covered with blood and bleeding heavily at the bottom of the steps, in an apartment building. I called for an ambulance and then did the best I could to stop the blood that was pumping out of several holes in this man's back. Upon the arrival of the ambulance, they informed me that this male's injuries self-inflicted. My assisting officer and I then followed the trail of blood, which lead to a bloody pick axe in the street, as well as into the apartment hallway, stairway and the victim's room. Inside the victim's apartment we observed the bed soaked with blood, the bathroom covered with blood, and the bathtub full of what appeared to be bloody water. We later determined that what had happened was that this man had recently been released from a mental institution. He was on a temporary three-week period to see if he could make it on his own. Well, apparently, he cannot. This man had said that the devil was in him, and he wanted to get the devil out of himself. His answer to this was to go out into the street with a large pick ax, which he swung the pointed end of the ax over his shoulder and into his own back. This male did this three times, in his attempt to get the devil out of himself. After doing this the victim went back to his apartment and wrapped himself in a blanket and laid on the bed trying to get the bleeding to stop. When this did not stop the blood, he filled the bathtub with water and got in it, trying to wash the blood away. When the blood did not stop, he ran down the stairs and out into the street screaming. When he was seen and heard by his neighbors, they called the police and ambulance.

2. He Slashed Me With A Butcher Knife.

   One evening another police officer and I were dispatched to an area up north of the river on a first-degree burglary, (which is a burglary where contact is made between the victim and suspect). Upon our arrival I contacted the victim, a 23-year-old white female.

This female stated that she had been home asleep on her couch, lying on her back with her knees bent, wearing just her T-shirt and panties. When she was suddenly awakened by a 25-year-old white male who was sitting on the end of her couch, pressing his hand against her crotch area. He was also holding a big butcher knife in his other hand. Without even thinking her response was to sit up and grab this male's hand that had the butcher knife in it. When she did this it surprised this male so much, that he got up and ran out the rear door of the duplex. Apparently, the male had pried his way in through the rear door, gone straight to the kitchen and pulled a large butcher knife out of a knife rack. He then had gone to where the female was sleeping on the couch sat down, and dumped her purse out on the floor. He then went through the purse's contents taking what he wanted. When he was through with the female's purse, he reached up between the females parted knees, and placed his hand on her crotch. That is when she woke up, grabbed his hand and he fled through the back door. This same type situation had apparently occurred one year earlier to another resident in these same duplexes. A white male had pried his way in through a rear door, grabbed a large out of a butcher block, and then raped the victim. I was trying very hard to quickly get all the information for my report from the victim, while my assisting officer and another officer, were still ogling this victim and her girlfriend. (From the other side of the duplex, who was also dressed only in a T-shirt and panties?) This neighbor was the first person the victim had called after the male had left. I then went out the rear door and started checking the area for evidence. All of a sudden, I observed a white male matching the description of the suspect that the victim had given me. This male was running out of the rear door of the connecting duplex. This was the residence of the female whom the victim had called, and who was still with the victim.

This female had run over to the victim's residence when the victim called. She had left her 2 small children asleep in her residence and her door unlocked. Apparently, the suspect was outside watching this happen, and when he saw this other female leave her residence, he went into it. I then pulled my service revolver out and ordered the suspect to stop. He did not stop so I started chasing him, while at the same time getting my walkie-talkie out and informing the dispatcher and my assisting officers of the foot chase. I chased the suspect about half a mile, through the duplexes and down the road. Just as I was getting ready to tackle him, he stopped in the middle of the road and swung around slashing the butcher knife right across my stomach area. (It had been about a half hour since I had gotten to this scene, I had even forgotten about this butcher knife, I did not even notice it when he started running.) My reflex was to suck my stomach in and bend over quickly as the knife went across my stomach. I then instinctively grabbed the suspect by the wrist and shoulder that he was carrying the butcher knife in, and threw him down to the ground. This sudden jar of his face hitting the pavement, sent the knife out of his hand and sliding down the road about 10 feet. As my assisting officers were catching up to me, they had only observed the butcher knife go across my chest and me go down with this person. They both stated later that they were sure that they were going to find me with my guts hanging out from being sliced. They both ran up and started kicking and pulling on the suspect trying to get him away from me. They had not seen the butcher knife fly out of his hand and they thought he still had it. I then quickly informed them that I was ok, and that I only needed assistance in handcuffing the suspect. I had felt this butcher knife go against my stomach and I believed at the time that I had been cut. However, there was only a mark across my shirt, I guess someone up there was looking out for me. As it turned out the suspect lived on and off with his sister in the Westport- Plaza area. An area of town that was also being plagued by a notorious rapist at that time. When the suspect was not living with his sister he was living in Colorado. This suspect was questioned about this burglary by our Property Detective's and about the similar rape case, that occurred one year earlier in these same duplexes. As well as the many rapes in the Westport/ Plaza area, by the Sex Crime Detectives.

3.   He Shot Him 30 Times, Then He said, Get My Guitar!

One evening while I was patrolling north of the river, another officer had just responded on a property damage call, near the area I was patrolling. He was sitting in his patrol car getting the information for the report from his victim. A 20-year-old nude white female ran up to him and said, "My boyfriends in this house and there is a man shooting him!" The officer stated that he had then heard some small popping sounds, like that from a small-caliber weapon, coming from the house this woman was referring to. This officer then called for some assisting officers. Our sergeant, another officer, and I, must have recognized the excitement in this original officer's voice because we were all there immediately, knowing inside that this veteran officer does not become excited that easy anymore. The original officer and the sergeant went to the front door of this house as the other officer and I went to the rear. As we both hurried to the north and south rear corners of the house, a 42-year-old white male came bursting out of the rear door of the house. This male had a long rifle in his hands, and was putting live rounds into the chamber as well as swinging it around like he was going to start shooting at anyone he could find. This weapon appeared to be a semi-automatic type; however, it was unknown at that time. The male seen me as I peered around the comer of the house not really expecting to see him coming out of the rear door. I really thought that he was going to shoot at me; however, I had my revolver pointed at him stating stop or I'll shoot, and he took off running instead. 100.

I guess that I could have shot him at that time; however, the other officer on the other corner of the house also had his revolver pointed at this male. Thank god we both must have realized that if we shot, we would also be shooting at each other. Neither of us pulled the trigger, but I got on the walkie talkie and told the other officers that an armed male was running out the rear door of the house. This male ran until he disappeared behind a big barn like shed in the back yard. The other officer and I again waited on the north and south comers of this shed, until the other officers arrived. Then I hesitantly peeked around the comer and noticed that this male had thrown his rifle down and was trying to hide behind this shed in some trash that was there. I said lets go and we rushed him. I grabbed his arm and put my revolver up to his head as the other officer came around the other corner and put his gun up to the other side of this male's head, The then sergeant came around the corner, grabbed the suspect by the hair, and pulled him over, face down on the ground, and we handcuffed him. The suspect later informed us that he had 300 and some rounds of ammunition on him. He had planned to get up in the loft area of this shed, and then shoot all the police officers that he could see, we were not supposed to take him alive. Well, he never got that chance because we already had him. This male stated that he would tell us exactly what happened in the house, if we would get him his electric guitar so he could play it on Death Row. I located this male's guitar in the loft area of this shed, and placed it where this male could see we were taking it with us. This male then stated that what had happened was, inside the house on a waterbed the 25-year-old white male shooting victim, and his girlfriend were nude in bed. The victim employed this suspect and several other street people. He paid them to cut tree limbs and stuff for him, which was the business he was in. These employees slept in the loft of this shed out back, but they used the restroom in the house, just outside of the victim's bedroom. The suspect stated that he had not been paid properly and he was very angry about this. The suspect had been in this restroom and could hear the sound of the couple apparently having sex, in the bedroom. The suspect stated that he just did not think this was right that the victim should be happy after he had cheated him out of his well-earned money. While the suspect was in the restroom, he noticed three loaded long guns in the corner of this room. The suspect then decided that the victim was not going to get away with this, and he decided he was going to kill the victim. The suspect then picked up a .22 caliber semi-automatic rifle, then went in the bedroom and started shooting the victim. The suspect stated that he first shot the victim several times in the legs and the victim still got up out of the bed, and came towards him. The suspect stated he backed out of the bedroom and the victim went into the bathroom and grabbed a shotgun. The suspect then reloaded the .22 rifle and started shooting the victim again. This time all over the body, trying to get the victim to put the shotgun down. The suspect kept shooting until finally the victim fell to the floor on top of the shotgun. The suspect then tried to pull the shotgun out from under the victim however the he taught the victim would not let go of it so he shot him a few more times. However, all during this time the suspect's rifle kept jamming so he was ejecting the unfired cartridges on the floor, then re-loading and firing some more. The suspect actually shot the victim approximately 30 times. The victim's girlfriend had somehow gotten out of the bedroom and ran outside after the suspect started shooting the victim. Immediately when she got outside, she seen the police car, and informed him of the shooting. Meanwhile the suspect had gathered up as much ammunition as he could carry, and was running out the back door loading the rifle when he was surprised by me. At which time he stated that he was scared and ran behind the shed, threw the rifle down, so he would not be shot, and for some reason hoped he could hide from us.

4. 1 Like My New Teeth.
    This is another one of the rare times that I had to use my night stick. 101.

I had pulled over a drunk driver on Prospect, in the inner city. There were four people in this vehicle that were related to each other. The owner of the vehicle, a 26-year-old black female who was driving was going to be taken to jail for drinking and driving. The other three black males in their mid-twenties were asked to leave the area because they were very belligerent and intoxicated. I was not going to release the vehicle to any of them, but have it towed to the tow lot for safe keeping. One of the males then walked away but the other two males refused to leave the area. I realized that this situation was going to get out of control, because these males were insisting, they were going to take this vehicle. I had another officer take the female arrest to the Police station while I waited with another officer for the tow truck. During this time these two males kept trying to get into the car and would not leave. I informed them that they were going to be arrested for hindering/interfering, if they did not leave right then. They however were persistent and they were advised they were under arrest and handcuffed. A patty wagon was ordered and when it arrived, they were placed in the back of it. It was determined moments later, while the tow truck was hooking up this vehicle that apparently one of the times the males had attempted to get into this vehicle. One of them had grabbed the car keys and put them in his pocket. I went to the back of the patty wagon and informed the males that I needed the keys to the vehicle because it was going to be towed. Both males then moved back, in the patty wagon and refused to hand the keys over. I then reached into the patty wagon to grab and bring out the person I believed had the keys to this vehicle; however, he started kicking me with his feet. I jabbed at him with my night stick and at the same time, pushed the other one back in the patty wagon as he was trying to get out. As I was pushing the second male back into the patty wagon the first male kicked at me hitting me under the chin, knocking me backwards. As I fell backwards however, I swung with my night stick, striking the roof of the patty wagon I thought. I must have blacked out for a moment, because when I woke up an ambulance was there, and I could not talk. The kick had knocked my jaw out of place and broken two of my front teeth. The patty wagon driver just slammed the patty wagon door when he saw me get kicked. He then called an ambulance for me. After the ambulance arrived the patty wagon driver took both of the males to Police

Headquarters. (Because these males had not stopped screaming since he had shut the patty wagon door and Police Headquarters is where we take violent prisoners.) When the patty wagon driver reached Police Headquarters, he opened the rear patty wagon door and observed both males to be covered with blood. Apparently when I swung my night stick and it hit the roof of the patty wagon, as I was falling backward, I must have also struck the first male in the head. This male's wound was not as serious as it looked, but it did require 13 stitches. Generally, I guess this worked out fairly well for me, because my front teeth had been slightly over lapped; now I have very nice straight teeth. I got new front teeth, but he ended up with 13 stitches in his forehead.

5.   Whoops! His Toe Was Caught In The Paddy Wagon Door.
I had been dispatched on a disturbance, again in the inner city. When I got to the scene, I found a very large, intoxicated, irate 28-year-old white male. His landlord wanted the police to make him leave because he was being very loud and abusive. When I asked him to leave, he refused and started trying to fight my assisting officers and myself. It took five Police Officers to get this large man shackled and handcuffed, and all five of us to carry him out to the paddy wagon. He was so big and tall, that each time we placed him in the paddy wagon he would kick the door open before we could get it closed. After about the third time this happened, we were becoming exhausted. We finally heaved him in the back of the patty wagon, and slammed the door shut and locked it.

He immediately started screaming even louder, but we did not intend to open the door again. I followed the patty wagon to the hospital where our intentions were to have this man checked out for possible alcohol poisoning. However, when we got him to the hospital, we noticed blood oozing from the patty wagon door. This man's big toe had been crushed in the patty wagon door all that time.

6. He Was Shot In The Leg, But It's Not Who we Thought Did It. Occasionally during the summer when the Homicide Unit gets terribly busy, some of us.

Property Detectives would be pulled out of the Property Units to help. I went to work with the Homicide Unit one day, and we were called out to the area of south Troost. At that location they had found the body of a 25-year-old white male lying in a puddle of blood, on the back porch of a restaurant. There was no gun to be found, however the body had what appeared to be a bullet wound in the leg. We had no idea what had happened, however we figured it must have been some sort of assault against him, in which he died. We found a trail of blood leading from the body, down a ramp, up to some bushes. The trail of blood then led back down to the street to the area underneath a bridge that had some steps leading up onto Troost. The trail stopped right there. We were able to determine the identity of the person and we found out that he had been to a bar on Troost with a friend the night before. We then went to this bar and found out who the friend was. We went to the friend's residence to find that he had left town. It appeared even more now that the friend was a good suspect in this death. We learned that there had been a disturbance the night before between the victim and the friend at the bar and the friend had taken the gun away from the victim. It sounded like an open and shut case, the argument between the friends, a gun involved, the friend had the gun, and the friend had suddenly left town. We checked outside this bar and found footprints of the victims' shoes in the mud leading down Troost towards the area where the bridge steps went down. We were finally able to locate the friend that the victim had been to the bar with the night before. He informed us that there had been an argument at the bar between him and the victim, the victim, was extremely intoxicated, and had a gun. The friend stated he took the gun away from the victim because he was so drunk. That is what caused the argument and a fight began, so the friend told the victim to just keep the gun and the friend went home. I just knew that the friend had to be guilty; there was just no other way. The victim was taken to the morgue; an examination revealed a gunshot wound to the inner thigh with powder burns around it. With this information we knew that the gun barrel had to be right up against his leg when he was shot. Not often if someone is going to shoot you, do they stick the gun barrel right up against your leg, they would put it up against your chest or head, but not your leg. So, we had to staff reevaluating the situation. We realized that the victim would have had to have started walking from the bar, went to the bridge, then down the steps where the trail of blood started. We figured that most likely he had had the gun tucked in the waist band of his pants. As he was walking down the steps, the gun must have started to fall down his pants or fall out, and when he grabbed it, he must have accidentally pulled the trigger and shot himself. This would explain the blood trail starting at the bottom of the steps. The trail of blood started there and led past the restaurant up to some bushes and then up a ramp leading to the rear door of the restaurant, where the victim was found dead. With the help of a police dog, the victim's gun was located in the bushes, which the blood trail had led too. We were then able to speculate even more about what had happened. Apparently, the victim had determined that since he was so intoxicated, and he needed to get help. He could not be caught with this gun, so he threw it in the bushes with the intention of coming back later to retrieve it. He then must have knocked on the restaurants rear door trying to get someone to help him.

When there was no answer at the restaurant door, he apparently laid down and passed out, then bled to death.

7.   1 Heard My Hand Break, When 1 Hit His Bald Head.
One below zero winter night up north of the river, I made an emergency call. This call was to assist a Police Officer who was having problems with a drunk driver he had pulled over who was

resisting arrest. When I arrived, I observed the Police Officer and the drunk driver, a 40-year-old bald white male wrestling in the middle off interstate 1-35. I helped the officer get the male under control an off to the side of the Interstate. I was holding this male's legs and shoulders down while the other officer handcuffed the males' hands and was trying to place shackles on the males' legs. As I was holding the male face down on the ground, he intentionally quickly raised his bald head and struck me in the face with it, as hard as he could. My instant reflex, after getting a fat lip, was to punch this male's bald head, with my right fist. However, I should have thought first, because when I hit him, I heard a 'crack" and I knew immediately that I had broken my hand. The cold does make bone's brittle, but it also kept the swelling down awhile. I am sure this did not even phase the man's head. It was purely a reflex reaction. This male was arrested for drunk driving, resisting arrest and assault on a Police Officer.

8.   (Rape) Same PJ's My Son Was Wearing.

I responded one summer night to a rape victim call in the inner city. It involved a 26-year-old black female who was eight months pregnant and her small son, about the age of my son, five or six years old at the time. The victim stated that she had earlier let her small dog out into her back yard. When she later heard a noise at her back door, she went to let her dog in. When she got to the back door the first thing, she noticed was that the rear outside light was not on and she remembered turning it on when she let her dog out. She opened the rear door to let her dog in when all of the sudden a black man about thirty years old with a gun in his hand forced his way into the house. This man went past her knocking her son out of the way. The little boy started screaming and the suspect hit the little boy in the head with the gun. The suspect then told the victim to get in the house and be quiet. The suspect then forced the victim into the living room at gun point and told her to take her under clothes off, because he was going to have sex with her. The little boy however would not quit screaming, so the suspect took the belt off the victim's robe and tied the little boy up and put him in a bedroom closet. The suspect then took the woman back into the living room and forced the victim to take her under clothes off. The suspect put his gun up to the victim's head and made her get on her hands and knees on the living room floor. This man then pulled his pants down to his ankles and began to have sexual intercourse with her. The little boy still had not stopped screaming in the closet, so the suspect became upset and he took the little boy out of the closet. This man then forced the little boy and the victim into the victim's bedroom. The suspect then ordered the victim to get her son to shut up, which she was able to. The suspect then told her to bend over the bed and he again entered her and had sexual intercourse with her while the boy watched. After the suspect ejaculated, he got dressed and told them both to stay there and be quite. The victim then heard the suspect moving things around in the other room, but she stayed in her bedroom until she heard her car start up and leave the driveway. The victim then called the police, after which she noticed that the suspect had taken her VCR, TV, and other belongings, as well as her car. Upon my arrival at the scene, the first thing I noticed was that the little boy was wearing the same kind and color pajamas that my son had on when I kissed him goodnight.

I immediately requested additional Police Officers and the Police Helicopter to search for the suspect. However, the suspect could not be located in the area, he had gotten away with all the victim's property and he abandoned her car about six blocks away. The victim and her son were taken to the hospital by ambulance, where the doctors collected evidence from the victim for a police rape kit. The victim was not further physically injured, nor was her unborn child. The victim's son was treated for a minor cut on his head, from being hit with the suspect's gun, and minor abrasions on his wrists from being tied up. This case was then turned over to the Sex Crimes Detectives. This case was really difficult for me to handle. Not only because the victims were so innocent, but they could have been any of our families. As in many situations the suspects go so far over board, what harm can a 5-year-old do to you, why would you have to tie them up. Why would you rape anyone especially an 8-month pregnant woman?

9. Shoot Me, Shoot Me.
    I was approaching the corner of 39th and Main early one morning when a 19-year-old white male ran out of a business and straight towards my police car. This male had his hands in the air screaming, "Shoot me, shoot me, shoot me, and kill me!" He was very combative, belligerent and out of control. I called for an assisting officer and I tried to get him to settle down, however he started going for my gun and I had to take him down to the ground and handcuff him. We took him to a local mental health center. I later learned that this male was a mentally ill person who was living with another mentally ill person, who was taking advantage of all of this male's money and possessions. This male had been to the business on the corner of where I first observed him. When he went to get money out of his wallet, the other male had already taken it, and this set the male off. Since this male could not mentally handle the situation, he just ran outside seen the police car and wanted me to shoot him, and put him out of his misery. He was admitted to the mental health center.

10. Animal Tranquilizer Death.
    Another very early morning in the same 39th and Main area, I responded on a noise disturbance call. This disturbance was in an apartment building however I could not get into the apartment building because of a secured outer door. My assisting officer had not arrived yet, and I noticed an apartment balcony door to the left of the main apartment building door with a light on inside the apartment. I was thinking that if I knocked on this balcony door, I might be able to get the residents of that apartment to let us in the building so we could check on the disturbance. However,

my thoughts quickly changed and I forgot the disturbance when I looked into the balcony door. Inside I observed a 34-year-old white male lying on the bed face down, and a 22-year-old white female lying on the floor face down, neither moving. I la-locked loudly on the balcony door and yelled a few times, but I observed no movement. I informed my assisting officer, who had just arrived, of the situation and then I notified our supervisor to respond to the scene. We then decided that we had better check the situation out to make sure the people inside were all right, and that we were not going to wait for our supervisor. My assisting officer and I climbed up over the apartment balcony, and went into the unlocked balcony door. Inside I found that the female on the floor was breathing but barely, and the male on the bed had very shallow labored breath. I called for an ambulance then I began to try to get the male breathing regularly, by loosening his clothing and trying to get him to wake up. My assisting officer was mean while trying to get the female to wake up.

While we were waiting for the ambulance, I got the male to wake up, but the female quit breathing on us and my assisting officer and I had to start giving her CPR. I remember feeling so bad when my assisting officer checked the female and said she was not breathing. He started giving her mouth to mouth, I had just checked her and she had been breathing, maybe I could have done something else. Upon the arrival of the ambulance the ambulance personnel immediately took over CPR on the female, and they asked me to find out from the male if they had taken any drugs. The male stated that they had both taken animal tranquilizers. The male and female where then both rushed to a local hospital, where I learned that the female had died on the way to the hospital. The male recovered and informed me that the female had been his girlfriend. He also stated that he was currently a Veterinarians assistant and he had been a Medic in Vietnam. This male stated that on this particular evening he had injected himself with animal tranquilizers and had given his girlfriend animal tranquilizer tablets to take because she did not like needles. This male stated that they had done this quite often, but this time apparently, they both overdosed on this medicine. This male was arrested and turned over to the Homicide Unit.

11. Foot Chase, Dog Bite In Swope Park.

After a car chase one night, where the occupants of a stolen car, had shot their guns into a crowd of several people outside a bar wounding several of them. The car chase ended in the middle of Swope Park where the stolen car had crashed into a tree. After this crash the black male occupants of this car had gotten out of the car and ran into the dark woods where we lost them. We then called the Canine Unit and requested their dogs to help us find the suspects in the park, since we had surrounded the park and the suspects had to still be in the area. After the police dogs and handlers arrived my supervisor asked me and several other officers to get back into service to handle other calls. This leaving the Police dogs and the Police Helicopter to search the park for the suspects. While I was waiting for another call, I went over to another area just outside the park. After a few moments I heard a dog barking and I saw one of our Canine Officers and his dog running across the field. I remember the Canine Officer had the dog on a long leash, but the dog was running so fast that the Canine Officer tripped and fell. The Canine Officer then let the dog go loose as he got back up. The dog ran over to a tree and jumped up apparently just in time to get a mouth full of a suspect. I heard a male screaming and the dog barking. This male was obviously in a lot of pain, being attacked by that dog. The Canine Officer was there within moments and he called his dog off then handcuffed the suspect. This suspect was the only one caught that night; he was taken to the hospital then to jail. For some reason it just seems like justice, when I hear the sound of the dog catching a suspect that thinks they can out run the dogs.

12. His Intestines Were Hanging Out, But He Wouldn't Stop Fighting Us.

One of the worst incidents I have experienced occurred before I even became a Police Officer. I had been riding along on calls with a Police Officer, which I was able to do because I was working as a volunteer at the Northeast Police Station. We had heard other officers get dispatched to a bar on Truman Road regarding a tavern disturbance. Usually at least three officers are dispatched to go to these tavern disturbances. Since three cars had already been dispatched there, we decided to go and see if we would be needed. When we got there two Police Officers were entering the front door and one female Police Officer was going in the back door. The situation looked so routine that the Police Officer I was with, figured we would not be needed, so he started to back out of the rear bar parking lot. All of a sudden, we heard the female officer whom we had watched go in the rear bar door, yell over her walkie talkie.

She yelled for the officer I was with to get in there quick they need his help. The officer I was with then quickly pulled back into the rear bar parking lot and we both got out of the police car and ran toward the rear door of the bar. As we were running, we noticed blood splattered all over the parking lot and on the rear door of the bar. The first thing we observed when we entered the bar was that the bar was almost entirely covered with blood, which was splattered everywhere. We then observed a huge 26-year-old white male on his back on the floor, swinging his fist up hitting the female officer in the head, her Police hat then flying in the air. This male had stab wounds all over him and his intestines were hanging out of his belly. On the other side of the room, was a 22-year-old white male with a broken pool cue sticking out of his neck. This male was picking up a table and throwing it at another female Police Officer. There was also a third 23-year-old white male by the second one who was hitting a male Police Officer with a chair. The officer I was with, handed me the walkie talkie and told me to get some more help as he assisted the first female officer with the huge male. I got on the walkie talkie and I am sure I frantically stated that the officers need a lot of assistance at this bar. It seemed as it took forever but it was only minutes before we had Police Officers coming in from everywhere. After I had called for help, I helped handcuff the huge male, I remember really being groused out by his intestines hanging out and blood all over him. It had taken myself and four Police Officers to get this huge male handcuffed because he would not stop fighting. The officers were telling him that they just wanted to give him first aid. The arriving Police Officers finally got the bar calmed down and the three males under control. I remember noticing at that time that all during this struggle the bartender had remained behind the bar and the bar full of customers had just remained at their tables. The Police Officers then shut the bar down and the officer I was with requested that I watch the rear door for him and not to let anyone in or out except the Police. When this situation was finally figured out, it turned out that the three males inside the bar fighting the Police were brothers. The huge brother had gotten into an argument with two of their cousins in the rear bar parking lot, over a girl or something. The two cousins started stabbing the huge male, who then went back into the bar followed by the two cousins. Inside the bar the two cousins also started fighting with and stabbing the other two brothers. During this fight one of the cousins broke a pool cue and stabbed one of the brothers in the neck with it. The two cousins apparently had just run out of the rear bar door as the Police arrived. It was not known if the brothers really knew they were fighting the Police or they taught they were still fighting their cousins. The first three officers at the scene were sent to the hospital for minor injuries. When I got back out to the Police car and we started making other calls this situation did not really bother me too much. I think it was because right then this was all new and exciting to me. However about two hours later, I finally settled down and realized what had happened and what I had seen, and I felt nauseated. I found that this is a very normal reaction and that you have to learn how to deal with these situations. Because in this job you can go from a situation like this, to helping a little old lady back into bed and you cannot carry your emotions from one to the other.

13. Mentally Ill Arsonist, Dressed Like A Mummy.
For a little over a year and a half I worked in the Bomb and Arson Unit, where my primary job was to investigate suspicious fires. On this occasion I had been called by the Fire Department to meet them at the scene of a house fire in the northeastern part of town. When I arrived at the scene of this fire, I found that no one was home at the time of this fire. Someone had however piled curtains, clothing, and a lot of paint from a shed, lighter fluid, blankets, and miscellaneous items on the living room floor and set it on fire.

In this living room there was also a collection of several hundred different kinds of knives. Some of the knives had a red substance on them that looked like fresh blood, as well as what appeared to be and smelled like some sort of excrement. The house still smelled like dog excrement, even after the firefighters put out the fire, with all that water. The strange thing was that no dogs or cats were found at or near the residence. I checked around the residence and found a couple of old addresses and a possible name of one of the residents who lived in this residence. We could not locate the resident, however after I finished my reports. I talked to a couple of neighbors and learned that a mentally ill 37-year-old white male, lived by himself in this residence. I also learned that the male was a good carpenter and a knife collector. One of the neighbors informed me that they had seen this male at this residence approximately one hour earlier and the male was chasing his dogs away. As I started driving away from this residence, long after everyone else had left, I noticed a white male walking towards my vehicle in the middle of the road. It was fairly cold outside and he had on only a pair of jeans, no shoes or shirt. This male was carrying a big stick using it like a walking cane, and he had his head wrapped in ace bandages with only his eyes visible. I just knew this guy had to be the resident of the residence where the fire took place. Regardless of that, I knew that this male needed to be stopped and checked out to see what was wrong with him, since this was obviously not normal behavior. I called on my Police radio and requested a uniformed Police Officer to meet me to check this suspicious person out. I stopped in the middle of the rode and this male just walked by staring at me as if he dared me to make a move, then he continued walking. I got out of my vehicle at that time and I asked the male if he was the resident of the house that had caught fire. This male became suddenly very angry and psychotic then he started to move at even a faster pace. He walked right past this residence that had the fire and he was screaming leave me alone as he went. I let him walk as I waited for an assisting officer. This male made it to a city park before a female assisting officer showed up. I explained to this female Police Officer that the male had gone into the park and might be dangerous. I also informed her that he was possibly my suspect, who collected knives and might have a knife with him. I made it quite clear that this male was obviously mentally disturbed, whoever he was. I was then ready to go into the dark park to find this male with the help of this female Police Officer. However, to my surprise the female officer refused to get out of her police car, and said she needed to protect her civilian ride-a-long. I was very unhappy about this situation but I did not want to deal with it at that time.

Luckily a male police patty wagon driver showed up right then. I then explained the situation to him and we then went down into the park and located this male hiding in the trees. We did have to fight this male to get him handcuffed and shackled so we could get him into the patty wagon. He did not want to go and he was carrying a knife. I cannot remember what things this male was saying, all I can remember is that they made no since at all. He was very much out of his mind. It was later determined that this male was the resident of the house that had the fire. We found out that the substances found on the knives in this male's residence were in fact blood and excrement. Apparently, someone had stuck the knives in their anus or that of some animal. This male had tried to burn down his house and then he did not know where he was or what he was doing. I did not do anything about the female officer. I did not want to deal with it or think about it. I thought I would let her handle it on her own.

14. Stranded Motorist, 1 Shot and Killed.
This incident happened on my first night as a New Property Detective out on my own. 1 had been driving my unmarked police car around learning the northeast area of town.

This story is still difficult for me to tell, but the story has been beneficial to many Police recruits because it gives them an idea of what it's really like out there. As well as showing them how the most innocent situation can turn into something very bad very quickly, so they should not be caught off guard. I had been driving my police car down Independence Avenue, when I noticed a suspicious male going into a shop that should have been closed that time of night. My plan was to circle around the block to see what he was up too. However, I quickly learned that north bound Chestnut Traffic way does not go around a block, but down to a lake, where there were no through streets, houses or anything for about a mile. I had driven about halfway to the lake, when I noticed a 26-year-old black male wearing red sweats walking south bound on Chestnut Traffic way. This male was also carrying something that looked as if it was rather heavy, which he had a sweatshirt or something over it. I could not tell what the male was carrying, however I thought that he looked rather clean cut and he might need some help. I thought that maybe his car had broken down or something and he did not want to leave this heavy item he was carrying in his car so he was carrying it. My intentions where only to stop and help this male, since he was so far from anything, that him having committed a crime did not really come to me. I was driving an unmarked police car, but it was obviously a police car because it had red lights in the front grill, a spot light, and a long antenna. I slowly made a U-turn to see if he needed help. I got out of my car, showed my badge and identification and said, "I'm a detective with the police department. Is everything OK?" He just looked at me. I repeated, "I'm Detective Hartman with the police department. Is everything OK?" He turned his head and started walking away again. I do not know if it was pride or what, but I walked up to him to get some acknowledgement and to find out what was going on. I repeated who I was and asked if I could help him. The male still kept walking. My intentions at this point where to go back to my police car radio to ask for an assisting officer. I wanted to check this male out to find out what was going on. I had by now gotten the impression when he looked at me that his attitude was, "Why are you fucking with me, because I am black?" Which was a very common thing back then, even if it was not true. When I turned to go back to my police car, the male all of the sudden said, "Just a minute, let me set this stuff down." Then he quickly threw the items he was carrying down and turned around and lunged at me and the fight was on. For some reason the man was flinging me around like a wet noodle. I thought he was much larger than me when he was fighting, although he was actually a little smaller. It was later determined that the man was intoxicated and had drugs in his system, which explained his strength. I was finally able to get the male face down on the ground, at which time I tried to bring his hands behind his back so I could handcuff him. However, each time I would get one hand behind his back and try to put a handcuff on it, he would pull his hand away and put it in front of him. He would then bring the other hand back, as if it was a game. This male was extremely strong, because I should have had the leverage to hold his hands behind his back. This game of his went on for several times, and then I somehow sensed someone was going for my gun. At that time, I carried a 2-inch Smith and Wesson .38 caliber 5 shot revolver, in a clam shell style holster on my hip, which the gun easily falls out of. When I reached back to check my gun I felt it leaving my holster so I and grabbed my gun putting my hand over the hammer as tight as I could. I remember it felt as if the hammer was ripping into my hand, but I knew I had to hold it back to prevent the trigger from being pulled, and me possibly being shot. During these brief moments we had both started to stand up. At this time, he actually had as much control of where my gun was pointing as I did and he was pointing the gun at my ribs, trying to pull the trigger.

We were turning the gun back and forth pointing it at each other, and both of us fighting for control over my gun. Neither of us had been able to stand completely up yet.

As we were both standing bent over, I put my finger over his finger that was on the trigger and I jerked back the gun. Then I pulled the trigger with his finger, while the gun was pointed at the red sweats he was wearing. He immediately fell to the ground with same expression on his face that he had when I first saw him nonchalant, no expression at all. The first thing I said to him then was, "Now look what you made me do, you son of a bitch!" I wanted to kick the shit out of him. I was so mad at him for making me do this. I ran back to my police car, and radioed for help, informing the dispatcher that I had been involved in a shooting. I then pulled my police car up to where the male was lying to make sure he was not going to try to get away. I immediately noticed a wet spot in this male's crotch. I thought that I had shot him in the groin and I figured he deserved it. I knew I should have probably tried to give this male some kind of first aid, but to be honest I was still scared. I did not want to take the chance of getting back into the same situation again, if he tried to attack me again. It seemed as if it took forever for a police car to arrive, even though I could hear a lot of sirens in the distance, but I am sure it was probably only seconds. My police department supervisors came and took my gun from me. Then they asked where my handcuffs and my Identification and badge were. My handcuffs were on the ground and my Identification and badge case was on the ground underneath where the male was lying. I was questioned on what had happened by every person on the department I thought, even before I was taken downtown and asked to give a formal statement. One captain wanted the evidence technicians to take all my clothing off me and put me in a paper gown, so they could use my clothing as evidence. However, another captain stood up for me and said I was a victim and there was no reason I should have to go through that as well, which I was really thankful for. I was then checked for injuries, I had only a couple of scratches and dirt on my suit, which they took pictures of. Finally, I was taken into the chief's office with a couple of my commanders. The first thing the Chief of Police said was that it was a good shooting, and that I had killed him. The Chief stated that the bullet I fired had blown this male's heart up, and he died instantly while he was still standing up. I remember at that moment raising my hands above my head and feeling nauseated, it was as if I was in shock, and everyone just looked at me like what is wrong with him. This was the last thing in the world I would have ever believed is that I killed this male, but I guess the commanders thought that I already knew that the male had died. The autopsy results showed that the bullet entered right below the males left nipple and it did not exit his back. It was hard to find out that I had killed this male. I am very glad that I was able to go home to my family that night. I also realize that this male also had to have had a family also, and pray for their understanding. I have told this story many times to show how the most innocent situation can become the worst situation you could ever imagine. It is something you never get over, but you learn to live with it as part of your job. Hopefully I can share these experiences with others, so that they do not end up in the same situations.

15. Mentally Ill, Nude Man in His Basement with A Knife.
    I was dispatched to this residence in the Plaza Area on a mentally ill suicidal male. The dispatcher had gotten the call from this male's doctor who informed her, that his male patient had called him and stated that he was ready to commit suicide. The Doctor also informed the dispatcher that this male was nude and armed with a knife. Several other police officers went to the residence with me, but he would not let us in. We could see him through the side window of his kitchen; he was a 45-year-old very large framed white male. He was just pacing back and forth in his kitchen, he was completely nude, all sweaty, and carrying a large butcher knife. He would occasionally walk across the room, talk to someone on the phone for a moment, and then continue to pace back and forth.

    We were trying to talk to him through the window, but he would not acknowledge our presence.

    This male's doctor was apparently whom this male was talking to over the telephone occasionally. The doctor had been trying to persuade the male to open his door and let us in. However, when this failed the doctor finally responded to this male's residence and the male let the doctor and us in. The doctor then all of the sudden stated get him; which we proceeded to do. Wrestling a nude sweaty person can get awkward, it's slippery and there is nothing to hold on to. We were finally able to get the male handcuffed and shackled, although we were not able to get him dressed. We covered him with a blanket and transported him to Western Missouri Mental Health Center where he was put in leather restraints and placed under a doctor's care.

16. The Shoe String Murders.
    Several summers ago, I was temporarily assigned to the Homicide unit. A 35-year-old Cuban male had been found dead in his apartment after his relatives noticed a strong odor in the hallway

of his apartment building. This male had apparently been dead about-a week. His tongue was hanging out of his mouth, his face was black and his eyes bulged. He had bled from his mouth and ears. His death was apparently caused by strangulation from a cord around his neck. The apartment showed signs of a struggle and drug use. The odor in the apartment was horrible! We contacted relatives and friends to determine who was the last one to see this male alive. It was determined that the last person known to have seen this male alive had seen him one week earlier. We discovered that he was a homosexual who sold drugs. We found numerous pictures of nude males and letters from presumably sexual partners. We also found drug paraphernalia. We determined later that he possibly sent drugs through the mail to Florida, in model airplanes and boats, cars, train sets etc.... We started our investigation to track down the people who had seen him last. One friend we were unable to locate was a bisexual who was in the military. We checked the friend's apartment and found that he was not there and that his roommate had not seen him for a while. We found nothing in his apartment to make him a suspect; however, we pursued trying to find this friend who was reportedly one of the last people seen with the dead male. I had located an address book in this friend's apartment and we called all the telephone numbers in this address book. No one knew where he was, except for one couple who said he was coming in for their wedding in the next few days. At that point my part of the investigation stopped. However, the next day I heard on the news that a 45-year-old white male had been killed in Kansas. I recognized the male victim's name and address, from one I had read in this military friends address book. Afterwards, we found out that the man killed in Kansas had been a lover of the Cuban dead males' military friend. Whenever this military friend needed help, the man murdered in Kansas would send him to a foreign country to help him get out of trouble. The military friend had apparently wanted to go to a foreign country to get out of the United States because he had killed the Cuban male over a bad drug transaction. The white male victim in Kansas apparently did not want to help him, so the military friend strangled the Kansas man with shoestring, killing him. Our Homicide Detectives apparently then went back to the military friend's apartment where they found a shoestring hidden in a rag in a closet. The military friend was tried and convicted on both homicide charges, in which he confessed to.

17.   He Raped Her While She Protected Her Baby.
This Westport rape case is another one that bothered me quite a bit. I had been dispatched to this apartment on a rape that had just happened. When I got there and knocked on the front door of the apartment.

A 22-year-old nude white female answered the door and said that a black male in his early thirties had just raped her, and he had just run out the back door. We were apparently too late because we could not locate the suspect in the area. This female had been home alone with her 3-month-old baby. This male had knocked on her apartment door and when she opened it, he forced his way into the apartment, with a knife in his hand. This male ordered her to put the baby on the bed then he told her to remove her clothes and get up on her knees on the bed. The victim stated that she pulled the baby under her to protect it from this male. As the male pulled his pants down to his knees and had sexual intercourse with her. This male had just held the knife in his hand during this time in a threatening manner. The only time the male talked was when he told her to lay down and take her clothes off and when the police came, he ran out of the rear door stating, if she told he would be back.

18.   He Died Foaming At The Mouth.
I responded to a Code One emergency call one night for a person having trouble breathing. Upon my arrival I observed a 42-year-old black male over six-feet tall and over 300 pounds sitting in a living room chair. A white foam like substance was pumping out

of his mouth, gushing out with every heartbeat. I did not really know what to do, however I surely was not going to let him choke on this stuff coming out of his mouth. So, I picked the male up and laid him on his side on the floor until the ambulance came seconds later. I later learned that the man was an alcoholic with previous heart problems and he was having a heart attack at the time and that he later died. The ambulance personnel informed me that no CPR or anything I could have done would have made a difference, the only thing I could have done I did by laying him on his side. I do not know how I picked this male up because he was so large. It must have been an adrenaline rush that enabled me to move such a large person, I had not even thought about it until it was all over.

31. I Broke My Toe Chasing A Window Peeper/Burglar.
A duplex where I used to live north of the river was having problems with a window peeper and sometime burglar. All almost every night I could look out my window and see a tall black male looking in windows running from house to house. Occasionally we were having burglaries but nothing would be taken. We were really having trouble catching whoever was doing this. One night this black male had walked into a residence where there had been a party. A 21-year-old white male had stayed, and was sleeping on the couch covered up with a blanket. Apparently, this black male did not know whether it was a man or woman asleep on the couch so he was trying to pull the blanket back to check it out. However, upon doing so, this male woke up and grabbed for the black male but he was able to get away and run from the residence. I started checking every night walking around the neighborhood and continuously looking out my windows trying to catch this black male. I had always before seen this black male looking in windows about 1 1 p.m. when I was waking up getting ready to go to work. I would never have any clothes on to chase him, and when I did get dressed, I could not find him. So, I started going to bed with a pair of jean shorts on at night so I could get up and

go right away. This black male did not show up for several days after the burglary. However, one night I finally did see him outside looking in a neighbor's window about the time I was getting up and getting ready to go to work. I took off out of my house in just my cut off blue jean shorts but I could not find him.

He had left the block where I was at so I went to check another block that was having the same problems. I did not see him so I just sat down out of sight where I had a good view of the area and I watched for him. It only took a few minutes and it was like I struck gold, here he came running from window to window looking inside each of them. I was determined that I was not going to lose him this time, I was fed up with this so I ran as fast as I could towards him and the foot chase was on. I was somehow able to catch him and I tackled him. During this foot chase I had been yelling for this black male to stop while I was identifying myself as a police officer but he would not. I did not know it or even feel it at the time I was chasing this black male but I somehow cut my foot open and broke my toe. When I tackled this black male and handcuffed him, I yelled up at a neighbor who was looking out her window. I asked her to call the police, and I again identified myself as a police officer. I did get some help, a lot of help this neighbor called 911, and stated that there was a police officer down, yelling for help outside her window. Police cars were coming from everywhere red lights and sirens on. It turned out that this tall black male was only 15 years old and his mother worked nights so he would sneak out each night after she left for work. This black male juvenile admitted to peeping in the windows every night, and going into some people's residences but was all for sexual gratification not to take anything or hurt anybody. This juvenile was ordered into counseling and I was given a commendation for catching this window peeper that had been bothering the neighborhood for months, and that nobody else could catch.

32. She Said that He Was Sending Messages To Her Over Her Car Radio. While serving as a Detective north of the river. I had a 38-year-old white female (Crazy Lady) that I had been trying to help out. I was just trying to pacify her, to get her to stop bothering me. She was always having problems, like when it was her birthday, she baked a birthday cake for some neighborhood boys that did not even like her. When she gave them the cake the boys threw the cake against this female's screen door as soon as she went back inside. She could not understand why they did this. She was having all kinds of problems with these boys because they were always harassing her and prowling around her house at night. These boys were also breaking into neighbor's houses and damaging everyone's property. This is how I met this lady, while I was trying to determine who these boys were, and to clear up these cases. However, when I met this female, my life became hell at work. She would continuously stop by the police station wanting to see me or be telephoning me. At first, I was just trying to get her to leave me alone by helping her. It got deeper than I thought, this lady started saying that her house was bugged and the mafia was following her. This female stated that her boyfriend could hear everything she said on her telephone. She believed that all of her electrical appliances were bugged so she did not want to go in her house. This female would always go to a pay telephone to call me. However later on she believed her boyfriend had also bugged her car so she would leave her car away from the pay telephone when she talked. When her boyfriend started bugging her car, he also got people to send her messages over her car radio, so she was scared not to turn her radio on. One day she told me that somebody had told her about taking a magnet and de-magnifying all these listening devices. She stated that a magnet would erase the tapes so nobody could find out what she was doing. This female even came up to the police station one day and stated, "Yeah, I even put the magnet on the wire under my bra, just in case he had a listening device there." This female always wanted me to check out car license numbers of people she said were following her. I would always check the license plates but

they would come back to ordinary citizens and I would always tell her that we did not have a record on these license plates.

This female was always concerned because her boyfriend always knew what she was doing and where she was. This female believed that her boyfriend was into drugs and that he frequented prostitutes. This female believed that the mafia and her boyfriend were trying to get her to become a prostitute. This female also believed that the people where she worked were corrupt and they were trying to set her up so she would be fired. This female came to me one day and informed me that she wanted a police report made. She stated that one of the people she works with made a face at her in the mall and she considered that harassment. Luckily, I was finally able to get rid of this female, this is how. I had been telling this female for a few months that I could not help her any further with her problems and I had been referring her to others, including her mother and her doctor. I tried many times to get her to give me her mothers or her doctor's name but she would not because she did not want me to call them. Finally, one morning she called me and stated that she wanted to meet me somewhere. She stated this, because she could not talk on the telephone and because I had asked her not to come to the police station any more. I as usual told her I could not help her with her problems if they did not involve property crimes and that I was not going to meet her. I thought it was all over but then the police station clerks came back and advised me that this female's mother was at the front desk and that she wanted to talk to me. I was very happy to hear this; I thought finally I could explain to this female's mother what her daughter was doing so she would get her some help. Boy! was I wrong, her mother was just like her and her mother handed me a subpoena to go to county court to testify for the female against the female's boyfriend. That was all I could stand, it was the last straw. I informed this female's mother that I wanted absolutely no more contact with her daughter. I tried to get out of this subpoena but I could not so I had to go to court. I observed this female, her mother, and this female's boyfriend (whom I had never seen before), all in the waiting room. After about three hours of waiting this female's legal aid attorney came up to me. She wanted me to go up to the judge and tell him what I knew about this female's boyfriend, assaulting and abusing her. Also, about his frequent use of prostitutes, drugs and his harassing her by having the mafia follow her and plant listening devises on and around her. I quickly advised this attorney that I knew nothing about this boyfriend. I informed her that if she put me in front of the judge, the only thing I was going to say was that this female was a crazy lady. Amazingly, this attorney returned to me a few moments later after talking to this female, and she informed me that I would not be needed to testify for this female in court. I have not been bothered by this female since (knock on wood).

33. He Was Bleeding, But He Would Not Let Us Treat Him, Until His Lover Arrived.

When I was going through my final stages before getting on the police department. I remember an officer on the review panel asking me, what I thought I would not like about being a police officer. I remember telling him, dealing with child molesters and homosexuals. Well, child molesters I am still not crazy about, I still do not like dealing with them. As far as homosexuals go, I have learned to treat those situations like any other boyfriend/ girlfriend situation. This case was a good example of that. I was dispatched on a 22-year-old white male who had cut his wrists and locked himself in his apartment bathroom, because his male lover had broken up with him. When I got there, this suicidal males 25-year-old white male gay roommate, let me in the apartment. This roommate explained that this male had locked his self in the bathroom after his lover had broken up with him over the telephone. This roommate stated he heard this male crying loudly so he went to console him. This suicidal male then informed his roommate that he was cutting his wrists and he was not coming out of the bathroom until his lover came over. This roommate stated that he then called the police.

I tried to talk this male out of the bathroom for about 10 minutes, I legally could not force the bathroom door open, and I did not even know if this male was really hurt. I then requested that this roommate call this male's lover on the telephone and ask him to come over. When this suicidal male heard his roommate talking to his ex-lover on the telephone, he unlocked the bathroom door and opened it. This suicidal male had beaten on the bathroom walls and had broken a bathroom mirror. He had been walking around on the bathroom floor barefooted on the broken glass. This male had also taken and broke the razor blades out of five disposable razors and had slashed each of his arms about twelve times. None of this male's cuts were very deep but he was losing a lot of blood because he also had a lot of cuts on his feet. He had apparently been bleeding for a while, because there was a lot of blood on the bathroom walls and floor. The paramedics had been dispatched to this call with me; however, this suicidal male would not let them touch him, unless his lover was there. In Missouri you cannot treat somebody without their permission, unless they are unconscious or mentally incapable of making this decision. This male's ex-lover however did not want anything to do with this male anymore. Finally, I got on the telephone with this males, 23 year old white male ex- lover. I requested that he meet us at the hospital, he originally refused, but I told him that his ex-lover might bleed to death so he agreed to meet us at the hospital. This suicidal male then let the paramedics wrap his arms and feet in gauge and transport him to the hospital. This suicidal male's ex-lover had not shown up yet, so this male again refused to let the doctor touch him. The doctor finally gave up trying to get this male to let him treat him. The doctor stated to me "were very busy here, let someone know when he passes out," and the doctor walked away. When this male's ex-lover finally walked into the emergency room this suicidal male jumped up and ran over to him. This was quite a picture this bleeding male running over to his ex-lover and jumping up and wrapping his legs around his ex-lover's waist and his arms around his neck. They both hugged and kissed then the ex- lover held this male's hand as he let the doctors stitch him up. This was the most obnoxious, sickening thing I have ever seen.

34. We Got A Standing Ovation, After Sprit Festival Tackles.
I occasionally work off duty during the Spirit Festival each year. A couple years ago was one of these times. I was given one of the better jobs finally. All I had to do was to drive a golf cart around the festival with my partner, and respond to calls when needed. On this occasion we were riding around on the golf cart, when we heard over our walkie talkie that there was a foot chase going on. (3) Hispanic males in their early twenties were observed selling drugs and they were being chased by several officers. I was driving along the side of a hill on the west side of the festival. There was a crowd beginning to find places to sit in this area because a concert was getting ready to start. When these 3 Hispanic males ran right in front of our golf cart. I then drove the golf cart right between two of them. My partner and I, without even saying anything to each other both dived off the sides of the golf cart. We were able to tackle two of the Hispanic males. The other officers chasing these suspects just kept running after the third Hispanic male. We had tackled these two Hispanic males on the side of this hill where all the crowd was gathering. Both of us had to wrestle the Hispanic males we had tackled because they were still trying to get away. Both of these Hispanic males also had long steak knives in their waist bands. The Hispanic male my partner had tackled was trying to throw baggies of marijuana into the crowd to get rid of them. We were both able to restrain and handcuff the males we had tackled. We then picked up the knives we had taken from these two and we put the knifes in our waist bands. We then further patted these males down for other weapons.

We found drugs on them, mostly marijuana and pills, etc. . . . Once we had the males under control and we started to escort them to a patty wagon that had just arrived. The crowd all of the sudden stood up and gave us a standing ovation, we thought that was pretty exciting. Now that I look back on it, I guess we did put on quite a show for them.

35. He Had $10,000 Dollars in His Socks, and His Cheek Was Slashed open.

I had been dispatched on a disturbance in the street, one night in the inner city. Two black males in their mid-twenties were fighting in the street. One of them had been cut with a broken beer bottle. It was raining pretty hard but we got out of our patrol cars and broke up this fight. I ordered an ambulance for the male who was cut. The side of his cheek was cut open and hanging completely down below his mouth. When he talked you could see his teeth, tongue and everything moving. Just a little bit of his lip was holding the whole side of his mouth together. He acted as if he were in no pain at all. This fight had started over a bad drug deal and this male that was feeling no pain had been using drugs. This injured male was not wearing shoes and there were holes worn in his socks. Because it was raining this male's socks were soaked. There were $100 bills sticking out of the holes in his socks, as well as a few of them on the ground around him. We were able to get this male in the ambulance and his socks off. We found (10) packs of $100 bills, $10,000 total, from what was on the ground and what was in his socks. When he was running, he was wearing holes in his socks and the money was getting wet and it was falling out. I asked this male where he had gotten this money and why he was carrying it all in his socks. This male stated that he had just cashed his social security check. This male was not really at all concerned about his injuries, only the money we had recovered from him. This male was found to be a drug dealer; the Drug Enforcement Unit was advised of this situation. This injured male also stated that he did not want to assist in the prosecution of the male who cut him.

37. Trash Bag Harley, Life Flighted.
I was patrolling my area one dark early morning up north of the river. I was driving my police car across the bridge southbound over North Oak on 1-29. All of the sudden I noticed what looked like several large black plastic trash bags in all three lanes of the interstate. I also noticed that at the other end of the bridge several vehicles had pulled over and their occupants were running back towards me on the bridge. I remember thinking to myself that these people were going to get ran over because it was really so dark that you could barely see them. I was thinking that these people were running back to get these trash bags off of the interstate, and I thought that it was a nice jester but a stupid move. I then quickly stopped and turned on my red lights, I started backing up to where I had seen the first trash bag, hoping that traffic coming from behind us would stop so that these people did not get hurt. However, as I was backing up my red lights lit up the interstate enough that I noticed that this was not trash bags on the interstate but pieces and parts of a human body and clothing. I then blocked off the entire interstate and requested an ambulance and traffic officers. I then got out of my police car to see what I was dealing with. Sure enough, what looked like trash bags in the middle of the road were body parts and clothing from this 26-year-old white male. The people that were running on the bridge stated that they had seen one car hit this male and keep going then the male's body had come out from under the first car and two of these people's cars had then run over him. This male had been drug under three cars almost all the way across this bridge.

I thought that this male was quite obviously dead at this time. It appeared as if the hood ornament from a vehicle had gone right up this male's rectum, splitting him right in half from his rectum right up his back. Because all of these people were watching me wanting me to do something, I went up and put my hand on this male's neck to check for a pulse. Just as I put my hand on this male's neck his body jerked and he made an Ahhhhh sound, which scared me to death and made me jump, I really didn't expect that. When the ambulance responded I explained what had happened and the paramedics stated that this is a command response to a violent death. The paramedics did however order the Life flight Helicopter to transport this male to the hospital because they stated that even though this male was unconscious and most likely brain dead that his heart had not yet stopped beating. This male's heart did stop beating in the helicopter and he was then pronounced dead. Just as the helicopter took off a sergeant came up to me and stated that he thought that my hit-and-run driver had returned to the scene. The sergeant then pointed to a white male and a white female in their early twenties sitting in a car at the end of the bridge. The white male was hysterical and he could not talk however the female stated that her boyfriend had struck this male as the male was walking in the center lane of the bridge, and that it was so dark that he could not see the male. This female stated that her boyfriend had gone directly to her house after striking this male because he was so scared. This female stated that her boyfriend explained what had happened and she made him return to the scene. We could not find any identification on this male but we did find a trucker's style wallet with a chain on it. This wallet contained no identification however it did have the words Harley Davidson stenciled on it. This is how we referred to this male as Harley, with his last name being Davidson. I turned this case over to the accident investigators and I am not really sure what happened from there, however I was later advised that this male had a very high blood alcohol level and that he was an ex-convict.

38. She had A Gun and a Knife, And She Tried to Use Both on Me, Thank You Lord.
I had a pretty scary one, one night in the inner city when I was parked outside of a bar disturbance. I was sitting in a parking lot

across the street from this disturbance waiting to see if the police officers handling the disturbance would need the patty wagon, I was driving for anything. All the sudden this white male in his forties runs up to the driver's door of my patty wagon. This male stated that there was a black female trying to break into his residence. This male also stated that he was an off-duty deputy sheriff. This male then pointed to a residence behind me and across the street, and he said there she is up at my front door. This male stated that he had a trained attack dog just inside of the front door and that the dog will eat her. I turned my spotlight on the front porch of the residence this male was pointing at and sure enough there was a 24-year-old black female trying to get in this man's house. This female had already ripped open the screen door and she was kicking on the front door. Even though I had put the spotlight on her and she just kept on trying to get into the residence. I informed the dispatcher of what was happening and I requested a backup officer. I then got out of the patty wagon and ran towards this male's residence. This female seen me coming so she started to run off of this porch. I yelled for her to stop and she reached into the front of her pants. I was close enough by that time to grab her, and then I checked to see what she had been reaching for in the front of her pant, that's when I felt a gun. I pulled this females arms back behind her back then I escorted her to my patty wagon, where I had her but her hands on the hood of it. I then went into the waistband of her pants and I tried to get this gun out.

38. She had A Gun and a Knife, and She Tried to Use Both on Me, Thank You Lord.

I had a pretty scary one, one night in the inner city when I was parked outside of a bar disturbance. I was sitting in a parking lot across the street from this disturbance waiting to see if the police officers handling the disturbance would need the patty wagon, I was driving for anything. All the sudden this white male in his forties runs up to the driver's door of my patty wagon. This male stated that there was a black female trying to break into his residence. This male also stated that he was an off-duty deputy sheriff. This male then pointed to a residence behind me and across the street, and he said there she is up at my front door. This male stated that he had a trained attack dog just inside of the front door and that the dog will eat her I turned my spotlight on the front porch of the residence this male was pointing at and sure enough there was a 24-year-old black female trying to get in this man's house. This female had already ripped open the screen door and she was kicking on the front door. Even though I had put the spotlight on her and she just kept on trying to get into the residence. I informed the dispatcher of what was happening and I requested a backup officer. I then got out of the patty wagon and ran towards this make*s residence. This female seen me coming so she started to run off of this porch I yelled for her to stop and she reached into the front of her pants. I was close enough by that time to grab her, and then I checked to see what she had been reaching for in the front of her pant, that's when I felt a gun. I pulled this females arms back behind her back then I escorted her to my patty wagon, where I had her but her hands on the hood of it. I then went into the waistband of her pants and I tried to get this gun out.

39. Good Identification on Murder Victim, "Daaaad".

I was dispatched on a shooting call in the inner city at an apartment building. Upon my arrival I observed a 34-ycar-old black malc lying in the hallway outside of four different apartment doors. This male had a large hole in the top of his head and he was lying in a large puddle of his own blood, which had also flowed underneath one of these apartment doors. The male had no identification on, and he was quite obviously dead. I requested through the dispatcher, a supervisor, the Homicide Unit, a crime scene investigator and some assisting officers. We protected and secured the area, then I started knocking on these four apartment doors, to see if anybody knew this victim or if they had seen or heard anything. The apartment door I knocked on first was the door that the blood had flowed under. When I knocked on this apartment door a twelve-year-old black male opened the door. I was trying to hide the dead male's body from this juvenile by standing in a position that I blocked his view. However, this juvenile immediately seen the blood under his doorway and he looked around me and said, (Daaaad)! Needless to say, that is not the way we like to identify our victims or have the families notified of their death. I felt so sorry for this juvenile I wish I would have covered the body up before I knocked on that apartment door. The only reason I didn't cover the body up was that I was trying to get him identified and who would expect a 12-year-old to be up at 2 am in the morning. I hope that this never ever happens to me again. I was finally able to calm this juvenile down enough where he was able to get his mother out of bed. This juvenile's mother came running to the door, and she also identified this dead male as her husband. This dead male's wife stated that her husband had got paid and he had left one hour before to go cash his pay check. Apparently, somebody had followed this male home and shot and robbed him in this hallway. This dead male had no wallet on him and he had been shot with a .45 caliber weapon, in the head.

The real strange thing about this case was that everyone had been home in each of these four apartments when this a .45 caliber weapon was fired in this hallway and nobody even heard it. No suspects have been found in this homicide, as far as I know.

40. He Kicked The Dog In The Mouth And He Got Bit, Many Times.

I had an incident in Westport one night where a female K-9 security guard was trying to stop a fight between 2 white males in their thirties. One of the males that were fighting kicked this security guards' dog in the mouth. When this happened this female security guard ordered her dog to attack. It was obvious that this dogs jaw was hurting him; however, he still bit this guy all over as this female security guard requested assistance. Another female security guard showed up with her dog and she ordered her dog to attack this male because this male was still hitting the first security guard's dog. Both of these female security guards were telling this male to quit fighting and their dogs would stop biting. I had been dispatched to this disturbance, and upon my arrival I observed this male falling to the ground and both of these dogs biting him. After this male fell to the ground in a fetal position and he stopped -fighting the dogs, these security guards called their dogs off and I went up and handcuffed this male. I had to order an ambulance because this male was really chewed up. His hips, legs and arms were all bitten up. I followed the ambulance to the hospital and after the doctors removed this males clothing, I could not believe it, there were big chunks of flesh tom out of his upper legs and buttocks.

41. Full Blown Aids Carrier, Burn Victim Burglar.

As a detective in the inner city, I was assigned a burglary case, where a 35-year-old black male had broken into his 33-year-old black ex-wives residence, while she and his children were there. This male's ex-wife had called the police then as she observed this male coming through her bedroom window, she told him to go away, however when he kept coming so she went into the kitchen and grabbed a pan of boiling water and threw it on him. The police then arrived an ordered an ambulance because this male had very severe burns over most of his body. This male also told the ambulance attendants that he was dying because he had full blown aids. This male had been treated for a couple of weeks at the hospital for his burns then he was brought to police headquarters detention. I had to interrogate this male because of this burglary of his ex-wife's residence. However, I had no idea what I was in for, this male even looked contagious, he was covered in bandages but he still had raw sores everywhere. This male had to wear a surgical mask but I had to keep reminding him to leave it on because he kept taking it away from his mouth when he talked, and he was one of those people who spit when they talk. I remember hating every minute of that interrogation; I just knew

I was going to catch something from this male spitting on me. I really could not understand how the hospital could have released this male; he looked like they would have kept him quarantined. I was finally able to get the detention supervisor to look at this male and he immediately gave this male a signature bond on all the warrants this male had and let this male go. I'm not really sure what happened to this male after that, I know I have never had to go to court on him. When I got back to the police station, I requested that my sergeant let me go to the department doctor to be checked for aids. I was able to go to the department doctor however he would not give me the aids test because he stated that aids cannot be transmitted by saliva.

42. Let Me See If This Railing will hold me! It Didn't.

I was dispatched code 1 on an emergency call at an apartment building in the Plaza Area, on New Year's Eve a few years ago. Apparently, the occupants of an apartment in this apartment building were having a very large party. The people at this party had been drinking heavily and because it was a crowded party some of them went out on the balcony. This apartment was on the third floor of this apartment building. A 22-year-old intoxicated white male was leaning against the balcony railing, and he all of the sudden stated, "I wonder if this railing will hold me". This 180 1b male then started leaning against the railing putting all his weight against it and leaning back on it. Well, the witnesses stated that the last thing they heard this male say was, "look it holding me", just before the railing gave away and this male fell to his death. This male had fell three stories, and landed on a lawnmower in the storage area of a bottom floor apartment that was also having a patty at the same time. The witnesses stated that they had to really beat loud on this bottom floor apartment door to get someone to respond to the door because the music was so loud. The people in this bottom floor apartment didn't even know what was going on when these witnesses informed them that their friend had fallen from the balcony and into their storage area.

When these people opened their apartment sliding glass doors, they observed this male laying on top of their lawnmower dead. The ambulance attendants arrived about the same time I did, and they stated that this male was dead at the scene; his chest had been punctured and caved in.

43. Followed One Mile Of Blood Trail In The Snow.

One early morning I was dispatched on an alarm call on a business in the southern half of Kansas City, along with a new police officer who had just got off of his break-in period. Upon our arrival we observed that the front window of this business was broken out, and that there was a large enough hole in the window that someone could have gone into the business. We checked the business and found no one inside, however we did see a trail of blood leading from the broken window down the snow-covered sidewalk. We followed this trail of blood for about a mile. It was freezing cold outside and the blood was just beginning to freeze solid on the ground. So, we knew that this bleeding person could not be too far ahead of us. This trail of blood in the snow led us to a residence. Up on the front porch of this residence the blood had pooled a little as if this bleeding person had stopped there to get a door key or something. I knocked on this residence door for several minutes when finally, a middle-aged white female answered the door stating," what's wrong you woke me up, it's only 2:00 a.m. in the morning"? I informed this female that we had followed this trail of blood from a business with a broken window to this residence. This female then looked down at her porch and then inside the residence on the floor and she screamed," Oh my God". This trail of blood led up some stairs, so we followed this female up the stairs to a bedroom where this woman's 24-year-old son was laying on his bed passed out and bleeding. This male was intoxicated, high on marijuana and he had a deep cut on his arm. I called for an ambulance and they took this male to the hospital. As the ambulance attendants were lifting this male off of his bed and onto the stretcher a baggy of marijuana fell from this male's pocket, and the ambulance attendant handed it to me. This male was losing a lot of blood and he might have died if it had not been so cold outside, which slowed his flow of blood down, and us finding him in time. When the hospital personnel got this male stabilized, I asked this male what he had been doing, and this male stated he didn't really remember but he thought that he fell into a glass window breaking it and cutting himself.

Apparently, this male was so drunk that he couldn't stand up and he fell into the glass front of this business and cut his arm. There were no signs inside of this business that indicated that this male or anyone else had actually gone inside this business. We determined that this was not actually a burglary but at the most property damage. Which this male was charged with as well as possession of marijuana. This male might have gotten off easy with the law but you should have seen his mother's face when that marijuana fell out of his pocket, I feel very comfortable that he heard about that for a long time.

44. They just Dumped her Off, She Could Have Died.
I was working off-duty one Halloween night providing security for the vehicles and patrons of several of the haunted houses in the west bottoms. I was sitting in one of these parking lots with my lights out just watching for car prowlers when I observed two white males in their late teens carrying an 18-year-old white female over their shoulders. This female was hanging limp not moving a bit. When these males got the female to a van, they opened the side door and dumped her in, shut the door and they walked off. These males were laughing loudly and they appeared to be intoxicated. I waited awhile then I decided I had better go and check on her just in case there was really something seriously wrong with this female. I knocked several times on the van door but there was no response. I opened the unlocked side van door and I observed this female on the floor lying on her back face up between the rear seats. I shook the females arm and I said ma'am

are you O.K., but there was no response, then all the sudden this female started vomiting straight up in the air, covering her entire face. This female was obviously unconscious because she didn't even move when this happened. I knew that this female was going to choke on her own vomit, so I turned her over on her side and I radioed for one of the haunted houses to call for an ambulance. When the ambulance arrived, the attendants were able to get the female to come in and out of consciousness then they took her to the hospital. The two males who had dropped this female off arrived as the ambulance was taking this female away. These males stated that they had all arrived in this van together and they didn't think anything was wrong, that the female just had had too much to drink. I explained to them that she could have died in that condition, she had way too much to drink and she had drank herself into unconscious. I explained to these males that this was a very serious situation and I informed them what hospital this female was being taken to. These males acted like this was funny and the attempted to get into this van. I informed them that they were not getting into this van because they were both obviously very intoxicated. These males wanted to know how they were going to get home or to the hospital and I informed them to walk or to use a local telephone to call someone to get them. These males were very unhappy about this, so as they walked away, they started calling me all kinds of names etc... These same males only walked just a short distance then came back an asked me if they could just sleep in the van until morning when they sobered up. I knew, that this was the oldest trick in the book, and as soon as I left, they would drive away. I took their keys and I locked them inside of the van and I told them to get someone to come to get the van that had an extra set of keys and was sober. These males were so extremely intoxicated that they didn't even know what they were doing. I was going to arrest these males for public drunkenness however one of their sober friends came by and they all walked off together. I never heard anything more about this female because she was taken to a hospital in Kansas. However, the ambulance attendants informed me that if I wouldn't have checked on her, she would have most likely choked on her own vomit and died.

We had already been out there for about 45 minutes changing hands because our hands were freezing and the female officer comes out and she is only out there with me for about 25 minutes, when she was relieved by the Tactical Response Unit even before we were. The Tactical Response Unit provided cover for the two officers who were pinned down on these stairs and they were able to get them out safely. The next day this same female police officer took off work for the next 3 days, complaining of a back was sore because-she stood-there with her arm extended pointing her gun at the window for 25 minutes. There were a lot of other officers out there long before this female officer arrived however none of us took off work because we were sore. The Tactical Response Unit eventually talked this male and five other women and children out of this apartment. It was later learned that the male that had been shooting out of the window, had been shot at from a passing car and when the police officers were coming up his stairs, he thought that they were the people who had shot at him earlier. When this male realized that this was the police, he had been shooting at he became scared and didn't know what to do. This male stated that he was too scared to give up because he was afraid that we would have shot him and his family.

45. It Didn't Happen In this Bar!!!
I had been dispatched on a tavern disturbance in the northeast area. Upon my arrival I observed blood on the sidewalk in front of this tavern leading into the tavern door and around the comer of the tavern. I also saw two broken and bloody pool sticks lying on the sidewalk. There were no people around so I went inside the tavern and the first thing I heard was the bartender a white female in her late 40's stating it didn't happen in here. This bartender stated that she knew there had been a fight outside but she thought

that they must have made up and went home. I went back outside and followed the trail of blood that led around the corner and it led to the back parking lot of the tavern where a 35-year-old intoxicated white male was laying there bleeding from several head wounds. I ordered an ambulance and gave him all the first aid I could and then I asked him what had happened. This male stated that he was playing pool with another guy's wife in the tavern when for no good reason this other guy grabbed the pool stick out of his wife's hands and started hitting him with it. This male stated that he hit the other guy back with his pool stick then some people pushed them both out of the front door of the tavern. This male stated that just as they both got outside and the people shut the tavern door this other guy hit him a couple of times in the head which knocked him down. This male stated that the next thing he knew, some lady was dragging him down the sidewalk to where I found him. It is not unusual for the tavern owners to say this because if they have fights in their businesses the City Liquor Control Bureau needs to be notified and there is a chance that they could get their liquor license revoked. It is also typical that no one in the tavern had seen anything or even knew who the man and wife that were also involved were, so no charges were filed against anyone, however I did report this incident to the City Liquor Control Bureau.

46. My kids watched, As I Fought the Drug Crazed Man.
     I was off duty one day taking my kids ages 6 and 8 home from school when we observed a car quickly pull over to the shoulder of the road in front of us. The driver of this car, a white male in his late thirty's jumped out and ran over to the passenger side and opened the passenger door, it appeared as if the passenger was sick or something.

I stopped to see if I could help and as I was approaching the passenger side of the car the passenger a white male in his late thirty's jumped out of the car and tackled the guy that had been driving, and they started wrestling on the ground. I tried to help separate them, there was blood coming out of the passenger's mouth and nose and he was spitting and acting like he was a crazy wild man. It took both of us to get this guy down and hold him on the ground, and it was a struggle moment by moment, but thankfully a neighbor seen what was going on and called the police who arrived shortly after and helped restrain this male. The driver informed us that the passenger had overdosed on drugs and that was why he was acting this way and he was trying to get him to a hospital. We ordered an ambulance and after we got him strapped down and the ambulance left, I looked back at my kids who were watching all this as it happened right in front of our van. My kids appeared to be frightened but I am sure they had no idea what was going on. I remember thinking at the time should I have stopped and got involved, what If this guy had gotten the best of us and then got in my van and took my kids, there is no way that I would have been worth it. I know I became a policeman to help people, but I am sorry my family comes first, and now I strongly evaluate any situation I get involved in off duty especially when I am with my family:

47.   14-Year-Old Killed Him; Because He Thought That He Was A cop. One summer when I was temporarily assigned to the Homicide Unit, I was assigned to help investigate the death of a 20-year-old black male. This homicide occurred in the eastern part of the inner city and it involved a 14-year-old black male suspect. This 14-year-old boy was actually ruling the neighborhood or at least all the blocks that surrounded the block he lived on. He was the only source for drugs in the area, and he had the most money and power because of the drugs. He basically just told people what to do, older people, younger people and if they didn't do what he said he would have his drug user friends go take care of them (burn their home, car, beat them up, steal from them, etc...)ln exchange for drugs. Elderly people were afraid to come out of their homes and no one wanted to talk to the police about him because of the fear of retaliation. I did get one person to talk to me but I had to meet him at another location. This person stated that this 14-year-old

boy had went with 5 of his larger drug user friends in their 20's to one of the neighbors' homes where they forced the front door open and he told the 25-year-old black male inside that he was going to have sex with his 20-year-old black wife and there was nothing he was going to say or do about it. This 14-year-old did rape this 20-year-old wife, but one of his friends apparently broke down on him so the 14-year-old was sent away to a group home during the week and he was home only on weekends. This however didn't really even slow this 14 .year old down he just used the telephone at the home during the week to do his business. One of the weekends when this 14-year-old was home he went to a grocery store/gas station with several of his drug user friends, where this 20-year-old black male pulled his car up to him and asked to buy some drugs from him. During the interrogation of this 14-year-olds drug friends it was learned that this 14-year-old just pulled out his gun put it to the guy's head who had asked to buy the drugs, then he shot him. The friends stated that this 14-year-old then looked at them and stated that he shot him because he didn't look right, he thought he looked like a cop (the victim was not a cop). This 14-year-old was charged as an adult and sent to a special protected area of prison the last I heard. The best thing about this whole thing was that the neighbors were now all free to do as they pleased and they all informed the police about how it had been living there and about all that this 14-year-old had done to them. This 14-year old's mother's home, car and almost everything they owned was seized by the police department as unlawful gains through the sale of drugs. This 14-year old's mother had been just sitting back and enjoying the profits and the power her son had.

48. (2) Children Die In Lawnmower Fire.
While working one early afternoon around the 4th of July as a Detective in the Bomb and Arson Unit, I was dispatched on a fire at an older inner-city residence. Upon my arrival there were fireworks going off all around the area, and ambulance was at the scene and I was advised by the Fire Department Fire Investigator

that two white male children age's 3 and 6 had been badly burnt while playing with a lawnmower that caught on fire. I responded to the rear of this residence where I observed a lawnmower in the back yard and I noticed that it appeared to have been in a fire even thought it was not badly damaged only a hole was melted into the plastic gas tank. I then went into the basement that was underneath of, but could only be entered from the rear of the residence. This basement area was where the fire had occurred; it contained the washer/dryer, furnace, and miscellaneous storage items. This basement showed only miner burn damages however the smoke and water damage was heavy. The first fireman on the scene informed me that upon his arrival he observed an adult male spraying a water hose into the basement and onto a 6-year-old child that was lying across the top of a lawnmower. This second 3-year-old child was lying on the floor partially behind the basement door still on fire. The fireman explained that after they rescued the two children, they pushed the lawnmower out into the back yard where it was now located. This fireman showed me where the lawnmower had been sitting at the time of the fire and I noticed that a plastic gas can was melted to the floor right next to where the lawnmower had been. I started questioning the people at the scene and I learned that relatives had been visiting this family and they had brought their laundry with them. The resident of this residence had put his lawnmower into the basement and had put the plastic gas can on top of it, right in front of the washer and dryer. The female relative a white female in her late twenty's stated that she had moved the lawnmower back out into the back yard prior to her starting her laundry. This female stated that she had just started her laundry and went around to the front of the residence to visit when a few moments later they all heard the 3- and 6-year-old boys screaming. The 30-year-old white male relative stated that when he seen the boys on fire, he grabbed the water hose and tried to put the fire out as someone else called the fire department. The residents and the relatives all stated that the boys must have pushed the lawnmower back into the basement because it had been out in the yard where the female relative stated that she put it. The residents and the relatives also stated that someone's fireworks must have gone into the basement which set off the fire. This basement had one concrete step going down into it and the basement door would not even open all the way wide enough for someone to easily get the lawnmower through the door, leaving me to believe that the lawnmower was never pushed out into the backyard as this female relative stated. It appeared as if the boys had been playing with the lawnmower trying to put gas in it and they had dumped gasoline all over the floor and on themselves. It is unknown what ignited this fire however a spark from the washer, gas dryer pilot light, water heater kicking on, it could have been from several sources, and however it could not be determined. One 6-year-old boy was most likely the one pouring the gasoline as the 3-year-old boy watched, because when the fumes ignited the breath was probably sucked out of the 6-year-old causing him to fall over the top of the lawnmower where he was found. The 3-year-old was most likely thrown backwards where he was found on fire partially behind the basement door. The 6-year-old boy died at the scene and the 3-year-old was in very critical condition the last I heard. I believe that this case still continues today between insurance companies trying to figure out exactly what happened, and who or what they can blame this fire on.

49. Attempt Suicide in Car.

I was driving my personal vehicle to court in Clay County one winter morning. On the way I observed a car parked on the shoulder of the other side of the interstate. I noticed that this car had all the windows fogged up, and there was a hose going from the tailpipe into the passenger window of the car. It was quite obvious what was going on, but I did not know how long the person had been in the car like that. I had to turn around at the next exit and come back to this vehicle. I immediately opened the passenger door and pulled the hose out of the window. There was a 35-year-old white male unconscious lying across the front seat of this vehicle; he was trying to commit suicide right there on the interstate. He had hooked up a big hose to his tailpipe and put it in the passenger window and rolled the window up. I was able to pull the man from this vehicle as other citizens pulled over to see if they could help. I asked one of these citizens to use their car phone to call for an ambulance. This man must not have been in this car too long because when I pulled him out of the car the cold air immediately started to bring him around. This man was fine but the ambulance took him to the hospital and hopefully he was also checked out at the mental hospital as well. The local police handled this situation from there; apparently, he had not been in the car all that long, just long enough to go to sleep. I was really glad that I just happened to look over there and see him in time.

50.   Gang Style Assassination.
I had been dispatched on a suicide up north of the river. Upon my arrival I was contacted by a 33-year-old white female who stated that she had just gotten home from work. When she looked for her husband, she found him out in the back yard and he had been shot. I checked in the back yard and in the tree line I could see what looked like a man kneeling down on his knees with his head down. I checked on this 25-year-old white male and he was definitely dead however he had not been dead for more than an hour or so. This male had his head lying on his knees and his hands tied behind his back. This male had what turned out to be a bullet in the back of his head. This was definitely not a suicide; it was as if somebody had made him get down there and then they shot him in the back of the head assassination style. I never did figure out what the reason for this was but it was quite obvious that it was an assassination. I turned this case over to the homicide unit and my best guess would be that this case involved drugs in some way.

51.   Bag Lady Fire.
I was dispatched to meet the Fire Department at the scene of an apartment fire one early morning while I was working as a

Detective for the Bomb and Arson Unit. Upon my arrival I was advised by the Fire Department Fire Investigator that there was one 70-year-old white female dead and her 50-year-old daughter was badly burned. The daughter she had already been taken to the hospital. This apartment fire occurred in the older section of downtown where both victims lived as bag ladies. They used this apartment for the storage of the items they collected and for a home for their numerous pets. The older woman was still lying in the apartment hallway. It was quite obvious that she had died from smoke inhalation. Because there was a lot of soot around her mouth and nose, and the fact that her tongue was hanging out. She did appear to have some bums, which most likely occurred after she had died. The Fire Department personnel were still inside this apartment spraying down hot spots when I entered the apartment.

As I entered the apartment, I realized that I had never seen anything like this before. This apartment was stacked with papers, bags, trash, and clothing, everything imaginable. There was no bare floor or walls showing whatsoever, they had just worn a path down the middle of all this trash as they had gone from room to room. These two women must have just lain on top of the stacks of trash; they had no beds or furniture. They did have a small apartment kitchen stove but no food was visible at all, other than stuff you would pick up off the street. Each room I would go into I would find one or two dead pets, it was hard to tell if they were dogs, cats or what they had been burned so badly. One of these pets was burned so badly that we could not be sure that it was not an infant so we had to further examine it to make sure. This apartment had no water, electricity, or gas. These women had this stove hooked up to a butane bottle, they used candles for light, they used their bath tub as a toilet, and they must have carried their water from some other place. This place was a disaster waiting to happen and it did happen. This fire was caused by the older female apparently falling asleep. She had fallen asleep on top of some of this trash, with a burning cigarette in her hand. I did find several smoke detectors in a closet but they were broken and without batteries.

52. School Talent Show Shoot-Out.

I worked off duty at a school talent show in the southwestern part of the city and I thought it would be real fun and easy. We used to go to talent shows, and it used to be basically for people to show their talents or just to have fun. There were never any problems. I could not figure out why they hired 8 police officers, I soon found out. It turned out this talent show was more of a meeting for all the rival gangs or different groups of kids because there was nothing else to do. The whole school auditorium was full of gangs wearing their different colors and everything else. One fight would break out and then another one and there just was not enough police officers to keep up with all the fights inside the auditorium not to mention the hallways and bathrooms. Pretty soon fights started outside and there were kids shooting at each other with guns right outside the schools front door. I learned later that there had been two kids shot outside. We had to call on duty district police officers to handle the outside because all of us were overwhelmed inside trying to control the kids at this talent show. The fights were going on inside and outside and we just could not get it under control. The kids were smoking marijuana in the bathrooms, hallways and in the auditorium. Finally, it got so bad, that waves of kids would be rushing to get outside because of the fights inside the school. Then waves of kids were trying to get inside the school, because of the fights and shootings outside the school. These two groups ran into each other at the doors and everyone was pushing both ways like a tug-a-war but no one was going anywhere. Finally, a wave of kids would come in and a wave of kids would go out. We just kind of teeter-tottered them back and forth trying to get everybody out of there but everybody outside wanted in and everybody inside wanted out. It was really a mess, the last thing you would expect at a talent show. To be honest I can't say for sure if they even had a talent show I was too busy. .Should not make judgments about people until you know them.